ROMANCE ON THE ROAD

THE BACHELOR NEXT DOOR - BOOK FOUR

PAMELA FORD

AINE PRESS

BOOKS BY PAMELA FORD

BACHELOR NEXT DOOR SERIES

Love on the Lane

Dancing on the Drive

Breathless on the Boulevard

Romance on the Road

Kissing on the Corner

CONTINENTAL BREAKFAST CLUB SERIES

Over Easy

Fresh Brewed

Honey Glazed

OUT OF IRELAND SERIES

To Ride a White Horse

A Rush of White Wings

This is a work of fiction. Names, characters, places, and incidents are either the products of the author's imagination or are used fictitiously. Any resemblance to actual events, locales, organizations or persons, living or dead, is entirely coincidental.

A previous version of this book was published under the title, *Dear Cordelia*.

Cover design by Robbi Strandemo

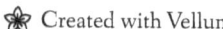 Created with Vellum

To my sons, Kristian and Sebastian. So many adventures already, so many more to come.

Dear Cordelia,

Freud had if all wrong. He should have asked: What do men want? Why is it that saying the L word practically gives men hives? Why does the merest hint of the word "commitment" catapult men into flight? Why will a man relentlessly pursue a woman, only to change his mind about her once she yields to his advances? I'm beginning to believe men think of women as they do fishing trips. Catch and release. Thank God it's January—the lakes are frozen over just like my heart.

Shivering in Chicago

Dear Shivering,

Things could be worse. You could still be dating a commitmentphobe. At least now you're free to find the right guy. In the famous words of Mae West, "A woman has to love a bad man once or twice in her life to be thankful for a good one." Don't give up yet. Cordy predicts that if you let the ice in your heart melt a little, you'll soon land the keeper you've been looking for.

Cordelia

1

ALL SHE WANTED WAS TO BE PART OF *BREAKING NEWS* instead of *baking news*. The chance to write about murders instead of menus. A little more pizazz and a little less pizza. Was it really so much to ask?

Liza Dunnigan scrolled through the three story ideas her editor had sent over—fast and tasty tortilla treats, winter dinners guaranteed to warm the soul, and waffle mania (whatever that meant). She let out a sigh.

Seven years of quick easy dishes and happy holiday entertaining and cool low-carb cooking and blah, blah, blah. *Enough.* She'd been working in the same job at the Chicago Sentinel since the day she graduated college—the small, private girls' school her parents insisted she attend when she'd really wanted to go to the University of Wisconsin with its wild parties and Big Ten football games. Instead, it had been sherry with the dean, charcoal blazers, and discussions of Thomas Hardy.

Well, no more.

She glanced up as one of her food section coworkers slid into the chair next to her desk. Kristin Coulter, every man's dream woman—tall, thin, blond, blue-eyed. She wore clothing effortlessly, making everything she put on look like a *Vogue* cover. Good thing she was as nice a person as was ever born. Because it kind of made her hard to despise.

"You look different today," Kristin said.

Liza looked down at herself. "Navy skirt. White shirt. Ballet flats. I don't think so." She reached behind her back to give a quick roll to the waistband of her skirt. Kristin probably never had to roll her waistband to make her skirt length fashionable. *Probably because Kristin had the good sense to buy new clothes when styles changed.*

The thought took her aback. Until this moment, she'd always considered Kristin's attention to fashion a frivolous waste of money.

"Not your clothes," Kristin was saying. "Your face. Seven years together in the food section and I can tell these things. You're hiding something."

Liza grinned.

"I knew it! What are you up to?"

Liza glanced at her watch with its plain black leather band. *How very mundane.* "In half an hour I'm going upstairs for an interview—"

"You're leaving the food section?" Kristin gaped at her.

A thrill ran through Liza that her announcement came as such a shock. Kristin's reaction was reinforcement of just how predictable she'd become. It was definitely time to put her new plan into action. As of today, her motto was: *Throw caution to the wind.*

Kristin leaned forward and waggled a finger at her. "This has something to do with Mark, doesn't it?"

Damn. "No. It's about me. I'm twenty-nine years old, in a rut twenty feet deep and a mile wide."

Kristin pushed herself up, put her hands on her hips and faced Liza, eyes sparkling. "It's about Mark."

Liza exhaled in defeat. "Fine. If it makes you feel better, I admit, Mark is the catalyst. But all he did was open my eyes. When he called me *practical and predictable*, it made me realize just how boring I really am."

"Honey, that was months ago. Just because he dumped you doesn't mean he's right. The world could use a few more practical people."

"Let it be someone other than me. I'm changing my life."

"Because of Mark."

"No. Because of me. When I took that Alaskan cruise with my cousin Tess—impulsively, I might add—it made me realize something. All my life I've followed the rules, taken the safe route even when I didn't want to. And what has it gotten me? Don't answer that. It's too late for sales pitches about yesterday's life. I've thought about this for months. It's *time* to shake things up. I'm going after the kind of job I've always wanted, the kind of job I should have applied for years ago."

"You're leaving the food section," Kristin repeated, almost dumbfounded.

"Cross your fingers," Liza said airily. "There's an opening upstairs for an investigative reporter and I'm going for it. With any luck, I'll soon be saying goodbye meatballs and hello mystery."

Forty-five minutes later she was seated across a large beat-up metal desk from Bill Klein, managing editor, a paunchy and wrinkled middle-aged man who looked as if he had left investigative reporting behind years ago. While his desktop was virtually empty, fat manila files and stacks of paper covered almost every other flat surface in the room.

Behind him, high-tech laser beams shot across his black computer screen.

He hadn't cracked a smile since the interview began, hadn't seemed impressed by her resume. And now, as she watched his bald head bent over her portfolio of sample articles, it was painfully clear that he wasn't impressed by her writing either.

"You've been with the food section for seven years," he said in a monotone. "Tell me about that."

Liza cleared her throat. The job hunting websites said to sell yourself, make your experience match the skills needed for the job. Food—investigative reporting. Now *there* was a match if she'd ever seen one.

"I get story ideas from almost anywhere. I might read something that inspires a concept for a series. Or a meal in a restaurant will trigger an idea. Then my first step is—" She paused for emphasis. *"—research and investigation.* I'll look into the history of a certain dish or the uses of a particular spice. I dig in, search to find the truth, and expose it to—"

A loud screech from the interoffice buzzer on his desk phone stopped her midsentence.

Mr. Klein sighed and picked up the phone. "Yes?"

Liza shifted in her seat so she could look through the glass wall behind her at the newsroom, awash in activity. She could picture herself there, phone squeezed between shoulder and ear as she typed the finishing touches of a gripping exposé into the computer. Her heart beat a little faster. This was where the action was, the excitement, the pulse of the newspaper. She had to get this job. She just had to. This was about as far from predictable as you could get.

After a long pause, Klein said, "You tell him the deadline is nine o'clock. If he's not finished by then, the story doesn't go in. It's not a big enough scoop to hold the presses. Got that? And Mary, hold my calls, I'm doing an interview right now."

He banged the phone onto the base and shook his head. "Sorry. We're using a freelancer until we can fill this position. The guy doesn't understand the meaning of the word *deadline*."

"I've never missed a deadline in the food section. I'd bring that same conscientiousness to investigative reporting. A reporter needs to know when the story is finished. I guess it's sort of an intuitive thing." An intuitive thing? Oh, please, she needed to learn when to quit talking.

He raised an eyebrow. "Tell me, does this intuitive thing help at all when you can't get anyone to confirm information on the record that someone has leaked off the record?"

A thrill of excitement rushed through her. Never once in all her years on the food section had anyone ever had to go off the record to answer her questions. *Off the record*. Let alone talking about leaking secrets. The very thought made her all the more determined to get the job. She sat up straighter.

"I guess ... intuition would help me choose just the right persuasive argument to get the source to go on the record. Or even help me decide whether I can push that person to give me names of people to contact who could confirm the information."

She leaned forward and felt the waistband at the back of her skirt unroll a bit. "Mr. Klein, I think I could do a good job for you and I'd do whatever needs to be done to—make sure I do just that." Babbling, babbling.

He drew a long breath and sat back in his chair. "I'm sure you work hard—"

"And I can even work harder—"

"But this isn't an entry-level job. You've no experience in this type of journalism. And you're used to the pace of the food section—we've got tight deadlines. We'll get breaking news late in the afternoon and you'd have to investigate it and submit your story in a few hours." He closed her portfolio and shoved it gently toward her.

"I can do that. If you look at the back of my portfolio there are some stories I wrote for my college newspaper. They're much more investigative. I didn't start writing about food until I graduated." Her words tumbled out in a desperate rush. "My goal has always been to write about something more meaningful, something more important to life than food. Not that food isn't important to life ..." She felt her dream slipping away with her prattling.

"I need someone who can hit the ground running. And with so many seasoned journalists out of work these days because people aren't getting the paper anymore ..." He shook his head. "Well, let's just say your competition is fierce. I'm sorry." He stood, signaling the interview's end.

Liza stared at him dumbly. It was over? Her one chance to break out, change her life, prove to herself that she wasn't so predictable after all? Defeated, she lifted her portfolio off his desk and stood to shake his hand. "Thank you for talking with me," she said.

He pulled open the office door and stepped back to let her pass, then followed her out. For a brief heart-stopping moment she thought he wanted to talk with her further, then she realized his attention was focused on a man heading across the newsroom in their direction.

"Are you getting anywhere on the interview with Dear Cordelia?" Klein asked when the reporter neared.

Liza hesitated, curious. Dear Cordelia, the advice columnist? She bent over a nearby drinking fountain and let the water run over her lips, swallowing every now and then so it looked as if she was actually taking a drink—a very long one. The back of her waistband unrolled a little more.

"Nope," came the reply. "Can't get near her. What a recluse. Her publicist says she doesn't want publicity. Just wants to be left alone to write her column and help people find *true love*. So if that's true, what does she need a publicist for?"

"True love for me would happen on the day she finally grants us an interview."

"At this rate, we won't have it by Valentine's Day ... and you know I'll be off for two weeks—"

"Yeah, yeah. Hell, let it rest until you're back from your honeymoon."

Still bent over the water fountain, Liza tipped her head slightly and watched Mr. Klein step back into his office. She straightened and dabbed at the water that trickled over her lower lip and down her chin. Reaching one hand behind her back, she surreptitiously rerolled her waistband to even out her skirt length.

So, he wanted an interview with Dear Cordelia, the purveyor of advice about romance and marriage, the author of the bestselling *Dear Cordelia's Authoritative Guide to Finding Love and Keeping It Alive*.

Well, well. This certainly presented possibilities. The practical, predictable person would go back to her office and write a story on the many uses of the lowly tortilla. Right. And Mr. Klein had already made it clear she belonged in the food section—not in investigative reporting. Uh-huh. She knew where her place was, where her skills were valued.

Before she could second guess herself, she spun on her heel and marched back into his office. "Mr. Klein?"

He raised his head; surprise flickered across his face.

"I couldn't help overhearing the conversation you just had ... about Dear Cordelia?"

He looked at her, silent, and a heat wave of mortification swept over her. She pushed forward.

"I love her column. I've been reading it for years."

He lifted an eyebrow.

"What I'm trying to say is ... I'd like to—I could—I mean —how about letting me try to get the interview for you?" The words rushed out of her, not at all professional like the websites advised. "I could do it on spec, to show you my investigative abilities, while that other reporter is on vacation. If I don't succeed, he can take over where I leave off."

The corners of his mouth twitched, the first sign all morning that she'd made any type of impression at all. Great. He was going to laugh at her.

"What about your responsibilities for the food section?"

Oh. "Well, you know ... vacation," she blurted out. "The new year just started. I could—I've got two weeks—I could take them off now to track down Dear Cordelia and get the interview." She mentally winced. Showing desperation was a definite no-no in the job hunting book.

He steepled his fingers. "I've been trying to get an interview with Dear Cordelia for ten years. She's never, by the way, given an interview to anyone, anywhere. In all my years of reporting, this is the only story I never got. I've assigned a dozen reporters at various times to get an interview with Cordelia. And everyone has failed."

Her heart dropped into her stomach.

"In other words, Liza Dunnigan, what makes you think you can succeed where nobody else could?"

Because this is the most impulsive thing I've ever done

in my life and if I don't try, then Mark is right about me. "Because I want this interview as much as you do," she said. "Because if I succeed, we agree that you'll hire me for the investigative reporter position, which is really what I want." Good God, did she just say what she heard herself say?

A slow grin slid across his face. He threw back his head and laughed. "Kid, you just might have what it takes."

"I know I can do it." She gripped the handle of her portfolio tightly to keep her hands from shaking at the enormity of her lie. Any moment the ceiling was going to open and a lightning bolt would shoot down from above and take her out.

Close the sale, the book said. *Ask for the job.* "Do we have a deal?"

"Oh, what the hell." He reached a hand across the desk and she grasped it with her own. "Deal. Let's go get the file so you can get up to speed on the first lady of the lovelorn, Dear Cordelia."

2

"You've got to be kidding me." Jack Graham shifted the telephone to his other ear and spun his chair round so he could stare out the window at the gray, blustery January afternoon. Today was one of those days that earned Chicago the nickname, the Windy City. "The caretaker kicked off before the dog?"

"Happened yesterday morning," Diane Cooper, his grandmother's neighbor, said with precision. "Heart attack right after church in the parking lot. Like the good Lord just didn't want Billy to leave, wanted to call him home right then and there. I'll go feed CJ and let her out, but you know I can't bring her over here. I have allergies ... and at my age even allergies can be dangerous."

Just what he needed—one more damn thing to take care of. Halfway across the country, in Maine no less. *Happy Monday*. He sighed.

As a publicist, he always had one fire or another to put out. And on top of all his usual work, next week he had an appointment with a wide receiver for the Chicago Bears who wanted to talk about Jack becoming his agent.

Representing this guy would be a huge step toward realizing a dream he'd had since college.

Except, the dog's caretaker had died. And now—hold the presses, stop the train—he had to drop everything and go to Maine to find a new caretaker for his late grandmother's basset hound.

"Jack? Are you still there? Did you say something? Speak up—I don't hear so well anymore. What do you want me to do? You'll be coming out, won't you?" Diane asked.

Guilt washed through him; his grandmother had loved that dog. She'd taken it in as a mangy, moth-eaten stray and given it a home—just like she'd done over the years with so many other dogs and cats, and a little boy named Jack. Before she died three years ago, she'd set up a trust fund to cover the cost of a caretaker for CJ so the dog could live out the rest of her days in her home.

"Uh, yeah, I'm here. Can you keep taking care of CJ for a few days? I have to clear my calendar, then I'll get out there as soon as I can."

"At some point, Billy's daughter is going to want to get his stuff."

"Maybe she'll want the job," he said hopefully.

"Hmmph. I know you always *see* her when you come back. And it's none of my business who you hire, but she's got all those boys—four wild—"

"Right. Forget I said it. Just let her in if she wants to pick up his things before I get there." He paused, thinking.

It had been hard enough to find the guy who took the job three years ago. Now, who the hell was going to want to take care of a fat, old, shedding, slobbering basset hound that had one bulging eye from glaucoma?

"You know it might speed things up if ... Can you put an ad on Craig's List for me? Something like ... *Live-in caretaker needed for twelve-year-old basset hound. Single person preferred. If interested, leave message at ..."* He paused, wondering if he could get Diane to field the calls.

"Craig's List? I can call the shopper paper and put something in the classifieds but I've never used Craig's—"

"Yeah, okay. You do the shopper, I'll set up Craig's List. Put in my phone number as the contact."

Jack's new administrative assistant stepped into the room and dropped a note on his desk, smiling prettily in her clingy little sweater and short skirt. He grinned back at her. She might be a bit light on gray matter, but she sure improved the office scenery. Maybe he should take her with him to Maine to interview candidates. They could call it a business retreat.

As she strolled gracefully from his office, he gave his head a shake. Not a good idea. Years ago, he'd given himself a rule to live by—never get involved with employees. Too much risk that the woman would learn more about him than anyone needed to know. If that ever happened, he stood to lose way too much—his income, his lifestyle, his reputation, his future.

He finished up the call with Diane, setting the phone back in its cradle as he scanned the note. A reporter from the *Chicago Sentinel* had called asking for an interview with Cordelia. This was the third call from that guy in as many weeks. He was just one of several reporters who had called.

"Not going to happen," he muttered, crumbling the paper into a ball and tossing it in his garbage can.

The month before Valentine's Day always brought the most requests for interviews with Cordelia. As her publicist, all the requests came to him. After so many years of turning them down, he'd have thought the media would have accepted that Cordy just didn't give interviews. Instead, the clamor seemed to be increasing.

"The worst thing you can do is run from the media," he said aloud, repeating the advice he typically gave other clients. Unfortunately, that advice didn't help in this situation at all.

Because Cordelia didn't exist.

He'd started the damn column himself in a local shopper paper to make some extra money in college. His grandmother's dog, Cordelia Jane, had provided his nom de plume—and he'd named himself Cordelia's publicist. Dear Cordelia had been a short-term financial solution—not a career plan.

But the column had taken off. A bestselling book followed. The more successful he got, the more important it became to make sure no one learned that Cordelia was a man. So he'd doubled down on his efforts to roadblock the media, and shoved his dream of being a sports agent into a dark corner.

Until now.

After ten years as Cordelia, he'd finally begun to go after his original goal. In the last year he'd become the agent for a couple of up and coming athletes. Now he just had to build his clientele until he was doing well enough that Cordy could quietly retire. He didn't want to risk the truth ever getting out, didn't want to take the chance that athletes might not want to be represented by him because they were afraid a guy who wrote a column for the lovelorn wouldn't be a tough enough at contract negotiations.

He walked over to the window to watch Mother Nature bluster outside as she tried to make it snow. In order to go to Maine, he'd have to reschedule his appointment with that football player.

As for the rest of his business, he could easily handle everything via cell phone from Maine for a week or two. His primary work still involved writing the column, and he was behind on that because he'd been putting so much energy into building his sports agenting business. At least in Maine he'd have no excuses not to get the column written.

Exhaling slowly, he headed out of his office to tell his assistant to book him a flight.

———

"Mr. Graham is out for two weeks?" Liza said into the phone as her voice rose several notches. She stared at her computer screen, still showing the home page of Jack Graham's business website.

"He may be back sooner, but it's too early to tell," his assistant said. She sounded very young. "Unless it's an emergency, you'll have to check back in a couple of weeks."

Liza would have stammered if only she could think of something to say. The man she needed to get to, had gone out of town during the two weeks she had to get to him?

"This *is* an emergency—in a sense," she blurted, mentally searching for an emergency that might help her learn where Graham had gone. She spewed out the first idea that came to mind. "You see, I'm on the class reunion committee and I need to talk to Jack as soon as possible. He volunteered to, ah—"

"Oh my God, what a coincidence. Are you calling from Coldwater?"

Coldwater? Coldwater, where? What was the right answer? She gambled. "Yes, I am."

The woman laughed. "I don't think he'll mind if I tell you—that's where he is too. He flew out this morning."

"Really? Oh, that's great. Could I get his cell number so I can call him?"

"I'm really sorry, I can't give that out. He'd kill me. But if you go knock on his grandma's door, you can talk to him in person."

Shit. "Good idea." She quickly Googled *city of Coldwater*. Damn, there were twenty-five in the United States. "I can't wait to see him again," she said, stalling. "You're sure I can find him at his grandma's?"

"He'll be there until everything is ... settled," the assistant said firmly in her very young voice.

Liza held herself back from asking what he was settling. She didn't want to cause any red flags to go up. "Okay. I guess ... I'll run over there. So, it's been a while, not sure I remember where—"

"I'd wait a little longer. He was flying into Bangor and renting a car. He's probably not there yet."

Liza let out a quiet exhale. Bangor? Bangor, Maine? Her fingers flew over the keyboard Google searching for Bangor. Please let there be only one Bangor in—

Her heart dropped. *Ten.* There were ten Bangors in the country. Seriously? What was wrong with people, couldn't they come up with original names in the olden days?

She decided to go for broke. "So, is Jack in Maine yet or still in the air?"

"Probably getting his rental car right now."

A smile burst across Liza's face. Bingo! Voicing thanks, she ended the call and drummed her fingers happily on her desk in celebration of overcoming her first investigative challenge. Jack Graham was in Coldwater, Maine.

Shit. She dropped her head into her hands. Jack

Graham was in Coldwater, Maine. For the next two weeks. And she had no way of reaching him.

How could this be happening? She'd never get an interview with Cordelia if she couldn't talk to the woman's publicist. At this rate, she'd be trapped in the food section for the rest of her life.

A desperate breath slid out of her. She had two weeks off. And she had two choices. Either give up on the story right now or go to Coldwater herself.

She lifted her head and stared at her Word of the Day desk calendar. Today she'd fully expected to make her first contact with Jack Graham, maybe even set up an appointment for next week. So much for advance planning.

Now the only way she'd get this assignment done would be if she tracked him down in Coldwater—admittedly one of the more impractical ideas that had ever popped into her head. Maybe even edging beyond impractical and into insane.

She mentally checked off all the reasons she shouldn't go to Maine. She didn't have the money for the trip, she'd never actually done a real investigation like this, and there was no guarantee she would connect with the man even if she went to Coldwater.

Her gaze landed on her desk calendar again:

Word of the Day: *Myopic.*

1: affected by nearsightedness

2: lacking in foresight or discernment: limited in outlook.

· · ·

Yeah, well, that certainly fit. If she were the superstitious type, she might be able to interpret it as a sign she should definitely go to Maine.

Or not.

If only she had more guts.

Her cousin, Tess, wouldn't even think twice about going. She'd been brave enough to start a personal shopping business in San Francisco. And how about Annie, her cousin up in Wisconsin? She was an entrepreneur, too, running her own bed & breakfast.

"What's the matter?" Kristin strolled up to her desk. "You've got two weeks off for a trial run of your dream job. Why the long face?"

"Dear Cordelia's publicist left for Coldwater, Maine this morning. For two weeks."

Kristin dropped into the chair beside her desk. "Ouch. No contact with the publicist means no interview, which means no new job."

"What do you think about me following him there?"

"And then what? Chase him around town and ask for Dear Cordelia's phone number?"

Liza rolled her eyes. "I could, ah, meet him, somehow. Kind of *undercover*. He's single. I'm single. We meet, *accidentally*. Then I could—put on the charm. We make plans to get together again. Maybe have coffee, go to a movie. Days pass. One thing leads to another, we meet for dinner. Soon, he's putty in my hands and sharing information that, unbeknownst to him, helps me track down Cordelia on my own. Voilà, mission accomplished."

"Let me make sure I have this straight. Liza Dunnigan, the woman who until quite recently referred to herself as practical and predictable, is going to go undercover to beguile Jack Graham, eligible man about Chicago, commonly referred to as a *player*, all to get an interview with Dear Cordelia?"

Liza lifted her chin. "You think I can't? Seems to me the only way to catch a player is to get in the game."

Kristin let out a laugh. "This new Liza is beginning to surprise me."

She wasn't the only one. Liza exhaled slowly. She could almost hear the pragmatic side of her brain lecturing: *Who are you kidding? You never put the moves on guys. And now you're going to do it to further your career?*

And why not? This was her chance, her one chance to prove she was more than just a woman who never broke the rules, more than just a woman who did everything exactly the way she was supposed to. Her new motto was *throw caution to the wind*. She wasn't going to blow it now.

3

JACK STARED ACROSS THE DINING-ROOM TABLE AT THE woman he was interviewing for the caretaker's job. She'd seemed promising on the phone and even more perfect once he saw her—tall, leggy, big green eyes and long, wavy red hair. Definitely his kind of woman.

Except, the more she opened her mouth, the more this third candidate was looking like strike three.

He'd been heartened to get seven calls about the job, and ultimately four people to interview about in living in his late grandmother's house and taking care of an old basset hound. It was certainly more than he'd expected for a town with a population of two thousand, four hundred. When he'd called each of the candidates back and explained the situation, all four expressed continued interest. Another good sign.

Which brought him to today and the interviews. Billy had died almost a week ago and Jack needed to find a new caretaker quickly. After so many days of living in the house alone, CJ had been starved for affection when he arrived. Diane had been great about coming over to feed her and let her out, but that wasn't a long-term solution. The answer was, one of these applicants had to work out.

Things weren't looking promising, however. Candidate number one arrived for the interview reeking of cigarette smoke—and Grandma's will had been specific about the caretaker being a nonsmoker. Candidate number two, after sounding promising on the phone, had spent most of the interview talking about remodeling the house.

Jack let his gaze drift around the 1920s home. Tall windows filled the rooms with sunlight. Wide oak crown moldings and baseboards framed the ceilings and oak floors, which were set off by old Oriental rugs. Nothing wrong with this old place—it was comfortable, lived in. *Homey*. Plus, it came completely furnished—from the furniture to the dishes to the linens. This was the perfect situation for ... someone.

Unfortunately, candidate number three, now sitting across the dining table from him, was not looking like that person.

"You have two cats?" he asked. He looked in confusion at his notes from the telephone calls. "Did you mention that on the phone?"

She shook her head sending her red hair rippling around her face. "You asked if I had any other pets. And I don't. I have two sisters. They just happen to be cats in this life."

O-kay. Definitely strike three. Jack nodded and scratched her comments on the paper next to her name. "I'll just mark that down here." He looked at her a moment, debating whether to ask the question burning in his mind. He knew he really should end the interview, but what the hell? "Any ... brothers?"

"Three."

He knew it. "Cats too?"

The woman leaned forward eagerly. "One actually was born a human in this life. But the other two are birds. Isn't that interesting?"

"Extremely."

"Because my sisters were born cats and my brothers were born birds. And you know, cats are predators toward birds, so it can create some real problems."

Jack stared at her, simultaneously fascinated and dumbfounded. "Especially at family get-togethers, I would imagine."

"You have no idea. I'm starting to wonder whether we should all go in together for counseling."

Jack nodded. "Where are your bird—ah—brothers?"

"Oh, they live with me."

Of course. He looked at his watch, then tapped it with his finger for emphasis. "We've gone a little long," he said. "So, we'll have to wrap it up—I've got another interview in just a few minutes. Thanks for coming." He stood, still talking so she couldn't try to keep the conversation going. "It's been great meeting you. I've got your number ... and I'll give you a call once I've made a decision." He walked her to the door and watched as she drove away, two cats sleeping in the rear window. They must be her sisters. He shook his head. He'd lied just to get her out of here—the next candidate wasn't due for another half hour.

CJ lay on her side in a patch of sunshine on the hardwood floor, sound asleep. He sat beside the old basset hound and ran a hand over her head and plump body, over the black and tan patches of short silky hair dotted with flakes of dandruff. She thumped her tail on the floor. Jack petted her flabby underbelly.

"Poor old dog. You wouldn't be so bad except for that

eye," he said. "Maybe an eye patch would help—make you look sort of dashing." He rubbed CJ's graying muzzle and she slurped his hand with a sloppy kiss. This dog was all gentleness. "You good old pupper. Don't worry. I'll find someone to take care of you. Someone normal. Someone who likes you just the way you are."

He frowned at the dandruff and brushed it away. No need to have too many obvious flaws for the next interviewee to see. He hoped she was a halfway decent, because otherwise today's interviews were a bust and he would have to start over.

This one had to be better than the last women. Now that he thought about it, even the first two candidates no longer seemed so bad once he compared them to the third one. Maybe he should quit being so picky. After all, the dog didn't care if there was cigarette smoke in the house. And if someone wanted to redecorate a little and paint the walls, well, truth be told, the place was looking a little rough anyway.

Still sitting on the floor, Jack rested his back against the wall. Maybe he'd been too businesslike in the interviews. Not open minded enough. He had to admit, as soon as he learned something he didn't like about a candidate, he'd immediately ruled them out.

He could almost hear his grandmother admonishing him to loosen up. *Don't miss out on making personal connections. Every person is just navigating life the best they can,* she would say. Stuff like that came out of her mouth a lot. "Okay, Gram, criticism noted. I'll take a new approach," he muttered. "I'll be friendlier, open-minded, and more willing to compromise."

The doorbell chimed and he glanced at his watch. Fifteen minutes early—a good sign. He appreciated promptness. He pushed himself to his feet and shuffled through the papers on the table to find his notes on the next interviewee. First name: Elizabeth, a nice classic name. Hopefully she was just a nice classic person.

———

Liza waited on the front porch of the large bungalow that used to belong to Jack Graham's grandmother and stared at the door knocker engraved with the name *Graham*. Shifting nervously, she tugged at the collar of her short down jacket and sucked in a breath of cold winter air to calm the pounding of her heart. This investigative reporting stuff took nerves of steel.

She drew in a deep breath. As soon as Jack Graham answered the door, she would put into action the plan she and Kristin had concocted. Earlier in the week, they'd used the newspaper's resources and the Internet to search out information about Jack's grandmother. It hadn't taken long to learn she'd died three years ago and that Jack now owned her house. Based on his assistant's comment on the phone, that he wouldn't be back until something had been settled, they'd quickly decided he must have gone to Coldwater to put the house on the market. It was as good a reason as any other they could come up with.

Granted, it was a little odd that he'd waited three years to sell. But some people took longer to grieve than others— maybe he'd wanted to hold onto the house until he had some sort of closure after her death. Or maybe he was selling to get closure. Who cared? The most important thing was, she had found a way to meet and engage with him.

And, she was dressed to catch him.

Kristin had taken her on a clothes-shopping spree like

she'd never been on before, during which they'd FaceTimed Tess in San Francisco for her personal shopper opinions. Out had gone the mantra she'd heard all her life from her mother: *classic shows class.* And in had come a new one: *fashion before comfort.* She'd never had so many pieces of clothing that were fashionable—and figure flattering—in her life. A finger of cool air slid across her lower back and she reached under her jacket to tug her sweater down over the top of her new jeans.

After a long minute of waiting, she took hold of the knocker and pounded it four times. Twenty degrees outside and her palms were sweating. She hoped he didn't want to shake hands.

She blinked hard a couple of times, as though the movement would clear away her panic and stop the question that was looping continuously through her brain: *What in the hell am I doing?* Every muscle in her arms and legs was tight. She squeezed her hands into fists and slowly opened her fingers in an effort to calm herself.

Why was she so nervous? She and Kristin had rehearsed this moment multiple times. As soon as Jack came to the door, all she had to say was that she'd heard his house was going on the market and she was interested in buying it. That little white lie would enable her to meet him. And meeting him was the first important step to getting an interview with Cordelia.

With any luck, Jack would invite her in for a quick tour. But in case he didn't, she and Kristin had brainstormed other ways to get a foot in the door, so to speak. Car trouble, needing directions, or frostbitten fingers—which was why she wasn't wearing mittens right now. She blew on her fingers. If the guy didn't hurry up and answer the door soon, she actually would have frostbite.

Exhaling slowly, she watched her breath drift away like a piece of steamy lace. She scrunched her shoulders up and down a couple of times to generate some heat. What if he wasn't home?

Just as she was about to give up, the heavy front door swung open. Jack Graham stood in the doorway in blue jeans, a ski sweater, and thick rag wool socks without shoes.

Her stomach flopped. In photographs, he always seemed moderately good-looking in a posed, self-assured sort of way. In person, he was—she had to hold herself back from gulping—ruggedly handsome. Tall. Brown hair, casually mussed. Hazel eyes.

What had ever made her think she could seduce Jack Graham into arranging an interview with Dear Cordelia? Men like him never gave women like her a second glance. Failure lodged a knot in her throat so big she couldn't speak Maybe she should just say, *Sorry, wrong house,* and run back to her car, back to her job, back to her predictable life.

And then, he grinned—oh God, what a grin, no wonder he was a player—and reached out to shake her hand. No man should be allowed to have a grin like that.

"Hi. I'm Jack Graham. Come on in." He stepped back to let her enter the house.

Come on in? She had no idea why he was inviting her in, but she was damn well going to make the most of it. Maybe these new clothes brought out an allure she didn't even know she had. She swallowed the lump and drew a breath—short and shaky, but at least there was oxygen moving into her lungs. No sense in passing out right after she'd made it through the door.

"I'm Liza. I'm here about the house," she said, mentally cringing at how she'd boiled down her carefully prepared statement to five cryptic words.

"Liza." He smiled like he knew her already. "Good to meet you."

She tried not to gape. She and Kristin must have been right—the house was for sale. Maybe they'd hit the jackpot with their advance planning. "Sure. I mean, good to meet you too."

He motioned at an old-fashioned coat tree in the corner. "You can hang your jacket there, then have a seat at the dining room table. Give me just a minute—I was going to get a water. Would you like one?" He lay an incredible smile on her that warmed her to the toes of her oh-so-stylish boots. She wasn't sure she could even answer the man—no guy who ever looked like him ever smiled at her like that.

More *maybes* filled her mind. Maybe this would all be easier than she'd expected. Maybe, now that she was an investigative reporter—with hot new clothes—she had some sort of aura that men found attractive. Maybe she'd been settling for guys like Mark, when all along she could have had guys like *Jack Graham.* The thought made her dizzy.

She settled into one of the dining-room chairs and tried to strike an appealing, open, seductive, friendly, trustworthy pose. Cordelia's book had said body language was so important. She shifted to the right and left, crossed her legs and uncrossed them, leaned an elbow on the table, then two elbows, then neither. She was still working out the details when Jack set a glass of water in front of her on the lace tablecloth and dropped into the opposite seat.

She froze. Ohmigod, please don't let him have noticed her extensive posturing.

4
_____

WARMTH CREPT UP HER CHEEKS, AND SHE REACHED for the glass just to have something to do. Ice popped in the water, startling them both and breaking the tension.

Jack laughed. "I'll start. That's CJ She was my grandmother's dog." He pointed at a roly-poly basset hound napping on her back in the sun under a big window, her floppy ears out to each side, like wings on the hardwood floor.

At the sound of her name, CJ roused and ambled over to say hello. Liza patted the dog's head. "Hi, CJ"

"I guess it's safe to assume you like dogs."

"Ah, yeah, actually, I do." Her smile faded at the sight of CJ's bulging eye, and she glanced at Jack.

"Glaucoma," he said. "My grandmother didn't notice it coming on and now she's blind in that eye. The vet says it doesn't hurt, so we just leave it alone ... I know it's ugly, but she's a really good dog."

"She has the most woeful expression." Liza ran a hand down CJ's neck, then turned her attention back to Jack. This was certainly an interesting home tour—water at the dining-room table and a discussion about the dog's glaucoma. Well, as long as she was inside the house and actually talking with Jack Graham, she wouldn't complain. She was already much further along than she had hoped to be fifteen minutes ago. She searched for something to say to build upon their camaraderie. "How old is she?"

"Twelve. Probably not too many years left."

CJ ambled over to her water dish in the corner for a drink. With each lap of her tongue, water slobbered out the sides of her mouth and splattered onto the dark wood floor.

Jack frowned. "Bassets are sort of naturally sloppy. When she drinks, it can get pretty messy. I hope that doesn't bother you."

Bother her? Why would she care whether his late grandmother's dog was a sloppy drinker? She was buying the house, not the basset hound.

He seemed a little fixated on the dog. Maybe he was really struggling with letting go. She could only imagine all the conflicting emotions he must be feeling over selling his grandmother's house. Once the house was gone, CJ might be his last remaining connection with her. It totally explained why, so far, he'd only talked about the dog and hadn't offered to show her around.

"I really like this house, the big front porch. Lots of curb appeal. Is there much of a backyard?" she asked as chirpily as she dared without sounding like a ditz.

He nodded. "Big enough for a dog, but it's not huge. An easy size to mow in the summer and rake in the fall." He glanced out the window. "And the driveway's short, so not much to shovel when it snows. The only other thing is ... it's always important to clean the gutters out in the fall and make sure the downspouts are attached. Since it's such an old house, it's good to keep water away from the foundation —to prevent leaks into the basement."

Jack Graham was obviously having trouble letting go of the family homestead. She felt a pang of sympathy. No wonder he hadn't put the house on the market for three years; the place was probably filled with wonderful memories. She gave him an understanding smile. "Do you mind if I look around a little?"

"Sure." He eyed her closely, as though appraising her in some way, but didn't make a move to stand. "So you live near UMaine right now?"

The University? She shook her head, a bit confused. Time to put the rest of her plan into action. She drew a breath for courage. "No, I'm new to town. I'm joining the staff of the Maine Culinary Institute over in Orono, so I'm just moving here." She swallowed hard and dove into another lie. "I've always wanted to live in a small town and decided this was the perfect opportunity."

He gave his head a shake. "I must be mixing you up with someone else. I thought you already lived in Bangor. Well, no matter. The commute to Orono won't be bad at all," he said. "You'd have time to let CJ out in the morning or even go for a walk. She gets a walk every day—fifteen or twenty minutes or so. She's getting slower but still gets around."

What was he talking about? Her brain started to race. Maybe he wasn't selling after all—maybe he was renting. But, no, that couldn't be right because he kept talking about the dog. He wouldn't expect a renter to take in his grandmother's dog ... would he? Maybe he was moving to Coldwater himself and looking for a roommate, one who would be willing help out with the dog.

Omigod, if that was the case, maybe she could move in

with Jack Graham, become his good friend, and surreptitiously discover how to contact Cordelia. As long as it all happened in the next two weeks.

"I like walking ..." she said slowly as red flags waved in her head. Something wasn't right. Jack Graham was too successful to need a roommate to share expenses. Even if he did, it was hard to believe he'd ever have to advertise for one. And then there was the way he'd acted at the door—way too friendly. He'd invited her right in—what was that about?

Practical and predictable. Mark's words echoed in her head, reminding her that being practical also made her overly cautious.

So Jack Graham had quirks. He was probably nothing compared to the types of people she'd have to deal with once she became a full-time investigative reporter. She might as well get used to it now. Besides, she didn't have a choice. Jack had the information she needed. He was the gatekeeper to Dear Cordelia. And Dear Cordelia was a requirement to her achieving her dreams.

"Actually, I love walking. In fact—" She jumped to her feet. "How about if you walk me around the inside of the house—I'd love to see more of it."

He stood. "Sure."

The doorbell chimed and Jack tossed her an apologetic look before striding across the room to open the door. She could hear the low murmur of conversation. After a moment, Jack stepped back to let a skinny, blond-haired young woman in torn blue jeans into the house. She couldn't be any older than nineteen.

Jack turned to Liza, his brows drawn together. "Are you here for the dog?"

"I'm here for the house."

"Yes, but the dog goes with the house. You can't have one without the other."

Now, *this* was a new sales twist. Or rental twist. Or roommate twist. *Whatever.* "Oh." She nodded as though she understood what was going on even though she had no idea.

Jack grimaced. "I'm a little ... confused. Did you call me on the phone?"

"No. I just knocked on the front door."

"And your name is—"

"Liza."

"Isn't that short for Elizabeth?" he asked, exasperation in his voice.

"It could be. But I'm not an Elizabeth. My mother didn't like nicknames—said they were pointless. I'm just plain Liza." Probably more information than he needed.

"Plain Liza," he repeated.

She bit her lip. Practical, predictable, and now ... plain? She didn't know if he'd intended to insult her, but she was getting sick of people putting labels on her. "No, not really," she began, but Jack had already turned his attention to the girl.

"You're the Elizabeth who called me," he said.

She nodded and looked around the room. "This place is awesome. How many bedrooms does it have? I can't remember if I mentioned I have three roommates." She peeked into the kitchen.

"No, you didn't mention—"

"Totally great. There's so much room. You said the furniture stays, right? We have a couch already, but not as nice as this one. We could put ours on the front porch—"

"And the dog?" Jack asked in a strained voice.

"Oh we love dogs. He'll be great." The girl bent over CJ

and gave a little wave. "Hi, puppy. We like dogs—all of us do."

CJ opened her eyes and clambered to her feet.

"*Oh. Oh.* What's wrong with his eye?" Elizabeth took a step back.

Jack's expression didn't change. "Glaucoma." He smiled at Liza. "Uh, Elizabeth, I'm sorry to tell you ... the position has been filled."

"Already? Are you sure?"

"I'm sure. Thanks for coming. I'll be in touch if the other person doesn't work out."

She looked around the room, up the walls and across the ceiling. "Okay, well, keep me in mind, because we really would, um, take good care of that old dog."

Jack shut the door behind her and turned to face Liza. "I'm sorry. When you said your name was Liza, I just assumed it was short for Elizabeth and that you were the person who called."

"That's okay. So, the dog comes with the house?"

He nodded. "More like the house comes with the dog."

"How does that get written into a sales contract?"

"Sales contract? I'm not selling the house—I'm looking for a caretaker for the dog."

Liza looked at CJ. The dog wagged her tail. "I thought the house was for sale."

"And I thought you were applying for the job." He grinned in a way that made her start thinking about things other than investigative reporting.

Her stomach flopped and she smiled back at him. "So you're looking for someone to live here and take care of the dog?"

He nodded. "It's in my grandmother's will. CJ gets to stay in the house, with a caretaker, until she dies. The man who had the job the last three years passed away last week." His face took on a hopeful look. "You wouldn't, by any chance, be interested in becoming a caretaker instead of a homeowner?"

Her mind raced forward. If she took the job, Jack would return to Chicago and she'd be stuck in Coldwater with no way to get at the information she needed to track down Dear Cordelia. On the other hand, if she turned down the job, he'd just hire someone else and go back to Chicago, and she would still be no closer to uncovering Dear Cordelia's contact information.

She'd have to go home in defeat. Once they were both back in Chicago, she couldn't very well call Jack and ask for an interview with Cordelia, not after lying about her profession, and about wanting to move to a small town— Coldwater, and about wanting to buy a house. He'd just hang up on her. And rightfully so.

She cocked her head. Somehow she had to slow this down, drag it out, figure out a way to keep him in Coldwater until she got the info she needed. "I might be interested. Do I have to decide today?" Omigod, she didn't know the first thing about caring for a dog—she'd never had one.

His mouth pressed into a straight line. "No, but the sooner the better. I really need to get this settled."

"This is such a different direction than I'd planned. I —I need some time to think about it. The responsibility and all ... of having a dog." She looked at CJ and pretended to consider the idea. If she was going to pull this off, she'd better find out something about dog care. And her cousin Annie was just the person to ask—she had a dog since she was a kid. "So the caretaker lives here ... free? Utilities included? In exchange for taking care of the dog?"

"That about covers it. Shovel the sidewalks, mow the lawn, rake the leaves."

She nodded. This had the potential to be even more beneficial to the cause than landing a date with Jack Graham. All she had to do was take her time making a decision, string him along, and play her cards right.

If only she knew how to play this game of cards.

She couldn't wait to get back to the inn and call Kristin to tell her everything that had happened—and get some advice.

Knocking on the front door drew both their attention. "Another candidate?" Liza asked.

Jack rolled his eyes. "You were the last one. Or rather, Elizabeth was."

He crossed the room but the door opened before he got to it. A tall, slender woman with short-cropped, blond-streaked hair stepped toward them, smiling at Jack like someone who knew him well. "Welcome back, stranger," she said, opening her arms.

"Ashley. How are you?" Jack reached out and the two embraced, their mouths meeting in a kiss that was definitely more than platonic. "I'm sorry about your dad," he murmured.

Ashley nodded and put a hand on his chest.

What was this? A firsthand look at *a woman in every port?* Hmm. Ashley could cause a little trouble in the *beguile Jack to get information about Cordelia* department. Then again, maybe not. If she remembered the Chicago rumor mill correctly, Jack had been known to juggle multiple women.

Liza watched, fascinated, as the two pulled back slightly to have a soft conversation. All Jack's focus was on Ashley and all hers was on him, each of them seemingly oblivious to anything outside their immediate circle. She felt a twinge of envy, wished that just once in her life a guy would make her feel like nothing in the world mattered except her.

Suddenly, four children piled through the doorway, arms laden with empty cardboard boxes, their vision obscured by other boxes upside down on their heads. They charged into the room, blindly banging into one another and falling to the floor, laughing hysterically. The smallest dropped the box in his hands, pulled the one off his head and threw it, giggling when it hit the window. He looked to either side, then charged into the dining room and hurled himself onto the floor beside CJ The dog rolled to her feet and ambled away as the kid wiggled across the floor behind her, repeatedly calling her name.

Liza felt dazed. Four boys. She'd never seen so much chaos in one spot in her life.

Ashley stepped away from Jack and clapped her hands together several times. "Boys! That's enough!" She glanced at Jack. "I thought we'd better pack up some of my dad's things and take them to Goodwill." Her gaze lit on Liza for the first time. "Unless you're busy."

The boys tumbled into one another sending boxes across the floor and smacking into walls and furniture. One boy stumbled back against Jack, almost knocking him over. Liza watched, awestruck.

"I'm just interviewing candidates for the caretaker post," Jack said.

Ashley's eyes grew round. "Interviews? I was thinking maybe I would take over Daddy's job. This house would be fine for me and the boys—"

"Uh yeah, how old are they now?" Jack took a step back.

"Well, you can see they're getting big. Eleven, ten, nine, and Jake over there's seven."

"Wow. And you want to be CJ's caretaker, too, huh?" He turned and looked at Jake who was once again writhing across the floor on his belly in pursuit of CJ The dog lumbered into the kitchen.

"The boys got to know CJ while Daddy was living here. They love her. They were over here all the time. Won't be like anything's changed for that old hound dog."

"So that's what happened to the walls," Jack muttered.

"What?" Ashley asked.

"Calls," Jack said hastily. "Just thinking about all the applicant calls I have to return."

He caught Liza's eyes with his own, and she knew he was begging her to agree to take the job. But much as she wanted to help him out, she couldn't. As soon as she said yes, he'd fly back to Chicago. And she couldn't let that happen yet.

Ashley took a step toward Jack and smiled, tilting her chin downward to look up at him flirtatiously. "Shoot, Jack, this'd be perfect. Anytime you want to come home to visit, you can stay here with us."

He nodded and raised one hand. "The thing is, I didn't know you were interested ... and I've already offered the job already to—Liza—uh—uh—"

"Dunnigan," she said.

"Liza Dunnigan."

Ashley stepped around him and looked from one to the other, her smile fading. The boys stopped jostling one another and fell silent, as if suddenly aware of a change in the room's tone.

"You're going to be the caretaker?" Ashley asked.

Liza felt a prickle at the back of her neck. Poor CJ didn't deserve to live with this woman and her four hellions. She opened her mouth to retort *yes* and stopped herself just in time. "I haven't decided yet," she said with decisiveness.

Ashley's mouth went tight.

"Hey Ashley, why don't you get started with the packing," Jack said in a pacifying voice. He slung an arm around her shoulder and walked her toward the staircase. "No matter who gets the job, we'll still have to move your dad's things. I'll give you a call later, and we'll get together."

Ashley smiled up at him and nodded. "Come on, boys." She headed up the stairs with the brigade behind her, five sets of feet clomping in military precision on the old oak steps.

As soon as they'd disappeared into the upstairs hall, Jack turned to Liza. "Sorry about that. I've known Ashley since high school."

"So I gathered."

He cleared his throat. "Yeah. Those kids would probably give CJ a stroke. If you take this job, it would make my life a whole lot easier."

She actually felt sorry for him. But what kind of investigative reporter would she be if she let emotion rule her decisions? She gave him an understanding smile. "I just need some time to think about it. Why don't you give me your number, and I'll let you know," she said with much more self-assurance than she felt.

5

Jack looked at the paper on which Liza had scratched her phone number and the place where she was staying—the historic Belleview Inn. The woman had excellent taste. The inn regularly landed among the top magazine picks for *discerning travelers*.

What a stroke of luck that she was moving to the area and had stopped by the house. Why anyone would want the slow pace of Coldwater was beyond him, but the fact that she did made her all the more perfect for the job. Besides that, she seemed *normal,* which was a key requirement. Plus, she liked dogs and hadn't seemed put off by CJ's many ... imperfections. And she was relatively attractive in an understated sort of way.

Oh right, *that* was critical requirement for the job. *Attractive* was undoubtedly one of the dog's most important criteria. He shook his head. *His* criteria maybe, if he were a dog.

Liza was no raving beauty, but there was something intriguing about her. Maybe it was the way her brown eyes sparkled when she spoke, or the way her light brown hair framed her face in loose waves. There had been a moment when they were standing in the living room, when he'd almost reached a hand up just to touch those waves. And then Ashley—and chaos—had bust in the front door.

Hopefully Liza wouldn't take too long to decide about the job. Because if things didn't work out with her, he'd have to start over—place another ad, wait for replies, screen the callers, conduct interviews. Either that, or offer the job to Ashley and her four bundles of chaos.

Good thing he didn't have a china shop.

Maybe when Liza said she needed time to think about the offer, what she really meant was that she was uncomfortable taking care of someone else's dog. Especially a dog with bizarre medical issues. Somehow he needed to show her that CJ was one of those dogs who grew you, so much so that soon you didn't even notice her eye or her drooling or her dandruff ...

He looked at the dog. "And the only way she's going to realize that is if she gets to know you better," he muttered. "Hell Ceej, could you turn on the charm a little? I know you can—you used to do it for Grandma."

He looked around the room, his gaze stopping at the small table by the window where his grandmother loved to work on crossword puzzles. He could still see her there, taking a break from the exercise bike she'd stuck in the middle of the living room so she wouldn't have any excuse not to ride it. He grinned. And still, she'd found excuses.

He drew a slow breath and exhaled. Sometimes he missed her so badly. Every now and then something would trigger a memory and he'd get a deep ache inside, a longing to see her just one more time, to tell her how his life was going.

Suddenly the house felt confining. He'd been inside all

day, interviewing candidates since early afternoon. What he needed was a change of scenery, to get outside and refresh in the brisk winter air. "Hey CJ, want to go for a walk?"

Five minutes later, he and the dog were crunching along the snow-covered sidewalk as the sun beat a late afternoon descent toward the horizon, delivering dusk like a gray wash. His breath curled white in the chill air and he hunched his shoulders against the cold.

"Jack! Jack Graham!"

His grandmother's neighbor waved at him from her front steps. Diane Cooper finished shaking out a throw rug, then pulled her heavy sweater close to her throat. He turned up the walk to her porch.

"How did the interviews go? Did you find someone to look after our beloved CJ?" Diane asked.

"Well, I'm—"

"I couldn't help but notice them coming and going all afternoon. That last one seemed awfully young—"

"College student. In her late teens—"

"But the one before her looked like a nice girl. And pretty, too. Not too pretty like some of those ones you date, but the kind of pretty a man should come home to. Did you give her the job?"

Jack held back a laugh. The last few years of her life, his grandmother had teamed up with Diane and another neighbor, Mary Sanderson, to find him a *nice girl*. They weren't impressed that he had no trouble getting dates with all sorts of *women* in Chicago. In fact, the more successful he got in Chicago, the more determined they seemed to find him a wife in Coldwater.

"She's thinking about it, so cross your fingers," he said. "She seems nice—you'd like her for a neighbor."

Diane narrowed her eyes. "I would?"

Jack nodded. "Pretty easy to talk to."

"You don't say." She looked at him for a long moment. "When's she going to decide by?"

"Tomorrow, hopefully. But I'm not sure. If she turns me down. I'm going to be a broken man."

Another gray-haired woman popped her head out the front door. "Hello Jack. Have you hired anyone yet?"

"Hi Mary. Not yet."

"Said one seems promising. She's easy to talk to," Diane said with a knowing nod.

Mary stepped out onto the porch. "She is? Which one? Not that last girl—"

Jack grinned at the replay of the conversation he'd just had with Diane. "No, the one before. That last one seemed pretty young—"

"That's what Diane and I said!"

"I was just going to tell Jack, maybe he should think about staying on. Do his business from Coldwater—then he could take care of Cordelia himself." Diane nodded at Mary.

"Ladies, you know I get claustrophobic if I stay here too long. It's too small a town."

Diane snorted. "It's all in your frame of mind. Now, if you were coming home every night to a pretty thing like that girl—what's her name?"

"Liza."

"If you were coming home to Liza, you wouldn't even notice where you were living."

Jack let out a laugh. The ladies had apparently decided to drop all subtlety in their quest to marry him off.

Mary wrapped her arms around her waist for warmth. "We'd better get inside before we turn into blocks of ice.

What I really came out for was to ask if you had plans for supper tonight."

"Figured I'd just hit a restaurant."

"No, no, no," Diane said.

"We'll be eating at six," Mary added. "You just come on over whenever you're ready. If you're early, we'll have a cocktail first."

"That sounds awesome. Thanks." Jack flipped up his jacket collar to cover the back of his neck and continued down the sidewalk.

As the darkness grew deeper and lights began to appear in windows, Jack admitted to himself that he was purposely taking a route past the inn where Liza Dunnigan was staying, that he had intended to do this the moment he left the house. After all, there was nothing wrong with casually running into her while he was out and about. Would give her a chance to see that CJ could be fun. He glanced down at the dog. Okay, fun might be a bit of a stretch.

He considered slowing their pace as they passed the inn, but realized that if he and his overweight basset hound walked any slower they would be standing still. Reaching the end of the block, he crossed the street and retraced his path, albeit on the other side of the road.

He stopped at the end of the next block, chagrined. So far he'd accomplished nothing he'd set out to do besides get some fresh air. He'd had no Liza sightings, no chance encounters, no opportunity to present CJ in a new light. He supposed he could walk past the inn again—night had fallen, after all, and the darkness would probably keep anyone from noticing him making a repeat tour.

———

Liza turned up the volume on her phone as she crossed her cozy French country room in the Belleview Inn. She sank into the window seat overlooking the street. "Annie gave me the lowdown on taking care of a dog," she said to Kristin. "Enough so I'll sound like I know what to say if Jack and I talk about it." She drew a breath. "But it still begs the question, what should I do about the job?"

"Nothing. Don't do a thing. Don't say yes, don't say no."

"But—"

"You have to keep him in Coldwater until you get some clues about where Cordelia is. Otherwise you're screwed. You can't just follow him to Chicago and start asking questions. How will you explain that you're there?"

"I quit the Culinary Institute?" Liza asked.

"Right. And, oh surprise, you're actually a newspaper reporter." Kristin snorted. "Liza, you show up in Chicago and Jack Graham's going to run from you as fast as he can. Your only hope of pulling this off is to keep him in Coldwater."

"It seems so disingenuous." Liza nervously pushed her hair back from her face. "I really don't like lying."

"Yeah, but what choice do you have? You said it yourself ten minutes ago. If you accept the job, he's going to leave town. If you turn down the job, he'll offer it to someone else and still leave town. The common denominator is that Jack Graham wants to leave town. Your job, then—"

"I know, I know. Is to make sure he stays in town. And the only way to do that—"

"Is to string him along about the job." Kristin sounded resolute.

Liza hesitated. "He might get a little upset when I ultimately turn down the job after all this stringing."

"Yeah, but cross that bridge another day. If you want

this story, you don't have a choice. So what are you going to say when you call him back tomorrow? Practice it on me."

Liza let out a troubled sigh. She really hoped Jack didn't hate her at the end of all this. He might be a guy who got every woman he ever wanted, but he also seemed like a decent human being. She cleared her throat and began her spiel. "Jack, I'm really interested in the job, but I'd like to get to know CJ better before making a decision. Would it be all right if I spent the next week or so getting to know the dog? I could stop by your house, spend some time with her, and take her for walks." She groaned. "I sound fake."

"No, you don't. You're fine. Just don't forget to say something about how you're concerned about her health and want to hear what the vet has to say. It'll give you a reason to postpone making a decision."

"Oh yeah."

"And that you want to talk to a groomer about her dandruff and drooling—"

"All these contingencies are going to make him think I'm too difficult. He'll rescind his offer and I won't even have a chance." Liza stretched her legs out on the window seat and rested her head against the wall.

"Okay, you're right. I'm done. So, is he as gorgeous in person as he is in pictures?"

"More. You would die if you saw his smile in real life." Liza gazed out the window at the narrow snow-covered street.

"I see. So, is he smiling a lot? At you?" Kristin teased.

"You wouldn't believe how quiet this place is compared to Chicago."

"Oh, smooth. Nice transition."

Liza laughed. "I'm serious. This street could be a picture postcard from a century ago. Picture this—night has fall, it's snowing, big white flakes falling on stately old brick homes, not a soul in sight except a guy walking his dog." She drew in a sharp breath as the man moved under a street lamp. "Kristin! Omigod!" Ducking behind the floral drape, she held one edge out to keep herself hidden, then peeked again to make sure. "Jack Graham is walking his dog down my street!"

"Do something!"

"Like what? Chase him down the street and ask for an interview with Cordelia?"

"Get out there! Hurry! Pretend you're on your way to dinner and invite him to join you."

"But I ate already."

"*Liiiza!* Go! Eat again! It's the ideal accidental meeting. The perfect step toward getting into his good graces."

"Okay, okay."

Kristin's words came fast and furious. "When you go out there, be interested in him. Smile. Look into his eyes. Touch his arm. Laugh lightly. Ask questions. Act a little coy, a little mysterious. Okay?"

"You're kidding, right?" Nerves jumped in Liza's stomach. This was uncharted territory for her. "I don't know if I can do this."

"You can. Just think of your other option—going back to the food section. Just be available—but mysterious. He's single. He's right outside your door. Come on, you can do this."

"Right. Got it. Call you later." She dashed into the bathroom to and see if she looked all right. Hell, her makeup could use a touch-up and her hair was a wavy mess, but there was no time. He'd be gone in another minute and the opportunity would be gone with him. "He's right outside," she whispered at her reflection. "My own bachelor next door."

She knew this thing with Jack Graham wasn't what her grandmother had in mind when she'd said, "*Make sure you don't search so far and wide you miss out on the bachelor next door*," but who cared? If she pretended there were possibilities, it might be easier to act *available but mysterious*. Whatever that meant. The fact that she didn't have a clue was probably the reason why men weren't falling all over themselves to go out with her.

She grabbed her jacket off the chair, pulled hat over her messy hair, shoved her feet into her boots, and ran into the hall. Mark had called her *predictable*. The door banged shut behind her and she quickly locked it with the old-fashioned key before running down the stairs and out the front door. Any way you spun it, *predictable* was not a synonym for *mysterious*. Didn't mean she couldn't do it, just meant she had to figure out how—quick.

Jack and CJ had just passed the inn. Good thing the dog's short legs meant they weren't going anywhere fast. She stared after them a moment, gathering her courage before finally calling out his name.

He turned and smiled, surprise flitting across his face. "Hi." He shifted the leash to his other hand. "What are you doing here?"

6

"THIS IS WHERE I'M STAYING." SHE LOOKED UP AT the inn.

"I know. I'm kidding. CJ and I thought we'd get some fresh air."

"It *is* a nice night." What a moronic thing to say. It was freezing.

He nodded. "Are you off somewhere—or would you like to join us?"

She tilted her head, let a small smile touch her lips, and hoped she looked sort of mysterious—and not sickly. "I was going to get some dinner, but a walk first might be nice." She fell into step beside him and pulled on her gloves. "It's so quiet here. I'm used to a lot more noise."

"Me too. Where are you from?"

She hesitated, debating whether to make something up and deciding against it. The closer she stayed to the truth, the less likely she would get caught. "Chicago."

"Really? I am too. And you want to move to Coldwater?"

"I love the small town feel. Knowing your neighbors.

Getting away from all the city noise and dirt. I've always wanted to live in a in a place like this—this is just completing a dream for me." She was surprised at how easily the lie rolled out of her. Well, it would all be worth it if she got the information she needed.

"What did you do in Chicago?"

Careful, careful. "I used to be a writer. For the food section of the newspaper," she said nonchalantly.

"The *Sentinel?*" There was surprise in his voice and she could sense him mentally pull back. If she didn't play this right, their budding friendship would end right now.

"That's the one. Newspaper work is pretty dull. I'm not cut out for it—all that research and writing, sitting at a computer all day—borrring."

"That's why you're switching jobs."

"Exactly. So, what do you do?" she asked, purposely taking the focus off her life.

"Nothing too exciting. I'm a publicist, small firm—just me and a part-time administrative assistant."

"Sounds a lot more interesting than writing about food. Do you have any famous clients?" She held her breath, hoping she'd managed to push them into some mention of Dear Cordelia.

He hesitated. "Mostly small companies, some public service ..."

"Anyone I would have heard of?"

He hesitated as though weighing his answer. "Probably not. So where were you going for dinner?"

Well, guess he didn't want to tell her he worked for Cordelia. Which was odd because it wasn't a secret. "I thought I'd wander downtown, maybe stop at that little café and get a sandwich. Unless you have a better recommendation."

He slanted a sideways look at her as though debating something. "I might. My grandmother's neighbors invited me to dinner tonight. I'm heading over there once I drop CJ at home. You want to join us?"

Her heart skipped about five beats. Jack Graham, a man certifiably worth drooling over, had just asked her for a date. Sort of. Or not. Regardless, it was exactly the kind of *in* she'd been hoping for. Kristin's words came back to her: *Act a little coy, a little mysterious.* "That's really nice of you, but I don't want to impose. What would those neighbors think when you show up with an uninvited guest?"

"They won't care. Believe me—they'll be happy to see you. Besides, if you take the caretaker job, they'll be your new neighbors. You can get the lowdown on the neighborhood. Demographics, scuttlebutt, gossip, you name it."

Liza scrunched up her face. "Okay, but only if you go in and ask first—and make sure they aren't just trying to be nice."

"Deal."

Fifteen minutes later, Liza found herself being ushered through the front door by a short, round, gray-haired woman. "My gosh, don't think twice about joining us," Diane said. "We're thrilled to have you. We saw you arrive for the interview today and knew you'd be good for the job. Told Jack that right away, isn't that right. Jack?"

He nodded, a wry smile on his face.

"Oh thank you." Liza shoved her gloves in her pocket and hung her jacket on a hook by the front door. The warmth of the house was a welcome change from the chilly outdoors.

Another older woman hurried across the living room. "Hello! Welcome! I'm Mary. So nice of you to join us. I'm

Jack's neighbor from the other side. Or used to be. Diane and I decided to move in together when our husbands died. Now, don't you waste any time. Take your coats off and come right into the kitchen. Food's ready."

Diane nodded. "Mary's sort of bossy."

Mary popped her hands onto her hips. "And Diane's sort of a busybody."

Diane rolled her eyes. "But we've been neighbors practically forever—"

"And now they're roommates. So they overlook that sort of thing." Jack tossed his jacket over the banister.

Liza swallowed a laugh and followed the two women into the kitchen. She couldn't have asked for things to happen more naturally than this. With any more luck, she and Jack would be friends before long, and somehow she'd find a way to get him to open up about Cordelia.

"We're having chicken and dumplings, I hope you like them. They were one of Jack's favorites when he was young —used to finagle a dinner invitation from my boys whenever I made them," Diane said. She set a platter on the kitchen table and hustled back to the stove, while Mary laid out another place setting.

Jack looked chagrined. "You knew that?"

Diane scooped steaming broccoli into a serving bowl. "Don't think for a minute I minded it. You were just like one of my own."

"Yeah, I remember the spankings."

"Oh, I didn't spank you but once."

"Once was enough." Jack slashed the air with one hand.

Mary laughed. "And it was well deserved too."

Diane smiled at Liza and shook her head. "We'd just had the house repainted. There were four of them—Jack, my two boys, and Mary's son. They were all about nine years old—decided they wanted to be painters too. So they took old gallons of paint from the basement. By the time we caught them, the side of the garage was a mishmash of different colors. Those boys together were a handful, let me tell you."

Jack leaned forward and said in a stage whisper, "And she doesn't know the half of it."

"And I don't want to know. As long as you all made it safely to adulthood, there's no point fretting over the mischief you got into then."

"Amen." Mary nodded her head. "Fill your plates, everyone. Don't let the food get cold."

Liza put a dinner roll on her plate and passed the basket to Jack. "Where are the other boys now?"

"They're all over. My Dan's in Boston, Will's in Atlanta and Mary's son is down in Portsmouth. But they were all home for Christmas." Diane smiled at Jack. "Even Jack."

"And we didn't get into any trouble, either," he said around a mouthful of dumpling.

'Thank goodness," Mary said. "Back in the day, I was worried all the time."

Jack rolled his eyes. "Ladies, everyone gets into trouble when they're young." He nodded at Liza. "Tell her. What kind of trouble did you get into as a kid?"

Trouble? She never got into trouble. She lifted one shoulder in a shrug. "Oh, I don't know."

"Come on, Liza, back me up here."

She grimaced. "I—I never really got into trouble."

A laugh burst out of Jack. "Oh come on. *Everyone's* done something. Out with it. I can't believe you were a Goody Two-shoes."

She could feel the heat rising in her face. Goody Two-shoes was exactly what she'd been. She hadn't broken away from always doing the right thing—the proper thing—until two weeks ago. If her parents knew she was in Maine, lying about why she was here and trying to use some guy to get to Dear Cordelia, they'd be mortified.

She forced away the guilt. It was about time they got mortified about something she was doing. They'd probably had the easiest child-rearing job in the entire western hemisphere.

But she was done toeing the line they'd set out for her. As of two weeks ago, she was going to live the life she wanted to live.

"Liza, everyone's done something. You didn't have to get caught, just had to do it. Come on, your secret's safe with us." Jack leaned forward, eyes dancing, elbows on the table, a fork in one hand with a piece of broccoli speared on the tines. "What was it? Toilet-papering houses, smoking stolen cigarettes behind the garage, throwing tomatoes at passing cars on dark summer nights—"

"That's what happened to all my tomatoes?" Mary glared at him.

Jack opened his eyes wide, the picture of innocence. "Not *all* your tomatoes. We took equally from every garden on the block."

Mary clucked her tongue and continued to eat. Jack returned his gaze to Liza.

She shook her head. "I led a dull life. An only child, born to parents who thought they'd never have any children. I think from birth on, my every outfit matched perfectly. I was—"

"The little princess." Jack looked like he felt sorry for her.

"It wasn't that bad. You can't miss what you never

knew," she lied as she meticulously buttered her dinner roll and hoped the subject would change.

He shook his head, and for a moment she saw a flash of sadness in his eyes. "Yes you can," he said softly.

Mary cleared her throat. "Now, now, none of this. We each make the best of what life has handed us." She turned to Liza. "So tell me, dear, do you have a boyfriend?"

The knife slipped from Liza's fingers and clattered onto her plate. This unexpected reminder of Mark's unceremonious end to their relationship five months ago wasn't the change of subject she'd hoped for. She moved her knife to the edge of her plate. "Sorry. No. No, I don't."

"Jack isn't dating anyone right now either." Diane refilled her water glass.

"Diane, leave the poor girl alone," Mary said.

"They've taken over where my grandmother left off," Jack said, shaking his head. "Bound and determined to get me settled down."

"Single men are always lonely," Diane said as Mary nodded agreement.

Liza held back a laugh. If these two only knew how lonely Jack *wasn't* back in Chicago. And based on the welcome he got from Ashley, it didn't look as if he would be lonely in Coldwater either.

Mary waved her fork. "Jack, you know, I've been thinking. If Liza were to take the job and move into the house ... Well, I don't mean to overstep here, but—"

"It's never stopped you before." He rolled his eyes.

"You really should have the walls repainted."

"It's crossed my mind." Jack looked at Liza. "Remember, she's bossy, just in case you become her neighbor."

Diane frowned. "I have to agree with Mary. The place is getting dreary, and some of those colors—"

"And remember, *she's* a busybody." Jack leaned forward. "The colors didn't seem to bother Billy."

Diane ignored him. "The wall colors are dated—don't you think, Liza?"

"Oh, I didn't pay any attention." She quickly stabbed a piece of chicken and popped it into her mouth in an attempt to stay out of the conversation.

"You didn't notice the harvest gold in the dining room?" Diane looked appalled.

"Oh, well, that, that was a little—"

"And the avocado green in the kitchen?" Mary added.

"And the rust orange in the front hall, and the pea green in the living room?" Diane let out a sigh.

Liza gave up. "Okay, I noticed."

"But did it bother you?" Jack asked.

"Not if I'm not going to live there," she said, hedging.

Mary set her elbows on the table. "The house really needs updating. Neutral colors. Beiges, tans, grays, whites."

"Is your nephew out of work again?" Jack asked.

Mary looked offended.

"Oh, for God's sake," Diane said. "Of course he is. That boy's spent a lifetime getting by on good looks—and Mary's said it herself a hundred times. But that doesn't mean your grandmother's house couldn't benefit from freshening up. And Davey could use the money."

Jack groaned.

"The whole place would be done in a couple of days. You could help him out if you want," Mary said.

"Dave and I did some painting after college, while we were job hunting," Jack said. "I learned pretty fast I wasn't a natural at it."

"Good thing you got into publicity then." Liza hoped the comment would nudge the discussion onto Jack's work.

"Especially since I didn't intend to go into that field. My goal back then was to become a sports agent." He shook his head. "Funny, the paths you end up on."

"That happened to me too. Here I am writing in the food section—or was, I mean, before I left—" Liza stopped, mortified at her mistake. She'd almost blown her cover story. "Anyway, what I always wanted to do was work in a culinary school."

"And now you're going to," Jack said.

Liza nodded, anxious to change the subject once more. "You seem to have done well in publicity."

"I'd say he has. Dear Cordelia is his main client," Diane said with a proud smile.

"Seriously? That's amazing. I love her column." Now, *this* was a coup. Who would have guessed the ladies would help her out? She raised her eyebrows at Jack.

"She helps pay the bills." He forked some broccoli into his mouth and chewed slowly.

"What's she like?" Liza asked.

"Old, crabby, private." Jack took a big bite of bread.

The two women nodded.

"Do you ladies know Cordelia, too?"

"You could say we do," Diane said.

Liza's mind began to churn. If she couldn't get the information she needed from Jack, maybe she could make a connection through Diane and Mary.

"What she means is that we feel like we know her because Jack's been working for her all these years," Mary said.

"You don't need to interpret for me. I know how to speak for myself," Diane said irritably.

"I never said you didn't."

"Is Dave available to paint right away? I did notice the walls looked a little beat up." Jack smiled brightly.

Liza mentally groaned. Something didn't seem totally right about the ladies' answer, and now Jack had just made a quick switch away from Dear Cordelia. This guy was obviously determined not to talk.

"I'm sure he is. I'll call—he could probably start tomorrow if you get the paint."

"Tell him to pick up a nice off-white," Jack said as he spooned another dumpling onto his plate.

"That would be safest," Liza said.

"Predictable," Mary added.

Liza blanched. How quickly she fell back into old habits.

"It's not that important," Jack said.

"Well, then go with some neutral colors. They're all the thing. Your grandmother had color in every room." Mary gestured grandly with one hand.

"Look, ladies. I'm willing to help Dave out here, but let's not get carried away. I don't feel like picking out paint—"

"Liza can help you." Diane looked at Liza. "Can't you, dear?"

Jack looked at Liza and shook his head. "I'm sorry. Years ago they escaped from an asylum. They were harmless, so no one ever turned them in. But they're getting worse as they get older. It may be time to call the head administrator and have them readmitted."

"Oh, Jack, stop that nonsense. Liza, can you help him?" Mary asked.

Liza sat a little straighter. Of course. Whatever it took to get close to the guy. Dear Cordelia, here she came. "I'd love to."

Jack's mouth dropped open but not a word came out.

"Perfect. I'll call Davey!" Mary brought her hands together with a clap. "Jack, why don't you pick up Liza in the morning and go to the paint store. And I'll tell Davy he can start painting after lunch."

"And they wonder why I don't visit more often?" He looked at Liza, and for the first time she noticed how long his lashes were, how the skin crinkled in the corners of his eyes when he smiled, how a lock of hair kept falling onto his forehead … and how much she wanted to reach over and brush it to the side.

She jerked her eyes away and focused on her plate of food. She'd come to Coldwater to get information, and instead, she was falling for the mark.

This was no way to begin a career as an investigative reporter. If she fell for every good-looking guy she interviewed, she'd end up with all sorts of charming memories and not an interview to her name.

She had to pull her feelings into line or she'd be back in the food section writing about melt-in-your-mouth meatloaf and creative Jell-O molds for sensational summer picnics. The thought was enough to drive any ideas of romance right out of her head.

7

JACK SAT AT THE DESK IN HIS BEDROOM AND STARED IN frustration at the document open on his laptop. He and Liza had picked out paint earlier in the day, and Dave had already begun *refreshing* the downstairs walls, as the ladies called it. Liza had taken CJ out for a walk. And he was trying to get some work done.

Except, in the hour he'd already been up here, he'd managed to accomplish absolutely nothing. He forced himself to reread the letter on his screen.

Dear Cordelia,

I'm a thirty-five-year-old female and I always seem to pick the wrong guys. I'm a college graduate, have a good job and people tell me I'm attractive. So why do I always date guys who are going nowhere or have some problem like being in major debt, or out of work, or married, or alcoholic? You get the idea. I'm ready for true love. Just tell me how to find it.

Loser Magnet

The words blurred in front of his eyes and he dropped his head into his hands. He could hardly stand it anymore. He'd probably read three thousand variations of this same letter, had probably answered it dozens of times in the column. And no one ever figured it out.

There was no such thing as true love.

After years of reading dozens of books on love, romance, and psychology; years of monitoring other advice columns to glean tidbits of insight; years of getting input from his grandmother—all in an effort to be able to answer the questions readers sent to Cordelia—he'd reached the conclusion that true love was a myth. For all the millions of dollars being spent on love, hardly anyone was finding it. And he had a sneaking suspicion that those who said they had, were lying.

All the books and columns did was perpetuate the myth that true love existed. Hell, he was as much to blame as they were. Frankly, he was sick of it. Which was all the more reason Cordelia needed to retire.

Laughter drifted up the stairs and through his open door. He sighed. Liza must be back from walking the dog. And Davey must be turning on the charm.

Boy meets girl.

And whenever Dave met a new woman ... That guy hadn't changed a bit since he was a two-time, all-conference baseball and football star in high school. A ladies' man then and a ladies' man now.

Jack gritted his teeth and began to type.

Dear Magnet,

    You like men with baggage so much you should take a trip—to see a psychologist. And if that doesn't work, give it up. True love is an urban myth.

He stared at the screen for a moment, then hit the backspace key, deleting everything he'd just written. Clearly, time for a break before he let his cynicism get in the way of work. No matter how sick he was of writing the column, no matter how tired he was of keeping up the deception about Cordelia, he couldn't quit before he got his sports-agenting business on solid ground. Only then could Cordelia retire. Until then, he needed her to maintain his income, his lifestyle ... and his freedom.

His phone rang and he answered it eagerly, grateful for the interruption.

"Jack, this is Molly."

He recognized the voice of Molly Monroe, an up-and-coming beach volleyball player. It wouldn't be long before she was top-ranked.

"Okay, so I'm really giving serious thought to signing with you." She laughed nervously.

This was more like it. "I'm glad you are," he said smoothly, sitting back in his chair. "Because together, I think we'd be headed for big things."

"I like you," she said. "I like your style. But I can't base my decision on just that. This is *business*. People keep telling me to go with a name, an established place. You know?"

He'd heard this before. In fact, it was his number one stumbling block. He drew a breath and dove into his pitch. "Molly, all my years in publicity are going to work for you. I know the media. I know how to *work* the media. I took Cordelia to the top. I can take you there, too."

"What do you see for me?"

"Big names. A shoe company, a clothing line. Come on, you'd be perfect for athletic wear. How about a sunscreen manufacturer? Then there's bottled water or a soft-drink company." His voice went up a notch. "Molly, that's only the beginning—"

"Jack! Hey, Jack, come down here once, will you?" Dave shouted from downstairs. "Quick!"

Jack rolled his eyes and headed into the hall. "I can help make your name synonymous with volleyball. Long after you retire, everyone will remember who you are."

"That's all well and good, but long after I retire, I also want to be living off my endorsement earnings."

Jack reached the bottom of the stairs to find Dave giving Liza a painting lesson. All the dining room furniture had been moved to the center of the room and was covered with a big white drop cloth.

"You hold the brush like this," Dave said as he wrapped his fingers around Liza's to guide her hand.

This was almost as bad as watching Dave give a woman a golf lesson.

"Don't worry about those," Jack said into the phone as he tried to carry on the conversation with Molly and listen to Dave at the same time. "You'll have more than you know what to do with."

"This gives you the best control when you're cutting in around the woodwork." Dave moved Liza's hand along the wood trim that framed the window. She looked over her shoulder, spotted Jack and smiled.

He held up one finger in the universal signal for *hold on a minute.*

"But my earnings?"

"No worries there either," he said in a reassuring voice. "When you're ready to retire, you'll be set. I'll make sure of that. You just keep doing what you do best—give people something to take their minds off their day-to-day stresses, help them find happiness—and leave the rest to me."

"Do I do all that?" There was a smile in her voice.

Jack relaxed. "You bet. People love you. You're the best."

Molly gave a self-conscious laugh. "I know I'm probably driving you nuts—"

"Not at all—"

"I haven't made up my mind, but, like I said, I like you. I just need to talk the idea over with my dad one more time for another perspective. I'll call you in a few days."

"Great. Thanks." Jack shut off the phone and set it on a window ledge. If he could land Molly Monroe, he might finally light on the horizon. He'd been working on signing her for a while and, with any luck, all that hard work might finally pay off. It was almost too much to hope for—Molly and a Chicago Bears wide receiver in the same week. If it all fell into place, Cordy might be able to retire sooner than he'd thought.

He turned to Dave and Liza, a self-satisfied grin on his face. "So what's up? What do you need me for?"

"My assistant here thought we should make sure you like the color before we got too far." Dave put a hand on Liza's shoulder, and a shot of irritation coursed through Jack.

"Your assistant?" he asked evenly.

Liza set the paintbrush in the tray. "I got back from walking CJ and Dave asked me to help."

Same old Dave. Except the help he'd be looking for was probably different than the help she was offering. Jack gave a wan smile.

"I thought I might as well be useful," Liza said, beaming. "I was going to hang around and visit with CJ a while longer anyway."

"Don't worry, Jack boy. I'm going to teach her

everything I know. She'll be a pro by the time I'm done with her." Dave grinned.

Jack nodded slowly. That's what he was afraid of.

———

Liza watched Jack carefully. If she was a betting woman, she'd bet that phone call had been important. Jack seemed to be in pretty high spirits when he hung up. She thought back to what she'd heard of his side of the conversation. Dave had been talking at the same time, so she'd missed some of it. But Jack had said something about being *ready to retire*. And helping people find happiness.

If she didn't know better, it sounded exactly like the kind of thing you'd say to an advice columnist. *Dear Cordelia.* She didn't know who Jack's other clients were, but Cordelia had to be nearing retirement age. Her picture sure looked like it. And her name sounded like she was from another century. Of course, Cordelia could be a pseudonym. But if it wasn't …

The file Mr. Klein had given her back at the newspaper showed that Cordelia was Jack Graham's principal client. As far as she and Kristin had been able to discover in their research, he didn't have any other clients he would be complimenting for bringing happiness to other people's lives. The more she thought about it, the more she was convinced Jack had just finished a call with the woman Liza wanted to interview. The problem was, how did she confirm her suspicions?

"So do you like the color?" Dave asked.

"Looks great. Very … refreshed."

"That's all we need to know. You can go back to your

computer." Dave climbed onto the ladder and began to roll paint on the wall.

Jack didn't move. He narrowed his eyes at Dave's back, then looked at Liza. "You're not really going to paint, are you?"

"You bet she is. We're a team," Dave said over his shoulder before Liza could reply.

"I guess I am," she said with a smile.

Jack shook his head.

"I don't have to. If you'd rather I didn't—"

"No, no. Go ahead. I'll throw down some old clothes so you don't get paint on what you're wearing." He tromped up the stairs, and she wondered at his obvious irritation.

"Thanks," she murmured as she went over to the front windows and looked out at the gray afternoon. Dark, heavy clouds covered the sky like a low ceiling and light snow had begun to fall. She didn't need to see a weather report to know that at least several inches of snow was in the forecast. Her gaze landed on Jack's cell phone, still on the window ledge where he'd set it a few minutes ago. Her heart started to pound. If he'd been talking to Cordelia, her number would be the first one listed in Recent Calls. At the very least, she'd be in his Contacts List.

Theoretically, if she could get Cordelia's phone number, she would be a step closer to tracking down her address. And as luck would have it—she smiled to herself— Cordelia's phone number was sitting in front of her screaming to be had. This could be the break she was looking for.

She glanced at Dave, still up on the ladder, his back to her. Then she looked at the phone again, eager to grab it— and terrified of getting caught. She reached out a hand.

"Incoming," Jack yelled from upstairs, and she snapped

her hand back. Pivoting, she hurried toward the stairs just as an old pair of pants and a long-sleeved tee shirt landed on the bottom step. Scooping them up, she called, "Thank you," to Jack, but he had disappeared—already back to his room and his computer.

His computer. No doubt there was plenty of Dear Cordelia information on that machine. The only problem was, how did she get at it? When she called Kristin late last night to report she'd had dinner with Jack and his neighbors, Kristin had been beside herself with glee. Then, when she learned Liza was going paint shopping this morning, you'd have thought they won the lottery. To hear Kristin talk, getting into Jack's computer was just the next simple matter to accomplish.

Right now, the cell phone seemed the easier mark. Arms wrapped around the clothes, Liza looked across the room to the window ledge holding Jack's phone. *Now. Go now.* Heart thudding, she peeked into the dining room. Dave was still on the ladder, his back to the door.

She stepped gently across the living room, cringing as the floor creaked twice despite her efforts to be as quiet as possible. In one quick motion, she seized the phone from the window ledge and shoved it into the pile of clothing.

"I'm going to change," she called casually in Dave's direction, then raced down the hall to the bathroom. After locking the door, she pulled out the phone and set it on the counter as if it were the Holy Grail.

8

SHE QUICKLY CHANGED INTO THE CLOTHES JACK HAD gotten her. One look in the mirror and all of Kristin's admonishments about making sure she looked stylish every moment she was here came roaring back. She groaned. She had *never* looked this bad before, even in her own clothes.

Hopefully the phone would deliver the information she needed, and she could skip town and never have to worry about Jack finding her appealing again. Hands trembling in anticipation, fingers mentally crossed that she didn't need a password to get into the phone, she opened the Recent Calls screen. The last call was from someone named Molly. Liza scrolled down the list; Jack had made and received several calls with Molly over the last week. Molly, huh?

She threw a nervous glance at the door as if expecting Jack to come barging in at any moment, then looked at the phone again. Could Cordelia's real name be Molly? Or could Jack have her listed Cordelia in his phone under an alias to protect her contact information?

She opened his Contacts File and scrolled through everyone listed under the letter C. No Cordelia. Then she went to the top and scrolled through his entire contacts list from A to Z. Jack had a long list of female names, phone numbers, and email addresses—and none of them Cordelia.

Cordy was his most important client; there was no way he wouldn't have a phone number and email for her in his phone. So, thinking like an investigative reporter, the odds were decent that Molly could be Cordelia. The only way to be sure was to call the number.

Later, of course. Not right now. Right now she just had to copy it.

Great idea. Brilliant. Copy it on what? Toilet paper? She let out a sharp exhale. Her phone was in her purse in the front hall, and she was in the bathroom without anything to write on. Or with. If she was going to be an investigative reporter, she really had to get her act together.

Cautiously opening the door, she stuck out her head and looked down the hall in either direction. She'd never get to her purse without Dave spotting her. The only option was to dash into the kitchen, write down the number, and return the phone to the window ledge before Jack came looking for it.

Feeling a little like James Bond, she stepped down the hall and into the kitchen. She tore the corner off a piece of junk mail on the counter, grabbed a pen from the table, and started to write down the number. No ink. Hissing out a breath from between clenched teeth, she scrabbled through a drawer until she found a pencil stub, scratched the phone number on the scrap of paper, and shoved it into her pocket.

Who said she wouldn't be good at investigative reporting?

She grinned. And then the phone began to boisterously ring and she jerked, juggling the phone, panic ripping through her as she fought to keep from dropping it to the floor. Forget James Bond, she was more like Inspector Clouseau.

"Is that my phone?" Jack shouted from upstairs.

Her heart clutched. She needed to get this baby into Jack's hands before he came downstairs and caught her with it. Taking the stairs two at a time, she drew up short as she met him in the hallway. "It's your phone," she said smiling inanely, her breath coming a little hard. "You left it downstairs. I found it. Here it is!" *Shut up.*

She handed it over and dashed to the first floor before he had time to notice the guilt that was, undoubtedly, written all over her face.

Two hours later, back in her regular clothes, Liza stood between Jack and Dave as all three surveyed the finished room. "It's gorgeous," she said as both guys nodded.

"Are you coming over tomorrow to walk the dog?" Dave asked her. "Wanna stick around and help me do the living room? Maybe we could catch dinner afterward."

Liza mentally winced. She didn't want to make any commitments until she found out whether or not she'd gotten Cordelia's phone number. If she'd been successful, she wasn't hanging around Coldwater. She felt a twinge of remorse. Jack Graham thought he was about to get a caretaker, and she might be about to burn him in a big way. "Maybe. I may have to run over to the culinary institute for a while."

She'd better hash this out with Kristin tonight. At least Kristin had experience letting guys down gently. Even though this wasn't a romantic letdown, surely some of the same principles could be applied.

She checked her watch and scraped a couple of paint spatters off the face with her fingernail. "I should really get going. Can I walk to the inn from here?"

"It's snowing pretty hard. I can give you a ride," Dave said.

"I'll take her." Jack said in a voice that implied the subject was closed.

She glanced at him in surprise. "Okay. Thanks."

Out in the car, Jack looked directly at her before backing out of the driveway. "Liza, I just want to warn you. Be careful with Dave. He gets around."

"You mean he's a player?" Obviously, it took one to know one.

"That's one word for it."

"Why, Jack Graham, are you worried about my reputation?" she teased.

"I just don't want you to get hurt."

For a moment, she was speechless. Jack Graham, lady-killer, was trying to protect her feelings? "Don't worry about me, I'm resilient," she quipped. And then, because it actually wasn't all that true and she had no idea why she'd said it and she didn't want Jack to start asking questions, she began to babble about the weather. "This snowfall is just beautiful. A winter wonderland. Is it always like this? What a great night for sitting by a fire and reading a good book."

By the time Jack pulled up in front of the inn, she felt like a moron. His unexpected concern had caused her to regress to her typical self-conscious self—as far from coy and mysterious as anyone could get. She sure hoped she'd nabbed Cordelia's phone number because the odds that Jack Graham might want to spend time with her had probably dropped to from zero-to-none.

Inside the lobby, she shook the snow out of her hair and allowed herself a small fantasy about telling Mr. Klein that she, of all people, had gotten the coveted interview with Dear Cordelia.

She hurried to her room, already ringing Kristin's cell phone as she pushed through the door.

"I think I might have got it," she sang out when her friend answered the call.

Kristin gasped. "Got what?"

"Cordelia's phone number. I'm not totally sure it's hers, but I overheard Jack on the phone and he was saying the kind of stuff you'd expect him to say to her."

"Seriously? How'd you do this?"

Liza briefly recounted the day's events. "The only issue is that in his phone, the number is listed to someone named Molly—"

"That's okay. I seriously doubt Cordelia's her real name."

"Exactly. It's a 312 area code, so if it's her, she's right in Chicago somewhere. Which will make it easier for me to come home and track her down."

"Hold on a sec. Let's say it is her. How are you going to explain where you got her number?"

"Yeah, I know. I was thinking I would say something like, Jack gave it to me before he left town and asked me to call her directly." She did a little two-step in front of the mirror.

"What if she wants to clear it with him first? Just to be sure."

Liza frowned at her reflection. "I'm hoping she won't."

Kristin let out a snort. "You can't take that risk. You've got to have a reason to see her that's so good she won't be able to say no."

"And that would be what, oh wise woman?"

"Give me a minute," Kristin said.

"Couldn't I just say—"

"I've got it!" Kristin said. "I'll make the call and say I'm a new employee at Mr. Graham's office—calling from my cell phone because I'm not in the office. That he wanted her to know the media is getting so persistent he thinks it's time to throw them a bone. That he recommends she do this one Valentine's interview to get the media off her back. And that he asked me to set everything up because he's out of town."

Liza nodded to herself. "It could work—as long as she doesn't call Jack to confirm."

"We have to risk it. It works in our favor that her phone number is the world's best-kept secret. I'll mention something about why Jack is in Coldwater, maybe something about those ladies next door, stuff no one would know who wasn't in contact with him. It'll help—"

"Give you legitimacy."

"Exactly," Kristin said. "You think I should call right now?"

"The sooner the better. It's just five o'clock in Chicago anyway. Not like it's late," Liza said. "Besides, I need to know tonight if I'm leaving town—the boys want me to come over again tomorrow."

"The boys?"

"Jack and Dave. Dave's the painter."

"My, my, my. How things do change."

Liza grinned. "Will you go make the call, please?"

"Okay, okay. But later I want to hear more about *the boys, and you going back over there again.* I'll call as soon as I have something to report."

Liza spent the next hour pacing her room and holding herself back from calling Kristin. She checked flights and discovered she could catch a morning flight to Chicago for just a seventy-five-dollar change fee. One glance out the window told her that morning flights might be delayed because of weather, so she checked afternoon flights as well.

Okay, she had options, she had a destination, and she had an interview—maybe. Her stomach rumbled. What she didn't have was anything to eat. Giving in to hunger, she ventured out into the storm, windshield wipers on high so she could see through the wet snow falling on her windshield. Not many people were on the road. Probably because everyone who lived in Maine knew enough to stay home when it was snowing this heavily.

She ordered a burger and fries at the first fast-food drive-thru she came upon, then returned to the inn, skidding so badly as she turned into the parking lot that she almost crashed into another car. "That's it," she muttered once she was safely in a parking space. "I'm in for the night."

As she wolfed down her food on the window seat in her room, she mulled over her next steps. Once Kristin confirmed they had Cordelia's number, she would call Jack and tell him she couldn't become CJ's caretaker, that it would be too much to take on when she was just starting a new job.

Guilt tried to make an inroad into her mind and she shoved it away. Maybe Ashley could take the job—she seemed to want it bad. Her guilt intensified and she tried to rationalize it away. It wasn't her fault Jack couldn't find anyone normal to take the job. She pressed her lips together. Not her problem—even if he was a pretty nice guy. Even if he had been concerned enough about Dave's intentions to warn her about him.

The sudden sound of rock music wrenched her out of her thoughts. She looked around, disconcerted for a second before realizing it was her phone. When she left Chicago determined to quit being practical and predictable, she'd switched her ringtone from classical to rock and hadn't completely adjusted to the change. She glanced at the caller ID. Kristin. *Finally.* "It's about time!"

"I called her."

"And?"

"And I said what we decided I should say—"

"Do I have an appointment?" Liza was almost giddy with anticipation.

Kristen hesitated. "No. That phone number wasn't Cordelia's."

"It wasn't?" Her joy evaporated.

Outside the window, a streetlamp illuminated the heavily falling snow, burying the ground just like Kristin was burying her hopes. "Who was it?"

"Someone named Molly."

"But maybe it's a fake name and she really is Cordelia."

"No. She's a beach volleyball player. Sounded like she was twenty-three, max. That would mean she started the column when she was ten. Trust me. It wasn't Cordelia. Of course, I only learned all that out once I introduced myself as being from Jack's office and asked to speak to Cordelia."

"Oh shit. I hope she doesn't ask Jack about the call."

"I think we're good. I apologized profusely and said I looked at the wrong number when I dialed. She was cool."

Liza let out a sigh. "Some investigative reporter I am. I'm no closer to getting to Cordelia than I was yesterday." Great. Just great. She hadn't played the player. In fact, she wasn't even in the game.

"You're closer to Jack. That's a big step forward. Now you just need a lucky break."

Suddenly the power went out and the room went black.

"So much for lucky breaks," Liza muttered.

9

THE POWER WENT OUT AT NINE-THIRTY.

Jack let out a string of curses as he felt his way along the kitchen wall, rummaging through drawers crammed with stuff as he searched for a flashlight. Grandma always kept a flashlight and extra batteries in the junk drawer. Unfortunately, it seemed that every drawer had become a junk drawer since Billy moved in. Hopefully, Billy hadn't run through all the batteries and never bothered to buy more.

This storm was turning out to be bigger than the weather service had predicted. When he'd let CJ out earlier, it was snowing even harder and the storm seemed to be growing—not letting up. All this wet, heavy snow couldn't be good for power lines. God knew how many were probably down already.

His fingers closed around the cylinder shape of a flashlight and he triumphantly pulled it out of the overstuffed drawer and switched it on. A weak yellow beam illuminated a small circle on the cupboard. The damn thing would be dead in twenty minutes.

He aimed the beam into the drawer to search for extra batteries, finding two 9-volt, two AA, a full pack of AAA, and one C. Unscrewing the bottom of the flashlight, he checked the batteries by feel. Three C batteries. He should have known. Maybe there were still some candles in the dining room buffet left over from when his grandmother was alive. He doubted Billy had hosted many candlelight dinners since moving in.

If he had to, he could use the flashlight on his phone, but that had to be for emergency only; with the electricity out, he'd have no way to recharge it and the last thing he wanted to lose was the ability to make calls.

The buffet yielded six unused candle tapers, still wrapped in tissue paper. Perfect. At least he'd have a little light. But no heat. Once the house cooled down from the furnace being off, the only way to keep warm would be the fireplace. And he had a sneaking suspicion that when he went outside to check the woodpile, he'd discover there wasn't much of a woodpile anymore. He shrugged into his jacket, stuck his feet into his Sorel boots, and pulled on his gloves. CJ followed him to the back door, wagging her tail as if expecting to go for a walk.

"The snow is probably deeper than your legs, girl. I'll be right back." Jack gave the door a shove; it opened about six inches, then stuck in the snow. He put his shoulder to the door and forced it out enough to enable him to squeeze out.

Snow whipped ice cold against his face, and he turned his back to the wind so he could zip the front of his jacket up through the collar. Unbelievable. The storm was worse than it had been an hour ago. Head down against the wind, he trudged through the snow to the side of the garage where the firewood had always stacked. Just as he'd thought. No woodpile.

Hell.

He didn't have a caretaker for the dog, he had the wrong size batteries for the flashlight, no central heat, no wood for a fire, and the cupboards were only minimally stocked because he'd been eating most meals out. What else could go wrong?

He aimed the weak flashlight beam in the direction of Diane and Mary's house, then squinted along the light's faint path as though he would actually be able to see more than a foot in front of him in a blizzard. Those two old ladies were probably in a frenzy with the power out. The least he could do was go over and calm them down.

He set off across the yard for their porch. Wet snow smacked against his cheeks, melting from his warmth and running slowly down his cheeks in icy rivulets. His flashlight did little to illuminate the way, but memory served him well and a minute later he was ringing the front bell.

The door swung inward and he was momentarily blinded by the brilliant light of a huge flashlight. He threw his arm up to shield his eyes. "Hey, you're blinding me here!"

"Oh, Jack dear, it's just you!" Diane aimed the beam at the ceiling and took hold of his arm and half dragged him through the doorway. "Come in, come in. Can you believe this? When was the last time we had such a storm as this?"

"I think it was the winter I decided it was time to move further south."

Diane tsked. "You didn't get too far."

He let out a laugh.

Mary brushed the snow off his shoulders and arms. "Isn't this exciting? I can't remember the last time we lost power. Well, actually, I do. It was two summers ago—or was it three—no, I do believe it was two—well, it was summer anyway and lightning hit a transformer. You'd never guess how many babies were born nine months lat—"

"Mary, do stop. I believe Jack wouldn't be coming over in this weather if he didn't have a reason."

"Oh, yes." Both women looked at him expectantly.

"Actually, I just wanted to make sure you ladies are okay." He wiped his face with his glove.

"Lord, yes. Mary is in her glory—that bossy old thing. She's always saying we need to stockpile in case of emergency. Blizzard, ice storm, terrorist attack, tornado, power outage, you know, anything you can think of. We've got enough bottled water for weeks, batteries—"

"You have batteries? Could I borrow a couple?"

"We've got boxes. Come on in."

He followed her into the living room where a cozy fire burned in the hearth, red and gold and blue. *Blue?* "You ladies have wood, too?"

Mary laughed. "I've got a supply of those fireplace logs. I get them at the hardware store. The package says they're made out of sawdust. We like them because they burn so slowly—"

"And in colors too—blue and green," Diane said.

"We can be out of power for weeks and not have a problem," Mary added.

Of course. Jack shook his head. These ladies didn't need his help. Quite the opposite, it looked more like he needed theirs. "And to think I was worried about the two of you."

"What size batteries?" Diane went to a box in the corner and held two packages—one C and one D.

"C. Thanks." He moved closer to the fire as he unscrewed the top of the flashlight and replaced the batteries. "I should have known you two were okay over here."

"Of course we're fine. Two old ladies—what else have we got to do but prepare for emergencies?" Diane clucked her tongue.

"Have you got any wood, Jack? Billy was great with CJ, but if ever there was a man in need of a woman's organization, it was Billy. We can give you some of our logs if you like," Mary said. "You only need to burn one at a time and they last and last."

"No wood, no batteries, no food."

"Oh, that's terrible. Why don't you just stay with us until the power comes back on? It would be an adventure." Mary smiled.

"No, no. Diane's allergic to dogs—and I can't leave CJ alone in that cold house. I'll just borrow a couple of those logs if you can spare them, and go back."

A police radio crackled from the coffee table and they stopped talking to listen to an exchange about a multi-car accident on the nearby highway.

Diane shook her head. "I don't know why anyone would be fool enough to go out in this weather."

"Amen," Mary replied. "Jack, won't you stay a bit anyway? We can all have a glass of beer. CJ won't get cold right away—she's wearing that fur coat."

"Yeah, okay, a quick beer would be great." He followed the ladies into the kitchen.

Diane took three pilsner glasses from the top shelf in the cupboard and filled them with Miller High Life from the bottle. "The beer's a little warm," she said as she dropped a couple of ice cubes in each glass.

Jack gave the ladies a big grin. *Ice in beer.* Whatever. If it didn't bother them, it wasn't going to bother him.

Back in the living room, the scanner was cackling out a steady stream of alerts about cars in the ditch, accidents, and people needing help.

Diane turned the sound down a little. "Just before you came over, the scanner said a truck knocked down one of the poles that brings power into Coldwater—took out the whole southern half of the village. They're using trucks and snowmobiles to move people to the high school where there's a generator keeping the furnace going."

"The whole southern end is out?" Jack asked. "Liza's staying at the Belleview Inn." He didn't like the thought of her stranded, even if she eventually got evacuated.

Diane nodded. "Your new caretaker is probably sitting in the dark."

"My *maybe* new caretaker. She hasn't decided yet."

"No need to worry. I'm sure they'll be taking her to the high school too." Diane sipped her beer.

"Well sure, but what kind of a how-do-you-do welcome is that?" Mary scooted forward to the edge of the couch. "You can't just leave her to fend for herself. The poor girl is new in town, all alone, stuck for the moment at an inn with no light or heat. Why, they don't even serve food in that place, except breakfast—"

"She'll have no reason to want to stay in Coldwater after this storm is over," Diane finished.

Mary looked at Diane. Diane looked at Mary. Then they both looked at Jack.

"What?" Jack asked, even though he had a pretty good idea what this pair was about to insist he do. "Look, ladies, I know what you're up to and it's not going to work. Liza Dunnigan is a nice woman. But she and I aren't a match. In fact, here's a news flash—she wants to live in a small town so bad she's moving here. And I get the shakes if I stay in Coldwater too long."

"We're only talking about a neighborly gesture," Diane said.

Mary nodded. "We're not up to anything."

"But you'd better go get her quick. Who knows how long she'll be stuck at the hotel before they move her to the school."

"Have you looked out the window lately? This is a blizzard. I don't have a snowmobile or a plow. So I'd either have to get her on the old toboggan in the garage—or in my rental car. And without four-wheel-drive, I'd probably end up another one of those people stuck in a ditch." He took a swallow of beer. "Besides, didn't Diane just say anyone would be a fool to go out in weather like this?"

"Well, yes, but this is different. It's a rescue mission. And what's wrong with the toboggan anyway?" Diane said.

Jack rolled his eyes and drank some more beer, grimacing at the slightly watered-down taste from the melted ice cubes. He thought of Liza in the dark in the inn and wondered how she was holding up. She seemed like a relatively easygoing person, not the type to complain much when things went wrong.

"I've still got Charlie's old pickup in the garage," Mary said.

Jack tried not to laugh, remembering the blue GM truck Charlie used to tool around town in. That truck had been old for a long time. "What did you keep that thing for?"

"Emergencies," Mary said with a sniff. "And it looks like it might come in handy."

"I told her to sell it when she moved in but she refused," Diane said.

"Is it still full of his carpentry tools?"

Diane sighed. "No—those are in the basement. We're saving those for an emergency too."

"Yes, well, let's hope we never need them. Now, Jack, that truck will get you there in one piece. It may be old but I know it has four-wheel-drive. You go on and get her before she freezes—"

"Or starves. Or just plain gets scared," Diane said.

"We'll take care of CJ," Mary began.

"You go get Liza," Diane finished.

Jack held up both hands in surrender. "Okay, okay, okay. Where are the keys?"

Outside, he began to question his sanity. Only a snowplow driver—or an idiot—would purposely drive in this weather. And since he had no snowplow, it could only mean he was the latter.

He delivered CJ to the ladies, then headed out, not at all certain of success. The wind was whipping snow so violently against the windshield, there were moments he didn't know whether he'd end up the rescuer or the rescuee.

Though the inn was only slightly more than a mile away, it took him twenty minutes to get there. He pulled up in front—plenty of parking available—shut off the engine, and sat there a minute, watching as the heavily falling snow covered the windshield like a blanket.

10

Bundled against the cold, Liza waited in the small lobby of the Belleview Inn for a ride to the high school gym. Several other hotel guests sat nearby, quietly discussing the weather.

She wanted to cry. Not only had she not gotten Cordelia's phone number or an interview, but now she was bound for a stay at the high school while the storm raged and the experts tried to get the power going again. Her plans were falling apart by the minute.

Not long after the power had gone out, the front desk clerk had knocked at her door and told her about the evacuation, "for the comfort and safety of our guests." He said each person could bring along one small piece of luggage. So she'd put a change of clothes and her toiletries in the plastic laundry bag she'd found in the closet and come downstairs to wait for a ride.

The thought of spending the night in a gymnasium filled with strangers snoring, coughing, crying—as her own goals for finding Cordelia were moving further and further way—left her bereft. She stared morosely at the wall.

The inn's front door swung open, and everyone turned expecting to see the snowmobile drivers who would ferry them across town. Instead, Jack Graham came into the room covered in a layer of white. Liza's heart skipped a beat. Jack pulled off his stocking cap and shook it, sending sprinkles of snow flying, then brushed off his arms as he looked around the room. When he spotted her, his eyes lit up.

Impossible. Jack Graham's eyes couldn't be lighting up because of her. She looked to either side for the source of his enthusiasm. A middle-aged man was at her left, an elderly woman at her right. Somehow she didn't think either was Jack's type.

"Liza!" He headed straight toward her.

She stood, trying to contain her surprise. "Jack! Are you one of the snowmobile drivers?"

A blob of wet snow slid from his eyebrow down his cheek, and she had to hold herself back from reaching up to catch the migrating slush. He shook his head.

"So what are you doing here?"

"Rescuing you."

"Funny, that's what the guy from city hall said he was doing, too."

"Some rescue—to the high-school gym." Jack looked at the other guests, all listening in on their conversation. "Not that there's anything wrong with the gym. It's really nice. Awesome, in fact."

"I'm told what it lacks in atmosphere, it makes up for in warmth."

He laughed. "I've come to make you a better offer. Come home with me. Diane and Mary are so prepared, they can go weeks without power."

"Is this okay with them?"

"Okay? They sent me. Come on, let's get out of here.

The snow is probably up to the windows on Mary's truck already."

Liza made a face. "Mary doesn't strike me as the truck type."

"It was her late husband's. The truck's old, but it gets the job done." He looked around. "Where's your stuff?"

She held up the plastic bag. "They told us to pack light."

"Better bring your whole suitcase. Who knows how long the power will be out?"

"Really?"

As if to say, *get a clue,* he gestured at the big front window. Outside, the wind was wildly whipping the thickly falling snow.

"Right. Give me a minute to pull my stuff together."

"I'll carry your bag."

A sudden image shot into her mind—Jack Graham spotting the cotton bra and white cotton full-cover briefs she'd left out on a chair. "No, thanks. I can manage," she stammered.

She lugged her heavy suitcase to the lobby, bumping down every stair, then watched Jack lift it like it weighed next to nothing. He pushed through the front door and she followed, stepping outside just as the wind gusted and sucked her breath away. Dropping her chin, she grabbed hold of Jack's arm for support, glad she wasn't venturing out alone.

Head down, she lifted her eyes toward the faded blue pickup truck Jack had led her to. No way. He was driving that old wreck in a blizzard? "Is that what you came in?" she asked, appalled.

"Don't worry, it's safe. And drives great." He gave the passenger door a tug and it opened to the sound of old metal grating against old metal. Then he threw her suitcase inside and Liza slid across the cracked vinyl seat after it, grateful to escape the weather even if she wasn't convinced this truck was the best choice of escape vehicles. After a harrowing drive, they pulled into Diane and Mary's garage, and the ladies greeted her at the front door like she was a long lost relative.

Diane gave her a quick hug and drew her into the living room near the fire. "Jack was so worried you'd have to stay overnight at the high school."

He was? Liza turned to look at Jack but he had taken her suitcase into the dining room.

Mary nodded. "We have plenty enough for all of us to eat and lots of bottled water—"

Liza's mouth dropped open. "You don't have running water either?"

"Yes, of course we do. Pay no attention to her," Diane said. "Mary's stockpiled for emergencies so long, she just wants to use everything. I wouldn't be surprised if she starts putting plastic over the windows in preparation for a chemical attack."

Mary snorted. "One day you're all going to thank me for being so prepared."

Jack joined them by the fire and rubbed his hands together. "This is going to be a little like winter camping— hot by the fire and cold everywhere else." He patted CJ on the head. "Good old Ceej—thanks for protecting the ladies while I was gone."

Diane reached into the cuff of her sweater, pulled out a tissue, and wiped her nose.

"Are your allergies kicking up already?" Jack asked. "If you give me a couple of those logs, we can go over to my house. It's already pretty late."

"No, no." Diane lifted a cribbage board from an end table and held it up. "We're having an adventure. Anyone for game or two?"

"I'm in," Mary said.

Liza scrunched her face up apologetically. "I don't know how to play."

"Two-handed then. Partners. Diane and me against you and Jack."

"You're on." Jack took a deck of cards from a drawer in the coffee table. "They're still in the same place," he said, shuffling the cards from one hand to the other. "I'll get the card table and chairs. Still in the first floor bedroom?"

They pushed the furniture to the side to make room for the card table in front of the fireplace, then settled into the chairs.

Jack bent toward Liza and began to explain the rules of the game. She sucked in a breath at the nearness of him. He smelled of fresh air and pine, gorgeous man and knight in shining armor. It was all she could do to concentrate on his words. His forehead touched hers for a moment and she clenched her teeth to keep from sighing.

"Now, the goal," he said in a loud whisper, "is to keep from losing to these two sharks. I've been trying for upward of twenty years now. *I think they cheat.*"

The ladies giggled. "I believe we've been insulted, Diane," Mary said.

"We'll just let the card playing speak for itself." Diane shuffled the deck and dealt everyone a hand.

For the next couple of hours they played cribbage, ate potato chips, and drank hot chocolate they heated up in an old pan in the fireplace. Diane whipped up some dip from a container of sour cream and dry onion soup mix. And they played and laughed, and much to Liza's chagrin but not her surprise, she and Jack almost always lost.

As the night grew later and Jack left the room to take a bathroom break, Liza tried to steer the conversation onto Dear Cordelia. Based on the ladies' last comments about the columnist, she had a feeling they knew more than they were letting on. "You know," she said as she shuffled the cards, "I hope this doesn't sound nosey, but I've always been a big fan of Dear Cordelia. And with Jack being her publicist and you ladies knowing her, too—well, is there a chance she lives in Coldwater? Could I run into her at the grocery store one day and not even know it?"

The ladies exchanged a look.

"No," Diane said.

Mary got up and peered out the front window, shaking her head. "I can't remember a storm this bad—it's not letting up at all," she said.

"Desperate times call for chocolate." Diane pushed back her chair and hurried into the back hall.

What the hell? Why would no one talk about the woman? Their determination to avoid the subject only convinced her further that she was on the right path.

Jack returned, and she decided it would be better to wait until everything was back to normal tomorrow before pursuing the story again. Besides, the nearness of him put all sorts of fanciful ideas into her head, few of which were very conducive to investigative reporting.

Diane came back holding a bag of assorted bite-size candy bars.

"Are those left from Halloween?" Mary demanded.

Diane nodded, sheepishly.

"You little oinker. You told me they were gone, and now I learn you've been keeping them all for yourself."

"You were on Weight Watchers," Diane protested.

"So were you."

"But I quit before you did."

Mary shook her head. "Now I see why. You were hoarding all those treats for yourself, while encouraging me to stay the course."

Jack smiled at Liza, a grin that shot straight to her heart. She tried not to read anything into what surely had to be just a gesture of friendship.

"Dig in." Diane dumped the candy onto the table. "Liza, have you decided yet about the caretaker position?"

Good thing the only light in the room came from the fire in the hearth so no one could see the lies on her face. "Not really. I want to spend some time getting to know CJ better. I've never had a dog, so the idea of taking care of one is something I really have to be sure about."

She looked at CJ snoozing closer to the warm fire. "Although, she does seem like she'd be pretty easy."

Diane blew her nose. "Very easy. We'd take her on but she sets off my allergies. Any dog with dander is a problem for me." She blew her nose again.

"You could get those shots," Mary offered.

"Allergy shots? At my age?" Diane snorted out a laugh.

"You're only as young as you feel," Jack said.

Diane ignored him. "As I see the problem, Liza, how well can you really get to know what it's like to have a dog if you're only stopping over once in a while?"

"Especially now that the weather has gone and done this." Mary lay her cards face down on the table, as if the conversation was so important she couldn't play and talk at the same time.

"I'm going to be stopping over quite a bit in the next

week or so," she said. "That should help make my decision easier." Time for a change of subject.

"Why don't you just stay there?" Diane rearranged the cards in her hand.

Liza blinked. "Stay where?"

Jack laid his cards face down and looked calmly at Liza. "What she means is, instead of going back and forth, why not spend a longer period of each day at the house."

Diane shook her head firmly. "No, Jack. What I'm saying is that Liza should stay at the house. Overnight. Move in. It's the only way she'll truly know what it's like to have a dog."

Liza glanced at Jack. His smile had frozen. Omigod. She felt embarrassed for him—and mortified for her. "Oh, well, that's maybe a bit extra," she said as her cards slipped from her hand. She scrambled to pick them up.

"Use your heads, children." Mary clucked her tongue. "Diane's right. Here's Liza, trying to get to know CJ And then we have a blizzard. Everyone will be housebound for at least a couple of days. How on earth will she bond with the dog while she's trapped in a school gymnasium or her hotel room?"

Jack looked from Mary to Diane to Liza. "We just met," he said.

"No one's asking you to get married—although it's high time you considered the idea. Surely by now Liza can tell you're a decent person, trustworthy enough to move in with." Diane looked directly at Liza.

Married? How had they gone from caretaker to marriage? "Uh, yeah, of course, absolutely. I think he's a decent person." She looked at Jack and started to laugh at the inanity of the discussion. "I mean, actually, he's more than decent—he's very nice."

"Handsome, too, isn't he?" Mary prompted.

Liza could feel her cheeks flame. "Um, yes." She couldn't even bring herself to look in Jack's direction.

He cleared his throat. "Okay, that's probably enough about—"

"From that very first day, Mary and I could tell that you were a decent person too. It only makes sense that you stay at the house with Jack to get to know the dog." Diane smiled a bit smugly.

"Ladies, you're putting Liza on the spot—not to mention me."

"For heaven's sake, she's already going to spend tonight with you." Mary picked up her cards and looked them over.

The fire cracked and popped and no one said a word. Liza quickly scrolled back through the entire conversation. As bizarre as the exchange had been, the ladies had just offered her all-day access to Jack's files, a pathway to Dear Cordelia that she might not otherwise get. It was a perfect opportunity and she'd better jump before it got away. She cleared her throat. "You might be right. It's an idea worth considering."

Jack's jaw dropped.

She smiled sweetly at him. "I mean, staying at the house would give me a firsthand look at what it's like to have a dog all day, every day."

"It'd save you hotel money, too," Mary said with relish.

"So, Jack? What do you think?" Diane asked.

"I ... need a caretaker," he said slowly. He met Liza's gaze. "And the best one I've seen to date needs some time to get to know the dog. If she's up for it, I'm up for it."

Mary yawned. "Well, thank goodness that's settled. I need to go to bed and it doesn't look like the power's going to come back on anytime soon."

"Looks like we'll have to camp out around the fire. I'll get blankets and pillows," Diane said gleefully. She bustled from the room, while Liza helped Jack put away the card table and chairs.

Long after everyone else had fallen asleep, Liza lay awake, wrapped in a cozy down comforter by the hearth. She looked over at Jack slumbering a mere foot away. Kristin was going to die when she heard all this. Not only was Liza sleeping next to Jack Graham—well, okay, Jack Graham and his two senior-citizen neighbors and a fat snoring dog—but she was moving into his house tomorrow.

Her stomach hadn't stopped tumbling since the subject first came up. The whole idea was completely absurd. Single women did not impulsively move in with single men they'd just met. The man could be a lunatic or a serial killer or, or ... he could be Jack Graham, man about town, ladies at his doorstep, in his parlor, in his bed, and—with this move— Liza might just be next in line. A tremor of anticipation rippled through her.

Her parents would probably think their properly reared daughter had gone mad. Scratch that, if her parents knew what she was up to, they'd decide she'd gone mad last week.

A month ago, she never would have considered moving into a strange man's house. Now she was not only considering it, she was doing it.

Much as her parents tried to make it so, life just wasn't paint by numbers. You had to roll with the changes. The fact of the matter was, if she wanted to get the investigative-reporter job, if she wanted to change her life, then she had to find Cordelia. She fell asleep, convinced that the fastest way to finding Cordelia was to move in with the woman's publicist.

At four in the morning, the lights burst on like an

explosion of fireworks. Liza bolted upright and looked around in confusion. Oh yeah, she was at the ladies' house, *sleeping beside Jack Graham.*

Jack blinked several times and rubbed a hand over his eyes. "Did you have every light in the house on when the power went out?"

"It's hard to see at night when you get to be our age." Mary sat up on the couch and rubbed her lower back. "You'll find out someday."

Diane blew her nose and gave CJ a long-suffering look. "Well, as long as the heat's coming back on, I think I'll spend the rest of the night in my bed."

Mary stood. "A splendid idea."

Jack looked at CJ "I suppose I could get you out of here so Diane can breathe again."

Liza had a momentary rush of panic. Everyone was going somewhere—was she just supposed to follow Jack? Suddenly, with the lights on, the idea of moving into Jack's house seemed sort of silly. Obviously, now that there was power, the plows would get out, the roads would get cleared, and life would return to normal. She'd be able to stop over and visit CJ every day if she wanted to.

Jack looked at her as though reading her mind. "Are you still up for moving in?"

He was practically handing her access to his computer. Say yes. *Throw that damn caution to the wind.* Heart pounding, her brain roiling in disbelief, she opened her mouth and stepped further away from the well-ordered world to which she was accustomed. "I think it's a great idea, actually."

11

As soon as the snow stopped falling, the temperature had begun to drop. Jack paused at the end of the driveway, wiped his face and shifted the chute on the snow blower to blow snow in the opposite direction. Thirty inches had fallen since yesterday. Moving it all would be a major effort. He put the machine into gear and headed up the driveway again.

He looked over at the porch where Liza was shoveling off the steps. She grinned and tossed a shovelful of wet snow in his direction. He grinned back, more optimistic than ever that she would take the caretaker job. She had to be pretty serious about the position; why else would she move into the house?

The good news was, as long as Liza was here with the dog there was no reason for him to stay in town. He'd called the airport this morning and learned a couple of runways were already cleared. So he'd rescheduled his flight to late tomorrow afternoon, which meant he could set up a meeting this week with that wide receiver for the Bears.

From the corner of his eye he saw a motion. Diane was

leaning out the front door and waving him over. He shut off the machine and trudged through the snowy side yard until he was close enough to talk. "What's up?"

"Billy always did our walks, too. And with him passing so suddenly, we hadn't gotten anyone else yet," she said. "We've been calling all morning and can't find a soul to do the job. They're all too busy."

"Don't worry—I'll do yours next."

Mary stuck her head out the door from underneath Diane's arm. "Oh, thank you. We weren't sure who to call."

"It's the least I can do to thank you for suggesting Liza stay at the house with CJ"

Diane smiled knowingly. "A mother always knows best."

Mary disappeared into the house.

"Not only will Liza get to know the dog, but it'll really help me out. I've got some work pending back in Chicago and this will be perfect. I can go back for a few days and know CJ is being taken care of."

"Pardon me?" Diane looked confused.

"Well, think about it. Liza said she wanted time to *try out* having a dog."

"Yes, but—"

"If she spends the rest of this week alone with CJ, it'll give her a great idea of what it's like."

Mary's head popped out the door again, this time with a bright purple scarf wrapped around her neck.

Diane turned to her. "Jack says he's going back to Chicago."

"You are?" Mary's eyes widened. "Has Liza accepted the job, then?"

Jack shook his head and explained his plan again.

"But how will she know what to do with the dog if you're not here?" Diane asked.

"Come on, how hard can it be? Besides, you're right next door. You know what to do. As long as you two are willing to answer questions, give advice—that stuff you're so good at—she'll be fine."

They stared at him as though dumbfounded.

"Is it okay with Liza that you leave?" Mary said in a strangled voice. She loosened the scarf around her neck.

"I haven't told her yet. But I'm sure she'll understand. She'll probably like the idea—it'll be a lot less awkward for her if she's not sharing a house with a guy she hardly knows."

The two women continued to stare at him.

"Don't you think?" he asked. *What the hell was the matter with them? It was a great idea. Brilliant even.*

Diane finally nodded. "Is the airport even open?"

"A couple of runways are cleared. Besides, I wouldn't go until tomorrow. Plenty of time to get everything in order for Liza's trial week."

"What if she decides not to take the job?" Mary crossed her arms and shivered.

"I guess I'll have to come back and start looking again." He grimaced. "Or seriously consider Ashley ... and her brood."

"But what if Liza decides to take the job? Then you'll just stay in Chicago? And not come back at all?" Diane actually sounded alarmed.

"That's my goal. Now, don't panic, you two. Taking care of a dog isn't exactly rocket science."

The ladies exchanged a look.

"What's the matter?"

Diane pursed her lips and nodded toward where Liza

was industriously clearing the front porch. "That *lovely* young woman—"

"*Adorable, sweet* young woman," Mary continued

"Might think you're taking advantage of her," Diane finished.

Jack blew out his breath and watched it steam away from him on the frigid winter air. "No way. I'll put together a list of things to help her out—feeding schedule, snacks, walks, all that stuff. It'll be easy. Plus, she'll have the house to herself. She'll love it."

"Is your flight booked?" Diane asked.

"Tomorrow afternoon—five twenty-five."

Diane looked at Mary.

"Is there something I'm missing?" Jack asked. "You two seem a little concerned about this."

"No. Nothing," Mary said.

"It's too cold out here. Say hello to Liza for us." Diane stepped back and shut the door.

Now, what was that all about? Considering the busybodies they were, he would have expected them to love his idea. With him gone, they'd have plenty of opportunities to come over and get to know Liza.

Shaking his head, he tramped back to the snow blower. There were benefits to living in an apartment in the city. Big benefits—like not having to clear the walks. Getting snowed in there would have meant something entirely different from getting snowed in here.

For starters, Kate from down the hall would probably have come down the hall.

He grinned. They would have had an evening by the fire that wouldn't have involved cards at all—unless Kate insisted on a game of strip poker, which she'd been known to do. And then, instead of getting up early to let out a dog and shovel the walks, they'd have wiled away the morning doing much the same as they'd done the night before, while waiting for the sidewalks and streets to be cleared by plows.

Not that he didn't have fun last night. The ladies were, well, the ladies. And Liza was really a trouper, she never complained about the situation, just made the best of it. Kind of a nice change from some of the high-maintenance women he was used to.

He yanked on the starter. When the engine didn't fire up, he pulled the starter again. Nothing. He turned the choke on full, primed it a few times, and tried the starter once more. Silence. He let out a low curse. No, no, no. This was not happening. The snow blower couldn't have broken down after a blizzard. He took the cap off the gas tank and looked inside to make sure there was plenty. Yep, plenty.

He pulled the starter again with no results. "Shit!" This thing had to be twenty years old. Why the hell hadn't his grandmother ever gotten a new one? Why hadn't Billy said anything? Irritated, he pushed the machine down the half-cleared driveway and into the garage.

Thirty inches of snow and he was going to have to shovel it all by hand. Yeah, this was definitely different than apartment living in Chicago.

He lifted a shovel off a hook on the wall and hefted it in both hands. This was a really old one. Not molded plastic, just heavy steel ... with a corroded blade.

He carried the shovel to the front of the house where Liza was working. She looked up expectantly, a winsome picture. Her nose and cheeks were pink from the cold, and a handful of wavy curls had escaped her hat and were dancing around her face in the wind. *Good thing he wasn't interested in winsome.*

"The snow blower quit working. We have to finish this job the old-fashioned way."

She set her shovel in the snow and rested one hand on the handle. "Do I get time-and-a-half for overtime?"

"No. But I'll promote you to vice president."

"I'd rather have the money."

He let out a laugh. "Back to work, then. Break time's over." He put the rusty blade to the concrete and begin to shovel the snow off to the side. By the time he finished the rest of the driveway, each scoop of snow seemed heavier than the last. He'd unzipped his jacket ages ago. Now he pulled it off and threw it in a snowbank.

He leaned on his shovel and stretched his back. Hell, he exercised almost every day, but shoveling this wet snow was like working in a rock quarry—with a pickax.

Liza pretended to check her watch. "Another break already? Your contract only allows two a day."

"Easy for you to say—you've got the modern, lightweight, molded-plastic shovel."

"Yeah. And you've got the muscles. I think we're even." She began shoveling again.

Jack watched her for a moment, admiring her determination as she threw each shovelful of snow to the side. "How do you know I have muscles? I could be a ninety-pound weakling under all these clothes."

"Believe me. I know."

She knew? The idea that Liza Dunnigan knew—that she'd even noticed—made the corners of his mouth curve up.

———

Liza looked up as Jack trudged down the sidewalk toward her. His cheeks were ruddy, his hazel eyes sparkled in the brisk air. His old, faded navy blue Stanford sweatshirt was just tight enough to prove her right—the guy had muscles, nice ones.

She gave her head a shake. This wasn't the kind of information she needed to be gathering. Her mission was to get to Cordelia—not to Jack Graham.

He jammed his shovel into a snowbank and blew out his breath in exaggerated exhaustion. "Wow. Now, *that* was a workout." He held up a hand and she slapped him five.

No doubt every muscle in her body would be aching tomorrow. She probably wouldn't even be able to walk. "I'm starting to wonder if you got me from the inn not to rescue me, but to ensure you had help moving all this snow."

Jack held up both hands in surrender. "Listen, if you take the caretaker job, I promise to buy a new snow blower."

A plow rumbled down the street and they watched as it filled the base of every driveway on the block with two feet of wet, sloppy, gray snow.

Liza let out a groan. "If I become the caretaker, I'm hiring someone else to do this job."

"Smart woman," Jack said. "There should be a law about snowplows and driveways."

"I think I'll look into joining a culinary school in Florida."

"Hell no. You'll *love* Maine. It's hardly ever like this."

She threw back her head and laughed.

"Tell you what, you go on inside. I'll clean up after the plow." Jack pulled his shovel from the snowbank and swung into action.

Liza watched him for a moment. He'd be out here until

dark clearing the two driveways. Hardly seemed fair. With a sigh, she picked up her shovel and went to help him.

By the time they finished almost an hour later, both were breathing hard. As they started up the walk, an older mini-van pulled in front of Jack's house. The doors slid open and out tumbled Ashley's four boys, whooping and hollering as they threw themselves onto the mountains of snow on lining each side of the driveway. Ashley got out of the driver's door.

"Hey, Jack!" she called. "I've brought the boys over to help you shovel. Just tell them what to do."

One of the boys slid down the huge snowbank on his butt, depositing a pile of snow on the freshly shoveled walk. Two others followed his lead and the amount of snow on the walk grew.

Liza frowned. "I'll tell them what to do," she muttered. "How about—get lost."

Jack grinned at her. "I dare you to say that loud enough for her to hear."

"Darers go first."

Jack widened his eyes. "Okay. Okay." He waved a hand as though this was no big deal and stepped toward Ashley. "Get ..." He glanced back at Liza and made a face. "Get ... a shovel and clear off a place in the backyard for CJ to use."

Liza stepped right up behind him and whispered close to his ear, "Chicken."

He turned slowly. She looked up, their eyes met. She gulped.

Somewhere in the distance, she could hear Ashley clapping her hands and shouting, "Boys! Listen up—go clear out a poop patio for CJ in the back." She heard the van doors open again and the boys screeching as they grabbed shovels and raced up the driveway and through the gate into the backyard.

"Who are you calling chicken?" Jack asked, his voice teasing, his eyes twinkling.

She could swear her heart stopped beating as he spoke. Her last resort—Plan Z—to gain access to Dear Cordelia was to seduce this guy into giving up the information she needed.

At the moment, she was thinking there might be definite positives to pursuing that plan of action. *If only she knew how the hell to do it.* Where was Kristin when she needed her?

A snowball splatted against the back of Jack's neck, saving her from blurting out the only thought in her head: *Want to make out?*

12

He spun round only to get hit in the chest by another snow ball. "Hey!" he shouted.

Ashley grinned at him and let fly another snowball, missing him entirely this time. Jack scooped up a handful of snow and formed a snowball as Ashley took off running, laughing as Jack shot a snowball her way.

Liza rolled her eyes. Ashley had gotten just what she wanted—Jack's attention. And it was just as well. Those two could play outside while she sneaked in to nose around Jack's stuff. She started for the side door only to have Ashley's four boys jump out of the backyard and begin pummeling her with snowballs, while making kung fu motions and shouting, "Hi-ya!" She threw her arms up in defense and ran down the driveway with the boys in hot pursuit.

"Incoming!" she shouted.

"Over here!" Jack ran toward her, grabbed her arm, and dragged her behind a snowbank. He pounded a fistful of snow into a tight ball and fired it at the boys, reaching immediately for more snow. "Backup, Liza, backup!"

She swung into action, unable to stop laughing as the snowballs flew so fast and furious between the two sides it was hard to see. "I'll make a stockpile," she cried, as she crouched down to make snowballs and pile them up.

Jack grabbed them as fast as she could make them. After a couple of minutes, he dropped down beside her and began to make snowballs, too. "We'll do a blitzkrieg." He laughed wickedly.

Liza stuck her head up over the snow pile to check on the boys and spotted them sneaking along the sidewalk toward where she and Jack were hidden. "They're coming," she whispered. "A frontal assault down the walk."

Jack made a fist with his gloved hand and held it up toward her. Liza did the same, punching her padded knuckles against his.

A snowball landed on the ground nearby.

"It's showtime," he said.

Grabbing a snowball in each hand, they jumped to their feet and began firing. The boys shot back, diving and rolling down the banks to the sidewalk, throwing snowballs as they fell.

Liza reached for the last snowball, just as Jack did. Their hands met on top of it. "You take it," she said.

He fired it off, then grabbed her hand and started running for the house, all the while shouting, "Truce! Truce!"

Snowballs peppered them from both sides as they raced up the steps to the safety of the porch. They bent over laughing, breath rolling out of them in white puffy bursts. A snowball landed on the porch and Jack held up his hands in surrender. "Uncle, Uncle!"

Mouth tight, Ashley marched up the walk. A snowball smacked into her shoulder. She turned slowly as the boys laughed and pointed at one another, loudly proclaiming each other the guilty party. She shook her head. Two more snowballs landed nearby. She looked back at Jack, smiled, and shook her head. "Boys."

Liza couldn't resist murmuring, "Discipline," under her breath.

"Dare you," Jack muttered.

Ashley joined them on the porch. "So, what have you decided about the dog?" she asked Liza pointedly.

This was clearly not a woman who beat around the bush.

Jack looked at Liza and raised his brows. She cleared her throat, determined to come across strong and in control of the situation. "I'm, ah, going to take some time to get to know the dog better before I decide."

Ashley's face scrunched in disbelief. "What's to get to know? How are you going to do that?"

"She's moving in here for the next week," Jack said.

Ashley's jaw dropped. "With you?"

Liza nodded, mildly enjoying the woman's surprise.

Jack shook his head. "Well, not exactly. I've got to get back to Chicago ..."

Liza tried not to look incredulous as she turned toward him. In the yard, the boys were tackling one another, wiping snow into each other's faces, sliding down the snowbanks to the sidewalk, and shouting and laughing with glee. Ashley seemed oblivious to their antics.

"I'm going back to Chicago for a few days," Jack said almost apologetically.

What?

He looked at Liza. "You don't need me here to get to know the dog—"

"Wait—are you serious? You're leaving?" Her stomach

flopped in horror, and her visions of becoming an investigative reporter began to melt like a snowball in the desert.

He had the good grace to look at least a little guilty. "Yeah—"

"You're leaving Coldwater?" Ashley said, shocked.

"When?" both women asked in unison.

"Tomorrow. Five twenty-five flight. Now, Liza, don't worry—I'll write down the instructions about CJ And you've got the ladies next door if you have questions."

He was leaving? He couldn't leave Coldwater—she was just moving in. Her mind raced for an excuse, any excuse, to keep him in town. "But—but—I've never taken care of a dog."

"That's why this is so perfect. You can get a real-life trial without any interference. We'll talk at the end of the week."

Let him know at the end of the week? But Cordelia— what about Cordelia? She tried to figure out what to say, what to do.

Ashley smirked as though she was sure Liza's only motive was a romantic interest in Jack. "The boys and I would be happy to take the job without even a trial period."

"Thanks, Ashley, but I made this agreement with Liza first."

"But—"

"I'll let you know if it doesn't work out," Jack said.

Ashley set her jaw just as a snowball landed on top of her head. Wet chunks slid down the sides of her face like long white sideburns. She wiped the snow away and pointed at the van, growling, "Let's go. Now."

The boys tumbled down the sides of the snowbank into the street and piled into the van. Liza shook her head as they drove away. Poor CJ would probably choose to pass on to the next world after a week with that brood.

She let her gaze slide over the sidewalks and driveway they had just spent hours shoveling. The snowball fight may have been fun, but now they were left with more work. She closed her eyes briefly.

"Good thing Ashley brought the boys over to help clear away the snow," Jack muttered. He went down the steps, picked his jacket out of the snowbank where he'd thrown it earlier, and slipped it on. Then he put his shovel to the walk and began to scrape it clean.

Liza waited a moment before following him. How could Jack be leaving tomorrow? How could everything suddenly be falling apart just when it had seemed like everything was falling into place? Despair tried to skitter through her but she refused to panic. Not yet. She couldn't panic until she thought through all her options.

Right, options. *What options?* Insist he stay in Coldwater because she was afraid to be in the house alone with a dog? Oh, that would go over well.

Maybe she should fly back to Chicago, too. Right. And leave the dog unattended while she chased Jack around the city for a story. Now, *that* would make him want to spill his guts.

She pulled her shovel from the snowbank where she'd left it. Obviously, as far as options went, she *had* no options.

After a hot shower, Liza pulled on jeans and a cable knit turtleneck then waited in her bedroom until she heard Jack go into the bathroom and turn on the shower. She knew the moment he got under the hot spray because he let out a groan of ecstasy. Reaching for her phone, she quickly dialed Kristin to distract herself from the picture of him naked, reaching bliss in the shower. "We have a problem," she whispered into the phone.

"Now what?"

"He's leaving tomorrow, back to Chicago."

"How can he leave? What about the dog? Weren't you supposed to be getting to know the dog this week?"

"He says I can stay at the house and get acquainted with CJ while he's back in Chicago." Liza sat on the edge of the bed.

"Oh shit."

"Any brilliant ideas?"

Kristin sighed. "Not offhand. How can you make him stay when you hardly know the guy? The only option left might be to seduce him into staying."

"Excuse me? You mean like promise him favors for the week?"

"Something like that."

Liza's face began to burn. "I don't think so."

"Oh, come on. What happened to the new Liza?"

"Even the new Liza has her limits."

Kristin laughed. "I'm just kidding. Sort of. Well, if you're not going to do the week-long seduction thing—"

"I'm not."

"Then, I guess you'd better get the information you need tonight." Kristin let out a sigh. "Or tomorrow before he leaves."

"This much I could have figured out myself."

"Where is he right now?"

"Taking a shower," Liza said.

"Oh, the pictures in my mind ..."

"Been there, done that. Come on, help me out, Kristin. I'm desperate."

"For starters, you should be looking around his room right now instead of talking to me," Kristin said.

"Maybe I should give up on stealth and ask him outright—"

"That's a total non-starter. Look at all the reporters who've called him for an interview over the last ten years. It's never worked." Kristin let out a sigh. "I'm telling you, there's only one way to get answers out of a man who doesn't want to talk."

"I was afraid you were going to come back to that."

"What's to be afraid of? All you have to do is tease—no one says you have to go any further."

Liza's chest tightened. What had she gotten herself into? It was so easy to talk about beguiling answers out of Jack. But to actually do it? "Yeah, but what if he's not interested?"

"He's male. He's interested. Now, as long as he's in the shower, go dig around his room while you have the chance."

Liza swiped off the phone and slipped into the hall, pausing briefly to make sure the shower was still running before she went into Jack's room. She dropped to her knees on the floor next to the desk, unzipped his computer case, and began to riffle though the pockets and papers searching for any reference to Dear Cordelia.

After a minute, she stopped to listen for the sound of the shower—and heard nothing. She started to stand. Omigod. Jack was out of the shower. Almost hyperventilating from adrenaline, she zipped the case shut and raced downstairs, not even breathing until she was safe in the living room. She dropped onto the couch and tried to look relaxed as she gulped in air and tried to still the racing of her heart before Jack came down.

In the hearth, a bright fire glowed—and a piled of

packaged pressed logs stacked was neatly stacked on the floor. Apparently, Diane and Mary had stopped over while she was in the shower. Even though the heat was working again, the fire was a wonderful touch on this cold winter night.

Her investigation into Jack's computer case had been a bust, which meant everything she needed was probably stored on his computer. She stared into the fire, hashing over the discussion she'd just had with Kristin and their different approaches to solving the problem. Maybe she could ease into a discussion about Cordelia by asking Jack what it was like to work for the woman. Then she could ask if, as CJ's caretaker, she might be able to meet Cordelia. And from there she could go right into a request for the woman's phone number. That could work.

Yeah, right, and basset hounds could fly.

Or there was Kristin's approach, which would have her snuggling on the sofa with the man, arms around one another, his incredible mouth on hers. And when they came up for air, she could, somehow, ask the same questions, in a breathless sort of just-wondering way.

Even if she didn't get any information, she had to admit Kristin's plan had a lot more appeal.

———

The doorbell chimed and Jack bounded down the stairs, pulling a wrinkled twenty-dollar bill from his jeans pocket. "I ordered a pizza when you were in the shower," he said as he went to the door. "Hope you like a lot of toppings."

"I'm so hungry I'll even eat anchovies," Liza answered.

Jack set the pizza on the coffee table and tore open the paper packaging. Steam wafted up from a thin crust pizza covered with sausage, mushrooms, black olives and onions. He inhaled deeply and his stomach rumbled. "No anchovies," he said, "just one of the best pizzas around. Eat up."

He looked at Liza on the couch, light brown hair still slightly damp from the shower. There was that winsome look again. Winsome and cute. Not his type. Although, that didn't mean he couldn't enjoy the moment. "You want some wine?" he asked.

At her affirmative reply, he ducked into the kitchen for a couple of glasses and the bottle of pinot noir he'd picked up at the grocery store the day he arrived.

He presented Liza with a glass and she smiled up at him. "Thanks. After all that shoveling, I think this is the best meal I could have ever asked for."

"It's pretty simple."

"I'm a simple person. A pizza and a glass of red. I'm happy."

What a change from the last couple of women he had dated. Too bad Liza wanted to live in Coldwater, because despite the fact that she had that winsome thing going on, he found her really appealing.

He browsed through the CDs on a shelf near the fireplace, then chose a couple of big band era music and inserted them into the CD player. "This is about as modern as my grandmother gets. At least I got her into the new century with a CD player. Got her a laptop too, so she could send email."

As the music of Benny Goodman slid out of the speakers, Jack settled himself on the floor by the coffee table, Japanese-restaurant style. Liza took a slice of pizza and scooted down to sit beside him.

"I can't remember the last time I was this famished," he

said. "Shows you what hard work will do." He controlled himself from wolfing down his food so Liza didn't think he was a pig.

"Famished and sore." Liza rolled her shoulders and tilted her head from side to side. "That hot shower was only a temporary fix." She leaned back against the sofa and stretched her legs out on the floor as she ate her pizza.

He watched as she chewed slowly and swallowed, as her tongue flicked out to catch some tomato sauce on her lower lip, as she rolled her shoulders in that tight blue sweater. His heart began to speed up. "This wine is like a muscle relaxant," she said in a low voice.

Muscle relaxant? A specific set of his muscles weren't feeling exactly relaxed right now. Aphrodisiac, maybe. "Then more is definitely in order." Jack refilled both their glasses.

"I think so," Liza murmured. "No more one glass limits. Life is too short to never wear a lampshade. You know, I'm changing my life."

"Right. The culinary school."

She nodded and sipped her wine and he raised his glass in toast. "To success in your new life ... and may you find you have a great affection for basset hounds."

Liza clinked her glass against his and took another big swallow of wine. "Do you ever think about changing your life?" she asked.

He shrugged. *All the time.* "Once in a while. But so far things have gone pretty well for me—it's hard to complain."

"Owning your own business must be nice. Take time off whenever you want."

"Yeah, no one forces me use vacation days to come home and look for a caretaker for the dog."

"Unlimited vacation days must be awesome." Liza

smiled at him, all warm and nice, eyes shining in the firelight. She shook her head. Her hair, now almost dry, had softened into waves around her face, waves that he could slip his hands into, comb his fingers through—

"What? Right, it's awesome," he stammered. "In fact, I really need to plan a vacation—after I find a caretaker—" He broke off, stunned at his awkwardness. This wasn't like him, he didn't ramble.

Liza put her hands on her lower back, fingers splayed out across her buttocks, and arched her back to stretch her muscles. Her sweater tightened across her breasts, and his mouth went dry. He reached for his wineglass and took another drink. Liza was definitely attractive, but she wasn't the kind of woman men lust after ... at least not the kind of woman he lusted after.

So what the hell was with him tonight?

Maybe it was the wine. He held his wineglass up and looked through it at the fire. Who cared what the reasons were? He finished off his wine and emptied the last of the bottle into his glass.

"I'll get another bottle," he said and headed into the kitchen, his thoughts still rolling. So what if Liza wasn't his type. So what if he was going back to Chicago tomorrow and she was staying in small town Coldwater. All he knew was that there was heat in the room and it wasn't all coming from the fireplace.

13

THE FRONT DOOR OPENED AND BANGED AGAINST THE wall. "Hello, hello!" Diane's voice rang out.

Jack winced. So much for all the heat in the room. Probably was for the best; he hadn't actually known where he was going with that previous train of thought anyway. "Come on in. We're in the living room," he called.

He heard boots clunk to the floor, then Diane came through the doorway in thick socks, Mary hurrying behind her carrying a large box. CJ rolled to her feet from her spot in front of the fire and wiggled her body and tail in excitement.

Diane drew up short and Mary almost ran right into her. "Oh, dear, we're not interrupting anything, are we?" she asked.

Jack grinned at Liza. "Not a thing."

"Oh. That's good." Diane sounded disappointed. "I guess. We just wanted to thank you for clearing or walk."

Mary patted CJ on the head. "We could never have done it ourselves, so we brought you a present."

Jack waved a hand. "No present necessary. We were happy to do it."

"Even though you're young, to do all that without a snow blower," Mary said, ignoring him. "You had to have strained some muscles. No one can lift that much snow and not have their back hurt."

Liza smiled. "We were just talking about the same thing."

Mary turned to Diane. "You see, I told you. I knew this was the right thing to do." She held up the box she had carried into the house. "This was Charlie's. Being a carpenter, he often had a sore back."

"BackMaster," Liza read aloud. "Two-motor back massager helps soothe and relax your back. Powerful massage action. With heat." As she raised her brows at Jack, it was all he could do to keep from laughing out loud.

"Well, thanks," he said, "We can probably put that thing to good use."

Mary pulled out a gray rectangular cushion with an attached electrical cord and a remote control. "I'll show you how it works." She plugged the cord into an outlet and set the BackMaster against the back cushion of the couch. "Someone sit here now." She patted the BackMaster. "Sit, sit. Charlie just loved this thing."

Jack gestured with one hand. "Ladies first."

Liza sat with her back against the cushion. "Can I drink wine while I do this?"

"Just hold your glass tight so it doesn't vibrate right out of your hand," he said with a grin.

Mary tsked. "For heaven's sake, the whole room won't be shaking." She picked up the remote control and pushed a button. "Here comes the heat."

Liza sipped her wine and waited. After a minute, she made a silly face at Jack. "Ooohh. I feel it. I *do* feel it."

Mary beamed and pushed another button. "Here comes the massage. Slow." She pressed another button. "Or fast."

Liza let out a squeal. "How could I have not known these things existed?"

She took the remote control from Mary's outstretched hand and pushed the buttons herself. "Jack, you have to try this—after I'm done with it, of course, which will be in a couple of hours."

Diane nodded. "Well, Mary, I think our work here is done. Good-night all." She ruffled the top of CJ's head.

The dog followed them out of the room. "Jack, I think CJ wants to go out," Mary said. "You want me to let her out back?"

"Yeah, thanks." He winked at Liza. "Best neighbors ever."

Mary led CJ through the house to the back door, talking the whole way. "It's a cold one out there tonight, sweetheart, so you do your duty quick." As she returned to the front hall to get her boots and jacket, she stuck her head in the living room. "She's outside, so don't forget her. See you two tomorrow."

"Enjoy the BackMaster," Diane called from the foyer. The door clunked shut behind the two women.

Jack turned to Liza. "Now, where were we?"

"You were going to try the BackMaster." Liza scooted away from the massaging cushion and Jack took her place.

He let out a laugh. "Wow, this thing is great. I think Mary may be onto something."

Liza lips curved upward and he stared at her mouth and held himself back from kissing her.

"I've got an idea," she was saying. "If we sit back-to-back we can both use it."

He looked at her and blinked. *I've got a better idea. If we sit front-to-front we can do something else.* He shook his head to clear away the thought.

Don't go getting yourself involved here, he admonished himself. This was the woman who was moving from Chicago and to Coldwater, who wanted to live in a small town. He turned up the heat on the cushion and relished the warmth seeping into his stiff muscles.

"Well, do you want to?" Liza's voice jarred him back to the moment.

Want to? Hell, don't be asking me questions like that. "I guess it's worth a try." He shifted on the couch so he was sitting sideways.

Liza plopped herself down with her back to his, then reached a hand back to position the cushion between them. A light laugh rippled out of her.

"What's so funny?"

"I was just thinking how my parents would react if I told them I'd shared a vibrating cushion with a guy I hardly know. Probably have a stroke."

"This is something new for you? I do this all the time."

"I bet you do."

"What's that supposed to mean?" He twisted to one side so he could see her face.

"All those women you know in Chicago ... surely there's a kinky one or two in the bunch." Her eyes sparkled, teasing.

"Kinky is in the eye of the beholder. You know what they say, one person's kinky is another person's treasure."

"Actually, it's *one person's* trash *is another person's treasure.*"

He was starting to love the way her mouth looked, the way it moved, the way the corners tipped upward even when she wasn't actually smiling.

This was not productive thinking. He tore his gaze off her lips and brought it to her eyes. *Really unproductive move.* Her eyes seemed even darker in the firelight. Exotic almost ... seductive. Damn.

She brought a hand to her mouth. "What? Do I have food in my teeth?"

He twisted around abruptly so he was no longer facing temptation. "I think the wine is making me stupid."

"Yeah, me too. Let's have some more. To celebrate. After all, how often in one lifetime can you have a blizzard, power outage, and vibrating cushion all in the same day?" She leaned over to the coffee table to grasp the neck of the bottle and refill their glasses.

He stared at the wall, glass in hand, his back against Liza's, vibrating, warm, every inch of him knowing she was behind him— Damn, get a grip. He was leaving tomorrow. And taking advantage of this woman tonight could ... Could what? Be fun? There was no reason they couldn't enjoy tonight if she was willing. He didn't want to scare her away from the caretaker job, but if she was willing ...

She moved her head to the music and her hair slid against the back of his neck, the scent of kiwi wafting toward him. He thought of kissing her, of burying his hands in that hair as he took her mouth with his.

Except this was the weirdest situation he'd ever found himself in. It wasn't as though he'd just brought her home from a date and they were sitting on her couch saying good night. He leaned sideways, twisting until she was forced to turn and see what he was doing.

She raised her eyebrows in question. "Yes?"

Oh hell. He was leaving tomorrow anyway. How could he leave town without knowing what it was like to kiss Liza Dunnigan? Screw the discussion.

He raised one hand to touch her hair, run his fingers along her jaw. Her eyes widened, and he gently pulled her head toward his and kissed her before she had a chance to protest. As her mouth softened beneath his, the cushion fell to the floor still vibrating, massaging the coffee table leg, and he came to the realization that kissing Liza was like eating potato chips—he wasn't going to be able to stop with just one.

Outside he heard CJ bark to come in, but he ignored her. The dog could wait a minute or two. He shifted slightly, his sore muscles strained to their limits by the awkward sitting position. "Maybe we should get more comfortable," he said.

In the backyard, CJ barked again.

"Does she need to come in?" Liza straightened and looked anxiously at him.

Her lips were lush and soft and slightly parted, and he'd be damned if he'd let CJ interrupt them now. He pulled Liza up against him, repositioning them both as he nuzzled her hair. "She'll be fine. She's wearing a fur coat," he murmured, taking her mouth again. He slouched down onto the armrest bringing Liza with him, his hands exploring the soft heat of her.

She pushed back slightly and drew a shaky breath. "What I'm thinking, actually, is that CJ—" She drew another quick breath. "She's so old—she'll freeze to the sidewalk. Maybe you'd better get her."

"You'll do just fine in the caretaker's job." He pushed himself to his feet and put his hands on the small of his back to stretch the exhausted muscles. "Don't go anywhere." He opened the back door expecting CJ to amble right in, but she wasn't there. He squinted into the darkness, then whistled irritably into the cold night, his mind distracted by an image of Liza all warm and soft waiting for him in the living room. *Dammit CJ, where are you?* After another minute, he closed the door, put on his boots, and grabbed his jacket from a hook by the door.

"Is something wrong?" Liza appeared in the kitchen doorway, hair mussed, cheeks flushed pink, lips temptingly kissable.

He forced himself to open the door. "CJ's not coming in."

Liza stepped toward him. "Is she in the yard?"

He shrugged. "I'm kind of hoping she's not frozen to the sidewalk."

"Really?"

"No. I'm sure she's just off in a corner smelling something," he said as he retrieved the flashlight from the kitchen drawer.

Outside, his optimism began to fade immediately. He aimed the light around the fenced-in yard, across the area Ashley's boys had shoveled clean so that CJ had somewhere to move around. That's when he spotted the backyard gate swinging open.

"Oh, fuck," he muttered. "Those damn kids." They must have left it open—and Diane let CJ out without checking because why would she think the gate would be unlatched.

That old dog wouldn't have the stamina to last very long with the outside temperature so low.

He started down the driveway, sweeping the flashlight beam from side to side, hoping to spot CJ in the shadows. Good thing she was old and fat, she couldn't have gotten far.

And with her short legs, there was no way she'd be climbing into the snow. Reaching the front sidewalk, he shouted "CJ" several times in either direction—to no avail.

Diane's house was dark, the ladies already in bed. Just as well; he didn't want to make them feel too bad about not making sure the gate was secured. He glanced at his watch. Nine-fifteen. He took the porch steps two at a time and went into the house, slapping his hands together for warmth. Liza met him at the door.

"She's gone," he said. "The back gate is open. Ashley's boys left it open when they shoveled."

"Omigod, CJ probably *will* freeze to the sidewalk."

Jack scowled. "Don't remind me. It's too late to call the animal shelter to see if she's been turned in. But I'll call the police—maybe someone found her already."

Minutes later, he learned that the police hadn't picked up a basset hound but would alert all squads. Alert all squads for a missing dog? Somehow he didn't think that he'd get the same level of response in Chicago.

Liza pulled on her boots and zipped up her jacket. "I'll help you look for her. She couldn't have gotten far—you didn't wait that long to let her in."

"Obviously long enough."

Two hours later, after driving slowly down every block in a mile radius, with Liza hanging out the passenger window shouting "CJ" and him doing the same out the driver's window, Jack pulled the car into the garage. "I can't believe we lost my grandmother's dog."

"We'll find her." She reached out to pat his arm. "Tomorrow we'll put up lost dog posters."

He nodded. Tomorrow. He was supposed to be flying home tomorrow. "Maybe she'll come back tonight," he said with more optimism than he felt.

14

THE SUN ROSE BRITTLE YELLOW ON A BITTER COLD front. Liza wrapped both hands about her coffee mug and tried to forget what it had been like to kiss Jack last night. For all her bravado about seducing him to get the information she needed, she had to admit she'd been relieved that CJ disappeared because it had put an end to whatever it was they had started in the living room.

"I can't believe you're up earlier than me. That coffee smells amazing." Jack padded across the kitchen to pour himself a cup, then called both the animal shelter and the police department to see whether CJ had been brought in during the night.

Liza held her breath not sure what to hope for. The caring, empathetic old-Liza side of her brain wanted CJ to be found right away, but the driven, new-Liza side half-hoped the dog stayed lost—but safe and warm—until Liza got the information she needed about Dear Cordelia. It was starting to seem as if she had a dysfunctional family living a full and demented life in her brain.

Jack stuck his phone in his pocket and shook his head.

"No luck at all. I'm going to run next door to tell the ladies, then go out searching again."

"We should make some signs, too." Liza rolled her shoulders, stiff from all the shoveling. She couldn't believe her luck; Jack was leaving her alone in the house. This could be her last opportunity to look for Cordelia's contact information before he left town.

She watched through the window until he reached Diane's front door, then raced upstairs to his bedroom as fast as the painfully protesting muscles in her legs and lower back would let her go. Flipping open his laptop on his desk, she was overjoyed to see he hadn't logged out and she could get in without a password. Hopefully, he wasn't storing everything on the cloud because then she might be totally out of luck.

Breath coming shallow and fast from her sprint up the stairs, she opened his *Documents* folder and began to scroll through files, quickly scanning the contents. Okay, here were some drafts of old Dear Cordelia columns. That was a good sign. But columns weren't going to give her phone number for Cordelia.

"*Come on, come on, come on,*" she muttered.

———

Jack waited a long time for the ladies to answer the door. From the corner of his eye, he saw the drape in the front window slide to one side, but by the time he turned to see who was there, the drape had already swung back into place.

"Shit, I hope I'm not waking them up," he muttered.

The door opened and Mary stuck her head out. She was

wearing a long, shiny pink robe. "Oh, it's just you, Jack. Good morning, you're up early."

He nodded. "Yeah, sorry. I've got some bad news. Ashley's boys left the gate open yesterday and CJ went missing last night."

Mary's eyes and mouth opened in perfect circles. "No!"

"Yes—"

"Oh, our poor girl."

Diane appeared at Mary's shoulder, wiping her nose. "What's happened? CJ's missing?"

"Disappeared last night—"

Diane sneezed.

"You don't sound so good. Maybe I better come in so you can shut the door." Jack stepped forward.

"It's just a cold, but it's a dandy. I wouldn't come in if I were you. You might catch it." She shook her head. "Darndest thing came on during the night. Woke up with a sore throat, itchy eyes, sneezing, the works."

"CJ's escape wasn't my fault, was it?" Mary asked. "I'm so sorry, I never checked the gate when I let her out."

Jack shook his head. "No, why would you? It's always latched."

"Maybe someone stole her," Mary said.

"CJ? Old, fat, shedding, drooling, dandruff, one-glaucoma-eye CJ? I doubt it," he answered.

"She has a lot of love to give," Diane pointed out, wiping her nose.

"Love is a many splendored thing." Mary grinned inanely.

"Love will keep us together." Diane's expression mirrored Mary's.

"What's love got to do with it?" Jack said, getting into the spirit.

"Well, everything, dear. My gosh, it's about time you fell in love, you know." Mary tsked.

"It's a song. *What's Love Got to Do with It?*"

The two women stared at him. He shook his head. "Okay, never mind. Liza and I are going out to put up some lost dog posters—"

"Are you staying then?" Mary asked, a note of hope in her voice.

"My flight's late afternoon—hopefully she'll turn up before then. Otherwise, I don't know." He rubbed his hands together to warm them. "Can you keep an eye out in case she wanders back? Or someone stops by who might have found her? You've got my cell number—"

"Absolutely. Yes. Yes. Don't worry, we'll both keep watch, won't we, Mary?"

"Of course. Now don't forget to reschedule your flight if you decide to stay or you'll have to buy a new ticket." Mary wagged a finger at him.

Jack took a detour through his grandmother's backyard on the desperate hope that he might spot some footprints belonging to the dog. No such luck. He let himself in the back door, cut across the kitchen and dining room. "Hey, Liza?" Walking to the front of the house, he looked around, then shouted up the stairs. "Liza!"

She skidded around the corner from the upstairs hall and half limped, half flew down the steps. "Hi, I was just looking for something we could use to make signs. Any news?" she asked breathlessly.

He shook his head.

"What did the ladies say?"

"Not much. I think I woke them up. Diane's caught a cold so they didn't want me to come in the house."

"Maybe they were embarrassed you caught them in their pajamas."

Jack snorted out a laugh. "There were covered from neck to ankle. They couldn't have been less exposed if they were wearing mechanics' jumpsuits."

———

Two hours later, they had made stops at the animal shelter, the veterinarian, the pet groomer, the police department, and were back at the animal shelter a second time, just because.

Jack stopped next to a cage holding a golden retriever mix and reached in to pet the dog. The animal's tail wagged happily. A little schnauzer/poodle/bichon type of dog in the next cage pressed itself against the bars, and Jack stuck some fingers through the wire to pet that animal as well. He moved along the row of cages, his expression soft and caring as he gave each dog a minute or two of attention.

"You like dogs," Liza said.

He looked up. "Yeah. But, even more, I hate seeing them like this. Caged. Dogs are pack animals. When they're part of a family, the family becomes their pack. Here, they're all alone."

He moved to a cage holding two smaller dogs and rubbed the heads of both. "These poor guys just want a home, someone to love them."

Liza's heart wrenched. This man was becoming dangerous in the worst sort of way. Taking time to pet the dogs in the pound? Whether she was here on business or not, she wasn't feeling particularly immune to that kind of charm.

"When I was a kid, I used to come down here all the

time. I'd tell the lady at the front desk that I was looking for a dog to adopt—even though it wasn't true." He shook his head. "What I was really doing was making sure the dogs didn't feel abandoned. I'd stop in and pet them and hope it made them feel like they were wanted."

"I bet they did feel wanted." Liza reached a hand through the bars and ruffled the hair on top of a little terrier's head.

"I thought I was so sly, saying I was going to adopt a dog. Years later, the director told me they looked for me every Tuesday and Thursday after school. They knew the truth and just went along with my ploy."

"Did you ever get a dog?"

"We always had dogs. I just wanted more—to give them a home. My grandmother had a soft heart and lots of love to give. She'd take in strays for the night and end up keeping them for good. She didn't care if they were scraggly mutts. So many people want a purebred with the perfect pedigree."

He stopped in the doorway to the room, looked back at the rows of cages and shook his head. "A mix loves you just as much. Maybe even more," he murmured. "My grandma knew that. She took in whatever, whoever, needed her love —and made them whole."

She suspected he was no longer talking about just dogs.

"Let's go put up the signs," he said.

The frigid outside air hit her like a slap across the face and she sucked in a breath. She didn't know how long a dog could last in this weather, but it couldn't be days. Especially not for an old dog used to living indoors.

After hopping in and out of the car a dozen times and pulling her hands out of her gloves to help Jack tape signs to telephone poles, Liza's fingers were stiff with cold. She curled her icy fingers against her palms for warmth, and began to fantasize about taking such a long hot shower that she drained the water tank and wrinkled her fingers and toes.

"You look chilled," Jack said as they headed for the car after posting the last sign.

Understatement. "Justalidda." Her jaw was so frozen she could hardly form the words.

He put his arm around her shoulders and rubbed vigorously. "Get in. I know just what you need."

She looked at his rosy cheeks and the dark growth on his jaw and thought of a really fun way to warm up. Last night he had kissed her as if he meant it. Maybe a little more of the same would do the job.

Gaack! Had her common sense frozen too? She was here to track down Dear Cordelia, not have a short-term fling.

Jack slid into the driver's seat and pulled away from the curb, one hand deftly turning the wheel while the other cranked up the heat. "There's a little cafe downtown. Strong coffee and great hot chocolate."

Well, didn't that about sum it up. She was thinking about kissing, and he was thinking about food. She pulled off her gloves and wiggled her fingers in front of the heat vents. Jack reached over to wrap his hand around hers.

"Does this help?" he asked.

Help? Help what? Help her already racing libido go into overdrive? She nodded, more because she knew he expected an answer and less from an ability to think clearly. "Thanks."

She tried to breathe normally. This investigation was taking a disconcerting twist. Jack Graham had kissed her last night. Now he was holding her hand. Sure, Kristin had told her to beguile Jack into getting the information she needed. But they'd never even considered what to do if she actually started to fall for the guy.

Jack pulled up in front of the Bear Claw Cafe and Coffee Bar. "Forget the coffee," Liza said, following him inside, "it's hot cocoa for me today."

She wrapped her hands around her mug and let out a sigh of contentment as the warmth seeped into her fingers.

"I'm really worried," Jack said. "This is a small town. If someone found CJ, we would know already."

"Yeah, but there are always new people moving into towns," Liza said brightly to hide her own pessimism. "One of them might have found her, and she's safe and warm in their house. It hasn't even been twenty-four hours." She picked up a newspaper someone had left behind in their booth and started to flip to the want-ads in the back. "Push comes to shove, we can run a lost-dog ad." She stopped and turned back a page. "Hey, look at this, it's your client! Dear Cordelia." She folded the paper onto itself and held it up so Jack could see Cordelia's column.

"After ten years, I don't get excited seeing the column anymore," he said wryly.

"I get that. Do you ever spend personal time with her or is it just a business relationship—emails, phone calls?"

Jack frowned. "Well, sure, I see her. She's my client."

She couldn't believe he was answering her questions. She forged ahead, afraid to waste a minute in case he clammed up. "So why does she use a drawing of herself at the top instead of a photo like other columnists?"

"Says it's more romantic. Softer edges means she never ages, or something like that."

"Hasn't she heard of photo editing software? Her picture can be doctored."

Jack shrugged and took a drink of his cocoa.

"So how'd you meet her?"

He froze with his mug halfway to his mouth. "Through a mutual friend."

She warned herself to slow down. She had dropped into investigative mode and Jack was obviously pulling back. Adjusting the newspaper, she pretended to read Dear Cordelia's column, while actually trying figure out how to ask: *Does she live around here?* With Jack flying out this afternoon, she had nothing to lose by asking. Actually she had plenty to lose, but it was worth the risk. She opened her mouth.

"Jack Graham?"

They both looked up at a tall, thin man who had stopped at their table.

Jack nodded. "That's me."

The man extended a hand. "Terry Schultz. I'm a reporter with the local paper. I knew your grandmother."

Liza sensed a wariness come over Jack. He shook the other's hand. "Nice to meet you."

"I understand you're the publicist for Dear Cordelia. The advice columnist."

Jack nodded, a pained expression on his face. "Yes."

The reporter grinned. "I thought so. I'm working on a Valentine's Day story—"

"No kidding."

Liza winced at the edge in his voice.

"It would really make this month's issue a success if I could interview Cordelia—"

"You and every other reporter in the country," Jack muttered.

"Excuse me?" the man asked.

"Cordelia is very private."

"I've heard that. But—"

"She doesn't do interviews." Jack's words were clipped, his tone curt. And it told Liza all she needed to know—Jack Graham would never set up an interview with Cordelia, not for anyone.

Terry Schultz frowned. "But maybe if—"

"No maybes. No interviews."

The reporter looked taken aback. "Everyone has their price—what's hers?"

Jack glanced at the man's worn leather jacket and old jeans. "She has no price," he said matter-of-factly.

"How about if I interview you then?"

"Her publicist? What do people care what I have to say?"

"You could give some insights into what she's like."

"No. Thanks for stopping over. Good luck with your Valentine's edition." Jack turned his attention to Liza, his body language clearly stating the conversation was over.

The reporter stayed a moment longer as if deciding what to do next. "Okay, thanks. Hope you find your dog," he said before turning away.

"Damn. Reporters drive me nuts." Jack smiled and his expression lightened. "Except food reporters, that is."

Liza's stomach took a flop. "Yeah, we don't care about love, only about how good our next meal is."

"Investigative reporters are just so damn persistent."

"I think newspaper editors value tenacity."

"Tenacity? Maybe. All I know is, some aren't above lying to get their story."

Liza blinked.

"You wouldn't believe the lines I've gotten from people trying to get an interview with Cordelia," he said.

"Maybe they're feeling, you know, desperate. Don't you

think if Cordelia would grant a couple of interviews, they'd quit being so persistent?"

Jack's expression darkened. "Cordelia is entitled to privacy just like everyone else. If she doesn't want to give interviews, she shouldn't have to."

"Maybe some of the pressure would go away if she'd open up a little? Half the interest is because she's such a mystery."

"She doesn't want to do interviews. So it's my job to protect her right to make that choice."

There was a fierceness in his voice that Liza both feared and admired. God help her if he ever got wind of her real reason for being here. He'd never believe she was one of those reporters who had no qualms about lying to get a story. He'd never believe she'd never done it before. And truth be told, if their roles were reversed, she probably wouldn't either. But that wasn't what she was really like. It was just that this an unusual case with unusual circumstances, and if she wanted to have any hope of changing her career path, she had to get this story.

Dread settled into her stomach. She gave a weak smile and hoped Jack couldn't sense her nervousness.

"Sorry," he said. "I don't mistrust all reporters. I'm sure the food section reporters are ethical."

"Oh, sometimes I'm tempted to stretch the truth about how many calories are in a recipe. Especially the decadent ones." Her stomach tightened at telling yet another lie even if it was in jest. She didn't want Jack to think she was just like all the other reporters. She didn't want him to think she was a Goody Two Shoes either. She mentally sighed.

Who the hell *was* she, anyway?

15

THE WAITRESS REFILLED THEIR COFFEE CUPS AND asked whether they wanted something to eat. "We've got a batch of chili simmering in the back," she said. "Just the thing to warm you up on a day like this."

Her words made Liza realize how hungry she was. "I could go for a bowl—unless you want to get back out and search some more ..."

"Hell, it's almost noon—we might as well eat first. Make it two bowls," he said to the waitress.

"You're looking for that dog, aren't you?"

Jack brightened. "Yeah. Have you seen her?"

"Naw. Sorry. Lots of folks are putting microchips in their dogs so they can find them if they're missing. I guess you didn't do that?"

Jack shook his head. "No microchip. Maybe lots of potato chips, though."

The woman gave him a strange look and left to put their order in. Minutes later she was setting two bowls of chili on the table, along with little paper containers of cheese, onions and sour cream. "You know, I've been thinking about your dog," she said, straightening. "Maybe someone took her for ransom."

Liza focused on dumping cheese and onions on her chili. She sneaked a glance at Jack.

He cleared his throat. "Uh, maybe. But who would think an old, glaucomic dog is worth some sort of ransom?"

"Well, it's hard for me to know, since I don't hardly know you anyway. But, ever since your grandma set up that fund to keep the dog in the house, people have been talking about how much money that old woman really had. Not me, mind you, but other folks."

"Anyone in particular?"

The woman shook her head. "Look, I'm sort of like a think tank. I come up with ideas for people. It's up to them to follow through." She ripped their bill off the top of her order pad and set it face down on the table. "Tell you what. I'll keep thinking about your situation and if I come up with any ideas, I'll let you know."

"Great. Thanks." Jack stuck a spoonful of scalding chili into his mouth and Liza was certain he did it to keep from laughing out loud. He grabbed a glass of water and gulped it down.

"A think tank?" he said once their server was gone. "Give me a break. Nobody would be dumb enough to think someone would pay a ransom for that old dog."

"You would," Liza said softly.

He jerked his head up, eyes meeting hers. His expression softened, and he set down his spoon. "Yeah," he said with a nod. "If for no other reason than because nobody else would."

Liza smiled into his hazel eyes. He was such a good person. And she was lying to him more every day. What a mess.

But it would be over soon. He'd be gone by this afternoon, taking all his Dear Cordelia information with him—and she'd be back writing for the food section by next week. "I got a text from the Inn," she said, changing the subject. "The lot's been plowed and I can finally get my car out."

———

Liza climbed out of Jack's car onto the freshly shoveled sidewalk in front of the inn. "I'll be over in a bit. I want to pick up a few groceries first." She waved goodbye as he drove away. Thank God he was gone. She needed some advice. Ignoring the foot of snow piled on her windshield, she got into the car, started the engine, and hit speed dial for Kristin.

"You can't let him get on that plane," Kristin said once she heard the whole story.

"Easier said than done. His flight's in four hours and I can't come up with any reason to make him stay, other than the fact that his grandmother's dog is missing."

"Lay it on thick about the dog. Stuff like, his grandmother's cherished dog is now missing because he didn't let her in when she barked. In sub-zero temperatures."

Liza winced. "That feels unfair, a really low blow. He's a good guy—"

"You need to stop thinking of him as a *good guy* and start thinking of him as a *goal to achieve*."

Liza let out a long sigh. "Yeah, I know. The thing is, he hates reporters—well, investigative reporters like I'm trying to be."

"Who cares? You didn't go all the way to Maine to get him to like you."

Liza hesitated. "No, but—"

"What? No buts, no buts—"

"But—things have changed."

"No changes allowed. Don't get personally involved." Kristin's voice went up a notch and Liza could picture her slashing a hand through the air. "You're changing your life, remember? Why would you give it all up because you feel remorse over—?"

"I don't feel remorse."

"Oh yes you do. You're the nice girl. You were raised on guilt. You always do what you're told. You don't take advantage of anyone—you're too nice for your own good. You always let someone else have the empty seat on the bus, you save old bread crusts for the birds, you never tried smoking a cigarette, you never drink too much, or waste money on trendy clothes that will only be in style for a season, or—"

"Okay, okay, I get it. You don't need to rub it in."

"No, I do need to rub it in. You got fed up with your life and wanted to change it. You can decide not to change it when you reach the end of this project—but not now, Liza. You can't quit in the middle."

Liza fiddled with the heater controls to direct warm air onto the windshield. "Why not?"

"Because if you quit now, someday when you're an old woman you're going to look back and wonder what would have happened if you'd seen this through, what direction your life might have gone. And you're going to wish you could go back, just once, and see what would have happened if you didn't quit."

"And it'll be too late."

"Uh-huh."

Liza sighed. "I think I *like* him."

"Yeah, you and every other woman, single or otherwise, who meets Jack Graham."

"But he's such a nice guy—"

"Of course he's nice. He's a guy who needs, I repeat, *needs,* you to take the job to watch that old basset hound. He's a charmer, Liza."

"I think it's more than that. Under all those good looks and charm, he really is a genuinely nice guy."

Kristin exhaled. "Guys like Jack know just how to make women do what they want. In your case, he doesn't want you to fall into his bed—he wants you to take the damn job. I've seen it a hundred times before. Let me guess, he's probably doing stuff to show you what a great guy he is—helping the poor, or kissing babies ..."

Or petting abandoned dogs in the animal shelter. Liza's heart dropped. "You've seen this before?"

"What's he doing?"

"Uh, nothing, really."

"Spill it. Tell me what he's doing and I'll tell you what he's up to."

"He stopped to pet all the dogs in the shelter. Said he didn't want them to feel abandoned." Saying the words out loud made Liza realize how ridiculous it sounded.

Kristin began to chortle. "Now *that* is good—"

"We went there looking for CJ He just wanted to make sure she hadn't been brought in." Liza said defensively.

"All he had to do was ask."

"He did. But he wanted to make sure they hadn't somehow overlooked her."

"Ah. He didn't trust the staff to recognize a basset hound? So he went to check for himself?"

Disappointment slipped under her skin. "Yeah."

"Liza, Liza, Liza. This man is playing all the right cards to make you take the job. And that's okay—as long as you realize he's playing you."

Of course. No doubt Jack was amazing at manipulation. How else could he have gotten the reputation he had? Liza shook her head at her own gullibility. She thought about kissing Jack and wished it had meant something more to him than just trying to make her take the job. Bending toward the passenger seat, she retrieved the long-handled window brush from the floor.

"Hey Liza? You still there?" Kristin asked.

"Yeah, I have to get a ton of snow off my windows."

"This Jack thing really sucks, I know. But if you're going to succeed, you have to step over it and figure out how to keep him from leaving. Otherwise, everything you've done up to now be for nothing."

Liza shut off the phone and stared at her snow-covered windshield, her view of the parking lot as blocked as her view of her future. "Oh God, what is the matter with me?" she murmured. She'd been ready to throw aside her plan simply because she'd gotten a crush on Jack. But all she had to do was strip her emotions out of the picture and it was easy to see Jack was pulling out all the stops to get her to take the job. She needed to remember to keep her eye on the prize. She had to stop Jack from leaving town, get the information about Cordelia, and then get out of Coldwater before she lost her heart to a guy who probably had a row of hearts carved into his headboard instead of notches.

No problem.

———

Jack was home for almost an hour before he couldn't stand being there anymore. He hadn't received any calls about CJ, and the ladies next door reported no sign of her. All he could do was wait—and he didn't do well with waiting. Especially not after dredging up all those memories of his childhood and the animal shelter and his grandmother.

He'd lost his grandmother's beloved dog ... and the weight of that sin was heavy. Slipping on his jacket, he headed out to the garage, grabbed a dusty red plastic geranium from a clay pot up on a shelf and drove to the cemetery in a search for atonement. The moment he passed through the big iron gates, a sense of peace washed over him. The grounds stretched out in every direction like a sea of white, broken sporadically by the tip of a cross or an angel on the top of taller headstones. Under the gray sky, a gusting wind rolled across the grounds, swirling the snow into tiny tornados.

Jack pulled to a stop beside a tall pine tree and sat there a long moment before switching his phone to vibrate mode and stepping out of the car. He pulled on his gloves and flipped up his jacket collar. The hush of the cemetery enveloped him and he squinted across the nearby area as he tried to find any sign of his grandmother's headstone. The whole place looked different covered with snow—still the same, and yet the path he would have followed was obscured, the usual landmarks buried.

After a short trudge through the snow, he stopped to brush off the front of a headstone rising through the snow. *Anna Cook.* One of Grandma's cemetery neighbors. He went a few feet farther and dug away the snow obscuring his grandmother's headstone.

"Catherine Graham," he read aloud into the stillness of the day. "Love never fails."

It had been part of one of her favorite quotes. He didn't know the whole thing, just the beginning—*Love is patient, love is kind ...* When his grandmother died it had only seemed right to have a piece of that quote define her for the rest of time.

"I lost CJ, Gram." His words were sucked away by the wind. "I'm sorry."

No reply came—not that he was expecting one.

"She was out in the yard and then she was just gone." Now, if that didn't sound like the excuse of a guilty kid, he didn't know what did. "You wouldn't be able to get the big guy up there to help us find her, would you?"

The wind whistled past.

He sighed. He hadn't thought so. A lost dog had to be pretty low on heaven's priority list.

16

He stuck the plastic geranium in the snow by the headstone and grinned. It looked silly—and that was just the way his grandmother would have wanted it.

Gazing across the cemetery, he made no move to leave. His flight was just a few hours away. What should he do? Hell, what choice did he have? It would be ridiculous to leave with CJ missing. Ridiculous to expect Liza to continue the search when she hadn't even accepted the caretaker job. And it would be ridiculously unfair to CJ and disrespectful to his grandmother. He exhaled and watched his breath frost in the air.

A golf cart rolled up behind his car. Ernie Crawford, the cemetery caretaker, stepped out. "Oh hey, Jack," he called. "Didn't know who was wandering out here with all the snow, but when you started digging, figured I'd better see who it was and what was up."

Jack tramped through the snow toward him. "Thought I might be robbing graves?"

"You never know these days."

"I suppose not." Jack inhaled, and icy air raced through

his nose and down his throat. "You haven't seen a loose basset hound, have you? My grandmother's dog is missing—"

"I know CJ Haven't seen her around here, though. Kinda doubt she could make it this far, being so old and fat. Did you ask the ladies next door?"

"They're keeping an eye out," Jack said.

"They're good at that. Mary tells me you found a new caretaker for CJ I mean, once you find CJ, that is." Ernie pointed to another section of the cemetery. "Billy's right over there in case you want to stop by and say hi. Good thing we got him in the ground before this storm hit. Hate to have to move all this snow."

Jack nodded.

"Mary tells me Diane and him were getting friendly just before he passed on."

Jack turned to toward Ernie and tried not to gape. "Diane? And Billy?" He quashed the visual that leapt into his mind.

"Yeah, except it came to a quick halt because she was allergic to the dog. Apparently he said her sneezing wasn't so sexy."

Sexy? Diane? Way too much information. Here he thought his neighbors were two nice old ladies who did volunteer work. And now he learned that Diane was getting it on with old Billy. And Mary—

He cast a sidelong glance at the caretaker. "You talk to Mary a lot?"

Either the guy was blushing or the temperature had dropped even lower.

"Oh, well, enough. She's awfully sweet ... I mean, she makes a mean corned beef and cabbage."

Jack nodded as though hearing about his neighbors' love

lives was just a normal everyday occurrence. Diane and Billy. Mary and Ernie. This was almost as bad as picturing his grandmother with a boyfriend. Parents—and their friends—weren't supposed to do this stuff. He wondered if Mary got out the vibrating cushion for Ernie.

No! Don't picture it.

A gust of wind blasted across the cemetery, swirling snow up and over them. Jack wiped a hand across his face, the snowy granules melting as he brushed them away. He reached for the car door.

"When you see Mary, say hi for me." Ernie got back in the golf cart. "I'll keep my eyes peeled for CJ"

Jack made it all the way home before discovering a voice message on his phone. After that vaguely disconcerting conversation with Ernie, he'd forgotten to turn the ringer back on.

He listened to the message as he went up the steps, then excitedly burst into the house shouting the news—someone had found CJ Liza met him at the door and he grabbed her in a hug and twirled her around. "CJ's found! I just got a call!"

Liza let out a squeal. "Thank God! Where is she?"

"Milford. Three miles north. Some woman came into Coldwater to run an errand and spotted our signs."

Liza stopped smiling. "How did CJ get three miles away?"

"I know, huh? Pretty weird. Maybe some kids found her running loose and took her there as a prank."

"Some prank."

"The woman said they found the dog wandering down their street so they took her inside and gave her a hot dog."

"Are you sure it's CJ?"

"She said the dog looks just like the picture on the

poster." He checked at his watch. If he hurried, there was enough time to pick up CJ and still make his flight. "Cross your fingers. Come on, let's go."

"Oh, I don't need to come along."

"Don't you want to be there when we find her? Might be a good bonding moment for the two of you."

"Oh, well, sure, but—"

He lifted her jacket off the coat tree and tossed it to her. "Come on—we're in this together. This is all part of dog caretaking. Besides, I have some juicy gossip to share about the ladies next door."

Liza let out a snort. "Oh, well that changes everything. Okay, let's go."

As soon as they were in the car, he related what he'd learned about the Diane and Mary and their relationships with Billy and Ernie. "I thought those two were acting strange this morning when I stopped over—maybe Ernie was there and they didn't want me to know. Mary *was* wearing this silky robe thing."

"That doesn't mean she had a man in the house. If I recall correctly, you said she was *covered from neck to ankle.*"

Jack nodded knowingly. "Yeah, but it was silky. When men aren't around, women wear cotton and flannel. Enter a man, and in comes the shimmery, slippery stuff."

"This is a fact, huh?"

"Remember, I've got an inside line to Dear Cordelia," he said confidently. "She's taught me everything I need to know about women."

"That's a pretty broad generalization—even if Dear Cordelia says it's so. I'd bet most women just wear whatever they're comfortable in."

He smiled. "What about special occasions?"

Liza's cheeks began to pink.

"I can't believe you're all cotton and flannel, all the time."

Her face went from slight blush to flaming red, and she pursed her lips, her perfect heart-shaped lips. "Who said I'm cotton and flannel at all?"

"So you're silky shimmery?" he said in a strangled voice and turned to face her for a second.

She wagged a finger at him. "A lady doesn't discuss her *unmentionables* with a gentleman ... until such point as they are ... they are ..."

"Being removed by said gentleman?" Jack had to restrain himself from pulling to the side of the road and checking out what Liza was wearing under her blue jeans and sweater. The idea that this woman, with her matter-of-fact style and kissable lips, might be wearing something not-so-practical underneath was incredibly appealing. Appealing, hell. It was an incredible turn-on.

"No! Until such point as they are ... in a relationship."

"Oh, same thing."

Liza pushed the button to lower the window a few inches, and he thought to himself that all the five-degree air in the world wasn't going to cool down the car right now.

Maybe tonight they could—

What the hell was wrong with him? He was leaving Coldwater in a few hours.

Although, it would be easy enough to visit.

But maybe not so smart. Getting involved with the dog's new caretaker could create all sorts of problems—especially once the relationship ended. Unless ... they both agreed anything between them would be a no-ties, short-term thing.

That might work. He didn't get into long-term things

anyway. Especially not with women who were happy living in towns the size of Coldwater.

They passed a *Welcome to Milford* sign, and Jack took his foot off the gas pedal until the car slowed to match the lower speed limit. The GPS voice on his phone directed him along a series of turns that led to a small, white Cape Cod with a cracked concrete driveway and dirty windows.

A woman stepped out on the porch to greet them. "You looking for the dog?" Her voice had the twang of the Deep South.

"That's us."

She pulled open the door and shouted, "Dwayne, bring that dog out here now." She looked back at them. "My boy's taken a liking to her already. There's a reward on her, right?"

"A hundred dollars," Jack said.

A boy about ten pushed open the door and out bounced a brown, white and black ... beagle.

"There she is," the woman said.

Jack's brow furrowed. Same coloring, definitely not the right dog. What the hell?

The dog raced around the yard sticking its nose into the snow and snorting.

"That's a beagle," Jack said. "We're missing a basset hound."

The woman looked from the dog to Jack and back again. "Are you sure?"

"I thought you said it was the same dog in the picture."

"Sure looked like it. Floppy ears and all."

"But basset's ears are so much, you know, longer." Liza pointed at her ear and met Jack's eyes with her own.

The woman shrugged. "Since you can't find your dog,

do you want this here beagle? Because we could sure use that reward money."

"No thanks. I'm pretty attached to the other dog."

"Try calling the animal shelter," Liza said. "The beagle's owners may have left their phone number."

Jack returned to the car, irritated that his plans had just been officially scuttled. "I'm going to cancel my flight," he told Liza. "I can't leave Coldwater until we find CJ"

"Oh, Jack, I'm sorry. If it's any consolation, I bought the fixings for spaghetti and meatballs. I'll make you a dinner much better than the one you would have gotten in the airport." A smile flashed across her face sending a zing through him.

A zing? He didn't get zings. The last time he felt a zing he had been a senior in high school and madly in love with Martha Chadwick, a super-popular girl who had no idea he existed—except when she needed help unsticking her locker.

Suddenly his attraction to Liza made sense. Martha Chadwick with her wavy brown hair. He'd almost forgotten about her. "You know, when I was in high school there was this girl whose locker was two down from mine—Martha Chadwick," he said.

"Oh?"

"Her locker would stick. And I had a knack for getting it open. She had hair kind of like yours, and eyes ..." He looked at Liza and she looked back at him, confused.

Of course she was confused. Why was he telling her this?

"We never went out ... she wasn't my girlfriend or anything." *Why was he telling her this?* He gripped the steering wheel tighter.

"And I remind you of her?"

"Yeah." Suddenly he had felt like he had in high school, awkward around girls, saying all the wrong things, wanting to ask them out and terrified of the rejection. He hadn't hit his stride until college. That's when he'd discovered that the harder to get he played, the easier the women fell.

Especially women like Martha Chadwick. He'd had lots of women like her, all self-assured in their heels and latest-fashion outfits. All confident and high-flying in their careers. All secure enough to ask him to dinner and take him home afterward.

And none of them like Liza Dunnigan.

"Actually, you aren't anything like her—except the brown hair and eyes. And that's good."

She grinned and his heart sped up. Maybe he should do a short-term thing with her just to get her out of his system.

17

LIZA MADE AN EXCUSE ABOUT HAVING TO RUN OVER TO the culinary institute for a meeting, and cut out of the house before Jack could ask any questions. She still couldn't believe the conversation they'd had yesterday, discussing underwear as if such topics were a matter of course for her.

Cotton and flannel? Of course that's what she wore. It was sensible. She'd never given it much thought before. And the worst of it was, even when there was a guy in the picture —she thought of Mark and cringed—she still wore cotton and flannel. Jack was completely wrong as far as she was concerned. She'd never run out and bought new underwear just because a man had entered her life.

Until now, anyway.

For some reason, the thought of Jack finding out she was all cotton and flannel all the time bothered her tremendously. She didn't want him to know—and there was no need for him to find out. Because as of today, she was changing her cotton and flannel ways.

She'd arrived at the mall in Orono right when it opened and now was deep in a department-store lingerie department, more overwhelmed than she'd ever been in her life. Cotton was so easy—white, off-white, pastels. When she was feeling particularly daring, she might even get something in black.

Silky was a whole other thing. The choices were endless, the styles seemingly unlimited. Colors like lime green and hot pink and neon purple ... and brothel red. And then there were the prints—floral and zebra-striped and leopard and polka-dot. And the lace and embroidery and the Brazilian cut and—

Nervousness rolled over her. What kind of girl would Jack think she was if he found out she owned underwear like this?

Maybe the kind of girl he would date.

Oh God, was that what this was about?

No, no, of course not. Now that he was staying in Coldwater a while longer, she was simply refocusing her efforts on getting the information she needed about Dear Cordelia. And if the pathway to that information turned out to be through allure and—she gulped—seduction, well at least she would be prepared.

Upsetting as it was to have CJ missing, it sure was a gift to her investigation. She truly hoped they found the dog— just not too soon. She needed time to capitalize on this opportunity.

Turning a slow circle, she let her gaze roam over the nearby racks, then turned her attention to the bras. A few minutes later, she was safely hidden in a changing room with armfuls of undergarments that contained not so much as a thread of cotton.

She tried on the silky pink and the baby blue and the pastel floral. And frowned at the sight of each one in the mirror. They seemed a little safe, dull even, not much different from plain cotton. Besides she already had blue and green underwear. If she was going to throw caution to the wind, maybe she should really go for it.

Slipping out of the dressing room, she went back on the floor and quickly gathered a large assortment of bras and underpants the likes of which she had never even considered before. A clerk stopped to ask if she needed any assistance, and Liza looked at the neon colors and animal prints in her arms and declined, mortified to be caught trying on such things. She raced into the dressing room, firmly shut the door, sat on the bench and drew a breath.

Get a grip, she told herself. Other women buy this stuff all the time.

As if to prove it to herself, she texted Kristin: *What kind of underwear do you buy?*

Her phone rang a minute later. "Why do you want to know about my underwear?" Kristin asked.

"I'm out shopping for—" Liza dropped her voice lower. "Underwear."

"Is that why you're whispering?" Kristin whispered.

"Uh-huh."

"What happened to yours?"

"Jack likes silky underwear."

"What?" Kristin shrieked. "How do you know that? And how does he know what kind of underwear you have?"

"Calm down. He doesn't know. And he's never going to know if I can help it." Liza stripped off her jeans and slipped a pair of zebra-striped underpants over her white cotton briefs. Huh. There was nothing brief about them. She made a face at herself in the mirror.

"What exactly is going on in Coldwater?" Kristin demanded. "Are you and Jack Graham actually hitting it off? Getting it on? This is incredible—"

"No, no, no. It's nothing like that."

"Well, it's something. Because I've known you for seven years now and you're not the type to go buy new underwear just for kicks. Did you buy new underwear for Mark?"

Liza tried to tuck the massive amount of white cotton inside the tiny zebra-striped panties and rolled her eyes at her ridiculous reflection. She turned sideways and sucked in her stomach, but the sight didn't get any better. "What?"

"Did you buy new underwear for Mark?"

"No, but—"

"Aha! Liza, be careful. This isn't the kind of guy who falls in love and settles in for the long haul. Hot underwear does not necessarily a lasting relationship make."

"Don't worry. There's nothing going on—" She tugged off the zebra panties.

"Not yet anyway."

"You're the one who said I should seduce him to get the info I needed." Liza pulled on a pair of black underpants with lace panels on the sides.

"*No,* you're the one who said that the very first day. I was the one who said, *This new Liza is beginning to surprise me.*"

Liza waved a dismissive hand at the mirror. "Who cares who said it? The reality is, I need to get this stuff, and I need some help picking it out."

She turned sideways again and patted her stomach, grimacing at her little potbelly. "Do they make sexy underwear with a control panel in front?"

"How could it unless the underwear came up to your waist. And I can guarantee that no guy—least of all Jack Graham—wants to see you in underwear up to your waist. No matter what fabric it's made of. Those are granny pants."

Liza pulled her sweater down to cover her granny pants and examined the assortment of bras she'd brought into the dressing room. "Leopard or zebra?"

"Huh?"

"What's more ... irresistible?"

"Oh my God, I can't believe I'm hearing this come out of your mouth," Kristin practically shouted.

"Shh! You're so loud, the lady in the next stall will hear you." Liza took a breath and lowered her voice. "Now, come on, you gotta help me pick this out. I'll describe it—"

Kristin's laughter filled her ear.

After waiting several seconds, Liza asked, "Are you finished yet? I'm on a mission?"

"Okay, okay, okay. Describe away."

Liza held up a hanger and looked at the thong hooked to the ends. God help her. "Hot-pink thong." She hung the hanger on another hook and began to recite a list what else she had: "Red Brazilian-cut. Leopard bikinis. Tiger-striped bra. Black bikinis with side lace panels." She paused. "Do you think that lace will itch?" she asked.

"Liza, Liza! Have I taught you nothing? *Fashion before comfort.*"

The word *cotton* slipped into Liza's mind and she pushed it aside. "Rosebud print—"

"Forget that one. Stick with the classics—black, animal prints, lace—"

"I've got a cheetah print," Liza offered.

"Oh yeah, that'll work. How many are you getting?"

"I don't know. What do you think?"

"Well, you won't be wearing them every day ..."

"Weeelll ..."

"You will?" Shock resonated in Kristin's voice.

"At least while I'm here," Liza said. "Seems to make sense. You know, just to be prepared."

"Oh, right. O-kay, then in that case, get several. Those hot colors—pink, lime green, whatever—always come in handy."

"I suppose I should get the matching bras?"

"You can. Or not. Matching would be good, but once you're at that stripped-down point, he probably won't care. Just saying."

Liza nodded thoughtfully at herself in the mirror. "My mother always said to make sure your underwear is nice so if you get in a car accident the emergency room doctors won't discover you wear ratty underwear."

"My mom told me the same thing!" Kristin said. "She even told me about some old lady who got in an accident and made the first guy on the scene pull her old girdle off and throw it in the bushes before the ambulance arrived."

"Yeahhh." Liza pictured herself demanding a passerby pull off her granny pants. "So what happens when the emergency room doctors cut off my clothes and find leopard underneath?"

"Oh, they'll probably just think you're an exotic dancer."

"A stripper! Coldwater is so small, it would be all over town in minutes."

Kristin laughed. "You're not going to get in an accident. Now, go buy the underwear and get to work. And keep me posted—this is more fun every day!"

Liza dropped her phone in her purse and tried on everything she had in the dressing room. "It may be more fun for you, Kristin," she muttered, "but for me it's more stress. Like an all-time high."

In the course of a few days, she'd gone from practical

and predictable to practically a stripper. And most shocking of all was that she didn't really see a problem with that change. Well, not much of a problem—unless, of course, she got in a car accident.

She gathered the items she wanted to keep. Now that she was about to own beautiful lingerie, she was more than a little excited about wearing it. The names of the lines really said it all: Flirty Foundations, the Glamour Collection, Sexy Little Nothings. She had a feeling just wearing a hot-pink thong would make her feel more attractive even if no one else knew she had it on. Comfort? Now, *that* was another question.

On the way to the cash register, she stopped at a rack of nightgowns. Oh God, she'd been so focused on foundations, she forgot about sleepwear. Flannel was cozy on bitter winter nights, but she should probably give it up for the rest of her stay in Coldwater.

She flipped through the racks and picked out a short nightgown in a slightly sheer, silky fabric that gave her goose bumps as it slipped over her skin. Who would have guessed when she put this plan into motion last week, that throwing caution to the wind would bring this kind of change to her life?

18

Liza waltzed into the house with her bag of purchases, hoping to sneak everything up to her room before Jack spotted her. She was halfway up the stairs when she heard Dave call from the front of the house, "Hey, Liza. I'm painting the living room. Wanna help?"

"Sure, I'll be down in a minute," she shouted over her shoulder. Taking the stairs two at a time, she charged into her room and pushed the door shut behind her.

Heart pounding, she tore open the bag and began to cut the tags off her purchases using manicure scissors. She arranged everything across the bed, then let out a nervous laugh before stripping off her clothes and sliding into the leopard-print set.

She walked from one side of the room to the other, pausing in front of the full-length mirror to stare at herself. Was it her imagination or did her lips look fuller, more kissable, her eyes more sultry? She tossed her hair and gave the mirror a come-hither look.

Wow. Had all those women who always got the best

guys figured this out years ago? She spun in front of the mirror, then danced across the room to grab her painting clothes and pull them over her new lingerie. She looked in the mirror again. Even in paint-spattered work clothes she felt different, more attractive and enticing. The big question was—would Jack notice the difference?

She stepped into the hall and spotted the door to Jack's room half-open. Tempted to sneak in and snoop around for Cordelia clues, she paused in the hallway to listen. Was he in there or not? When she didn't hear so much as the click of a computer keyboard, she gave the door a small push and stuck her head forward to peer inside.

Jack looked up from his desk, cell phone to his ear. "Hi. I'm on hold."

"Oh, hi." She jerked back slightly in surprise and banged her shoulder against the doorjamb. At least the bruise would be a nice match for the leopard print. "Just wanted to let you know I'm back."

"Get everything done at the institute?"

"All set," she answered evenly. "Any news about CJ?" She wondered whether he could tell that her brain was screaming, *Leopard! Leopard! I'm wearing silky leopard underwear and I'm the only one who knows it.*

He held up his index finger, then said into the phone, "Yeah, that sounds good. Tell them I'll do whatever they think is best. They know their business better than I do. Just let me know and I'm there. Right. Cordelia will hype it in the column."

He paused. "Yeah. So how many adoptive parents are making this trip? Great. I should be back in a few days at the most. Okay, let me know."

Cordelia? Adoptive parents? Was Jack Graham about to adopt a child? Or was Cordelia?

Jack swiped off the phone and brought his gaze to her again. "Sorry. I volunteer for an organization that helps people cover the costs of overseas adoptions."

Every thought exited her brain. Was this a joke? Dogs *and* kids? It was like he was purposely positioning himself as the *best guy ever*. Kristin would have a field day with this information. "You help people adopt kids?" She tried not to gape at him. "Why?"

Bachelor, player, single guy, man about town helped people adopt kids? "I mean, it's wonderful," she added hastily. "It just isn't something you typically see a single person involved in."

He saved the document on his computer and cleared the screen. "One way or another, we're all a product of our childhood. I spent my first nine years bouncing around foster homes. And then I got adopted."

Liza's heart twisted for the boy he'd been.

"Catherine Graham adopted me. She didn't have any children of her own. She and her husband wanted them, but ..." He gave a shrug. "Anyway, after he died, Catherine became a foster parent. I was the first kid she got—angry, belligerent, hurting. And she told me to call her Grandma." His voice cracked. "I had just been bounced out of a household where the foster parents insisted on being called Mr. and Mrs. The more they tried to bend me to their will, the more I fought back. By the time I arrived here, I was one tough little kid."

He sat back in his chair. "Catherine Graham gave me back my childhood. I just want to help do the same for other kids."

Oh. My. God. Liza tamped down the guilt rearing its head over how she was planning to betray Jack's friendship by stealing information about Cordelia.

"Eventually, they terminated my birth mother's rights and Catherine adopted me. But I still called her Grandma ... because she was just like a grandma is supposed to be. She'd lived long enough to know everything wasn't of equal importance. *Choose your battles*, she'd say. *Is this a mountain worth dying on?*"

"Didn't you say she took in stray dogs too?"

Jack grinned. "Anything that needed love."

"She sounds like a quite a woman."

Jack ran a hand through his hair. "She was. That's why I can't leave until I know what happened to CJ"

————

Liza zigzagged the paint roller across the wall, covering the dirty white paint with a layer of a creamy beige that connected to the paint Dave had cut-in around the window trim, baseboard, and crown molding.

Dave stopped and let out an appreciative whistle. "This is a great color," he said. "And I think it's mostly because of your skill with a roller."

She snorted out a laugh. The good thing about painting with Dave was that it kept her from thinking too much about Jack. And his childhood. And his grandmother. And his missing dog. And the way that he kissed. "You think so?" she asked, teasing. "Maybe I should open a painting business on the side.

"Careful, I have a loaded weapon." Dave held up his paintbrush and took a step toward her just as the doorbell chimed.

"Saved by the bell." Liza opened the door and Ashley swept past her into the room like a wave.

"It's so cold," she exclaimed. "Is Jack here?"

"He's upstairs." Liza yelled up the staircase for Jack, then watched as Ashley went over to Dave on the ladder and rubbed his lower legs in greeting. Liza rolled her eyes. "Pffft," she said quietly.

As soon as Jack appeared on the stairs, Ashley deserted Dave's legs. "Oh, Jack, I came as soon as I saw the signs about CJ" She gave him a hug. "Then I ran into Diane at the drugstore and she said CJ disappeared right out of the yard." Still holding his arm, she looked up at him. "The boys are going to be devastated when they hear CJ is gone. What can I do to help? Should I bring a meal over?"

Dave let out a snort. "It's not a funeral."

"Yeah, we don't need any food. Just keep your eyes open for her," Jack said. "Spread the word."

"If you feel the need to cook, you can bring a meal to my house," Dave said, grinning over his shoulder. "Stay for a movie."

Ashley gave him a wan smile, then turned her attention back to Jack. "It's freezing out there. You don't think that CJ might have ... I mean when it's cold you can just fall asleep and never wake up."

"No." Liza could hardly contain her irritation. What kind of idiot came over and speculated about the death of someone's beloved pet? "She's fat and furry. Both of those things will help her stay warm."

"She's probably safe and sound in someone's house," Dave said.

"You think someone stole her just to have her?" Ashley asked, incredulous. "With that eye and her drooling and shedding?"

Jack disengaged his arm from Ashley. "What he means is maybe someone found her and just hasn't reported it yet."

"Liza, sweetie, break time's over," Dave called, "I'm getting way ahead of you."

She poured more paint into a tray and began to roll another wall.

"A bunch of us are going to the Mosquito Inn tonight," Ashley said to Jack. "It's Brian Dixon's birthday—you remember Brian? He'd be really surprised to see you."

Liza let her eyes slide to the ceiling. What an obvious ploy—Ashley was no master of subtlety.

Not like Liza and her new leopard *unmentionables*.

Dave turned and sat on the top rung of the ladder. "Jack, you should come out. It'll be like old times."

Jack was grinning at Ashley, clearly considering going. Well, and why not? What guy would turn down the obvious?

Liza dipped her roller in the paint tray, then pressed it to the wall and began to roll with ferocity. Wasn't important. Didn't matter. Jack was just the guy she was staying with for a few days, the guy who had the information she needed.

She turned slightly to look at Ashley—the woman had the look of a vulture going in for the kill. "Lots of people will be there," she said in a cajoling voice.

"Well ..." Jack glanced at Liza and she glanced away. She wasn't getting sucked into this discussion.

"Please say *yes*," Ashley said in a throaty voice that she probably thought was sexy.

Please say yes, Liza repeated snottily in her head.

"Did I mention it's South Seas night at the bar? I'll be in a floral sarong."

"In that case I may have to come," Jack said.

Liza smirked at the wall. All guys were the same. And Jack Graham was probably worse than most. He was so used to women throwing themselves at him. Ha! Well, no way was she ever going to do that. If she and Jack Graham ever got together he would have to do a lot of romancing before she—

Her thoughts screeched to a halt. What was wrong with her? If she and Jack Graham ever got together, it would be for one reason and one reason only—because it was a means of getting Dear Cordelia's contact information.

"Liza, you should come, too," Dave said.

"Oh—no—that's okay—" She shook her head. "I wouldn't know anyone—"

"You'll know me." He winked.

"And me and Ashley." Jack smiled and Ashley glared.

"No, really. This sounds like a reunion." Besides, if Jack went out, she'd have a few hours to search his computer. Yesterday she'd failed in her quest to stay home instead of going to Milford with him. Tonight, however, would be a whole other story. Her adrenalin kicked up its feet.

"It *is* a group of old friends," Ashley said.

"New friends are always welcome." Dave began to paint again. "Besides, this is going to be Liza's hometown now. She should meet some people."

Oh, no, not again. "I'd feel like the third wheel, or odd man out, or something. Really, no. I'll stay home."

"Nah, you have to come on out," Jack said. "Dave's right. This is the perfect chance for you to meet some people who live here."

Liza mentally sighed. The more she fought the idea, the more determined Jack and Dave seemed to get.

"Well?" Jack was grinning that killer smile at her and she felt her determination begin to crumble.

"What about CJ?" she asked weakly.

"I'll have my phone," Jack said. "Come on, it'll be fun."

"Oh ... all right," she said weakly. "But only for a while." And *a while* meant she would stay for one drink, meet a few people, then plead exhaustion and cut out, leaving Jack behind. He'd be at the bar partying, and she would have plenty of time to get into his files.

19

THE MINGLED SOUNDS OF MUSIC, VOICES, AND laughter escaped through the bar's open front door and shattered the frosty night. Jack motioned Liza in ahead of him. "Sounds like the place is hopping already."

Though he hadn't been to the Mosquito Inn in years, the décor hadn't changed—neon beer signs, colorful Christmas lights still up from the holidays, and turn-of-the-century modified gaslights hanging from poles on the ceiling. The only difference were the plastic blowup palm trees adorning the entire room; obviously a nod to the evening's South Seas theme.

Jack spotted Ashley, Dave, and some other old friends gathered around the tall tables near the bar. Moments later he was shaking Brian's hand, wishing him a happy birthday, and introducing Liza around.

Kate Wilson waltzed over in a revealing coconut bra and grass skirt that showed more of Kate thank anyone probably ever wanted to see. She hung a lei around each of their necks. "So you're the new caretaker," she chirped and stuck a hand out to Liza. "I'm Kate. I sat behind Jack in statistics. Got him through that class."

Jack nodded. "It's the truth. She's a math wizard."

"Welcome to Coldwater," Kate continued. "Ashley tells us you're joining the culinary institute."

"That's right," Liza said, nodding.

Jack bent close to Liza's ear and asked over the din, "What do you want to drink?"

"Just a glass of Pinot Noir—" She broke off and frowned, bit her lower lip as though suddenly making a major decision. "I always have Pinot Noir. How about a ..."

"Beer?" Jack gestured at a pitcher on the bar.

She wrinkled her nose. "Too mundane. I'm changing my life, remember?"

Kate leaned into the conversation and held up a large, fancy glass with a paper umbrella on top. "It's two-for-one specials on exotic drinks. Mai tai means *the best* in Tahitian," she said happily.

"Wanna go native?" Jack quipped. "With *the best?*"

Liza tilted her head back and pursed her lips and he had to shove his hands in his pockets to keep his fingers from tracing the beguiling shape of those lips. And then following his fingers with his mouth. And then letting his fingers slide down the V-neck of her tight sweater to—

"O-kay," she said.

Dave leaned over from his bar stool and held out his glass to Liza. "Try this. It's a Zombie. Fruity. You'll like it."

Liza's mouth shifted up at the corners, breaking into a brilliant smile. "I will?"

Jack frowned at Dave's gaudy Hawaiian-print shirt. "Aloha," he said, annoyance morphing into irritation the longer Dave's eyes stayed locked to Liza's.

"I guarantee it. Or your money back." Dave bent so close to Liza their shoulders almost touched.

Jack looked from Dave to Liza and back again. The blinking Christmas lights danced on the wall behind them. "Mai tai?" he asked, feeling deposed and not liking it one bit.

Liza dragged her eyes back to him and shook her head. "No, I'll have what he's having."

"The lady has taste," Dave said smugly. "It's a Zombie, Jacky boy."

Jack headed for the bar, more than a little out of sorts. "Hey, Jack, what'll you have?" he muttered to himself. "A beer would be great, thanks for asking."

He flagged down the bartender for the drinks, and returned to find Liza had moved to the barstool next to Dave and was cheerfully sharing his Zombie.

"How soon before you decide?" Dave was asking.

"This week. Of course, we have to find CJ or it's a moot point."

"Cocktail delivery." Jack handed Liza a tall glass spilling over with slices of pineapple and orange, a cherry on a stick, and an umbrella.

"Oh, it's almost a salad," she said brightly.

Dave laughed too hard, and Liza smiled at him in a way Jack had never seen her smile before. She pushed her hair behind one ear and put her lips around the straw to take a drink. Jack took a swallow of his beer and watched Dave's eyes fixate on Liza's mouth.

Mine, his brain whispered. I claimed that mouth last night—*it's mine.*

Dave wiped a drip of Zombie from Liza's lower lip, then plucked the umbrella from Liza's drink and tucked it slowly into the hair over her left ear. "You can wear this like a flower," he said, grinning.

Jack felt a tightening in his chest and resisted the caveman instinct to lay claim to this woman. He felt an arm slip through his and turned to find Ashley cozying up.

"Hey there," she said. Her eyes lit on Liza and Dave, and she smiled loosely, as if she'd already had a Zombie or two herself. "Looks like your caretaker has found herself a boyfriend."

"They're just talking." He heard the defensiveness in his voice. Liza couldn't have found a boyfriend in Coldwater. She had other more important things to concentrate on right now than meeting a guy. She needed to put her energy toward getting ready to start her new job, moving in, maybe even on finding CJ

But not on getting a boyfriend.

Ashley squeezed his arm, and he dragged his gaze back to her. "Do you want to dance?" she asked.

"Jack!" Liza said over the noise. "Did you know Dave played for the New England Patriots for two seasons?"

Jack's right hand tightened into a loose fist, then he forced his fingers to uncurl. Apparently, two years on the practice squad were going to carry Dave for the rest of his life.

He turned to Ashley. "Yeah, let's dance."

After a minute on the floor, Ashley danced in close. "You're so preoccupied—can I help?"

"Just worried about CJ," he said.

"Have you ever thought that she might have run away?"

No valedictorian, this girl. What had he ever found attractive about her? Oh, right, how available she was. "Uh, yeah. That's pretty much what we thought."

"I mean, ran away to ... escape someone."

"What? Like the dog *reasoned* this out first?"

Ashley smiled a little. "Well, yeah. I guess."

"No. I've never thought of that." He wondered how much longer the song would go on.

"I bet CJ would come home if you got rid of Liza."

Jack snorted out a laugh. "Ashley, give me a break. The dog isn't out there hiding, waiting for a change in caretakers."

"How do you know?"

"We're talking about a dog. CJ doesn't even know that Liza's the caretaker"

"The *maybe* caretaker. And how do you know? She never ran away when my dad was caretaker. What does that tell you?"

It told him she had a couple of screws loose. As soon as the song ended, Jack made an excuse about needing to get another beer. He glanced at Liza and Dave, cozying up at the bar, looking for all the world like a new couple. Envy stabbed at him so deep it took him aback.

Jealous? Him?

Unlikely. He had no reason to be jealous—there were plenty of women in the sea—or was that fish? Besides, he'd be a fool to want a woman whose dream life included settling down in a small town. Let Dave have her.

Out on the dance floor, Kate Wilson was doing some sort of bizarre dance, a combination of the swim and hip-hop, arms and legs whipping in every direction. She spotted him watching her and began to dance toward him, hair flying, breasts heaving in her coconut bra, hips shaking, grass skirt swaying. She never could dance. He grinned, remembering many boisterous good times with Kate during their high school and college years.

Gyrating wildly, she made her way toward him,

laughing when he rolled his eyes. "Jackie, Jackie, want to dance? I can see it in your eyes. We could win the dance contest—just like junior year."

The memory made him laugh out loud. How they won was still a mystery to him. At one point he and Kate had actually gotten down on the floor and done *the worm*.

"I just got off the dance floor," he said. "How about Dave?"

Kate looked at Dave, then gave Jack two thumbs up and a big mai tai grin. "I can do that. Hey, Davey, let's dance!" she shouted. She grabbed him by the arm, and despite his protests forced him out of his seat. The guy threw an apologetic look at Liza.

Jack tried not to take a turn at feeling smug. *Too bad, Dave. He who dances with Kate loses his chair.* He slid into the bar stool next to Liza. "How's your Zombie?"

"Sweet." She grinned. "How's your beer?"

"Hoppy." He paused. "Hey, Liza. Remember, Dave's not—"

"He seems like a nice enough guy."

"He is a nice guy. It's just that he ..."

"Has his way with women and then discards them?" she asked innocently. She drank more of her Zombie, and he tried not to pay attention to her mouth.

"That's a nice way of putting it."

"Well, don't worry about me. No one is going to take advantage of me." She wiped the back of her hand slowly over her mouth, and Jack swallowed hard.

"Not even me?" he asked in a low voice, every rational brain cell warning him to back away, and every instinct pushing him forward.

Liza swirled her drink with her palm tree stir stick and raised flirtatious eyes to him. "Especially not you."

His heart dropped.

"I have a sneaking suspicion, Jack Graham, that you and Dave Butler are two peas in a pod."

He looked at her, taken aback. No way was he as bad as Dave. *Was he?*

"I think you're confusing me with someone else." He took her hand. "Will you dance?" he asked, pulling her up with him as he stood.

Liza set her glass on the bar and looked up at him, her eyes sparkling, her expression so open he almost took her in his arms and slow danced right at the bar. He led her through the crowd, and they popped out into the cavorting mass of dancers. The dance floor was a writhing mix of Hawaiian shirts, bright colors and leis wrapped around wrists, ankles and necks. When the song ended and a slow one began, Jack pulled Liza into his arms.

"So tell me. How are you different from Dave?" she asked.

The scent of kiwi wafted off her hair and he thought about slipping his fingers in those waves and kissing her until she was senseless.

What was the question again? Oh, yeah. How was he different from Dave?

He could say that he wouldn't ever hurt her. But that probably wasn't true. Or he could say he would always be honest with her. But that probably wasn't true either.

How *was* he different, then? He bent close to her ear, his cheek brushing against hers, inhaled the sweet kiwi scent and said, "Because I see the person you are, and Dave sees only another conquest." He hoped it didn't sound like a line because he didn't mean it to be one.

He felt a tap on his shoulder and turned to find Dave standing at his side. The guy was cutting-in? Who the hell cut-in these days? He scowled and graciously moved aside to let Dave take his place.

Kate intercepted him on the way back to the bar. "I did my best to keep him busy," she said.

"What for?"

"So you had time with her." She gave him a loopy grin.

"I don't want time with her—she's just the caretaker."

"Oh, come on, Jack. You may not be twenty anymore, but I can still tell when you like someone."

"I don't like her," he said a bit too forcefully.

Kate waved a dismissive hand.

"Okay, fine, I lust her. But that's it—no *like*."

"Maybe. And maybe not. I don't see you enough anymore. But I did know you pretty well at one time. I've seen Jack Graham lust and this isn't it. Not to say that isn't there, too, but ..."

Jack glanced at the crush on the dance floor. "Pheromones," he said. "I'm attracted to hers. It's a physical thing."

"Okay, just keep repeating that to yourself." Kate sipped her mai tai.

They stood on the edge of the dance floor until the song ended and the deejay boogied onto the floor holding a long pole and shouting, "How low can you go?"

It was definitely time to return to the bar. Suddenly, Liza brushed past him saying, "Quick, let's get away before they make us limbo."

"You too?"

"Please. I have no athletic ability."

"How much athletic ability does the limbo take?" he asked, following her.

"More than I have. No flexibility." She plucked her glass off the bar and took a long drink through the straw, emptying the glass. Then she waved at the bartender, who went to work making her another Zombie.

She was so damn cute. He wondered whether she had the same effect on everyone.

Out on the dance floor, the limbo line had formed, the music was playing, and everyone was hooting and hollering. He slid onto the barstool next to Liza and hoped Dave was stuck on the limbo floor all night.

"The last time I did the limbo, I was eliminated almost immediately. I'm not flexible enough, apparently," Liza said, looking up at him, a big grin on her face. "I don't need humiliation like that again."

"Who needs flexibility?" he said supportively. Actually he could think of a couple of instances when flexibility might come in handy, but probably not something to discuss right now. He thought about kissing her again. It would be so easy, really. Here they were just inches apart—

In a bar.

He hadn't done that making-out-in-a-bar thing since college, but for some reason, it seemed like a really good idea right now. "You know, Liza. If CJ is gone for good—"

"Don't say that. We'll find her."

"But if she is and you don't become the caretaker, and even when I go back to Chicago—" Shit, what was he doing? He was about to tell this woman he wanted to see her again once he was gone—in direct contradiction to what he'd already decided.

"Yeah?" She looked at him quizzically.

He didn't reply for a long minute. Oh hell, what could it hurt? If he kept everything between them confined to Coldwater, that would be manageable. "I'm trying to say, I'd like to see you—" *Naked.*

Oh hell. That thought just proved Kate wrong—it *was* lust, pure and simple.

Funny, he actually felt disappointed.

20

"That's the mai tai talking," Liza said when her brain finally registered what Jack was saying.

"No, it's not. I'm drinking beer."

She laughed. "Jack, that line—*I'd like to see you*—is straight out of Dear Cordelia's book. You've got to be able to do better than that."

"I can." He leaned toward her. "You're bright and funny and—" His mouth hovered inches from hers. "And you have a mouth that makes me crazy."

"I do?" She couldn't remember ever reading anything like this in the Dear Cordelia book. "Why?"

"Say that again," he said softly.

"What?"

"No. *Why*."

She tilted her head in confusion.

"Come on. Say it."

She formed the word with her lips.

"Stop!" he said before any sound came out. He swept a thumb across her pursed lips and she sucked in a breath. "God, but you're made for kissing." Then he brushed his lips across hers, kissed her hard, and pulled back to grin at her.

Shock filled her—shock and uncertainty and attraction. Jack Graham had just kissed her in the bar in front of all these people? And that line he's used—*I'd like to see you—*what was that about?

Dave sauntered up, still swaying to the limbo song. "Liza, can I get you another drink?" He dragged over a bar stool and hoisted himself onto it.

"No thanks, I've got a full one." She held up her glass.

Jack scowled. "Hey, Dave, Liza and I are sort of in the middle of something right now."

Dave wasn't buying it. "Yeah? Like what?"

Was this a dispute? Over her? Never in all her life had two guys ever had a disagreement over her. Especially not guys who looked like these two. Guys like them never looked at girls like her. *This was crazy.* Kind of a nice crazy, but crazy nonetheless.

She leaned forward. "Jack, I think it's okay if—"

"We're working on vowels," Jack said.

Vowels?

"Vowels?" Dave asked in disbelief. "Like A, E, I, O, U?"

Jack nodded. "Who, what, where, when, and sometimes Y." His gaze dropped to Liza's mouth and her heart started to pound. She whetted her lips with her tongue.

Dave's brows pulled together and he looked at her for confirmation.

She blanched. "Well, that's exactly what we were doing. We just did *why*—or Y—and it's all about proper form and pronunciation."

"If you need help with vowels, I can help just as much as Jack can. A, E, I, O, U, and sometimes Y," Dave slurred slightly.

"What're you guys talking about?" Ashley pulled a bar stool over from another table and plopped down.

"Vowels," Dave said.

"Like A, E, I, O, U?"

They all nodded. Jack winked at Liza.

"Why?" Ashley asked.

"That's right," Jack said. "And sometimes Y."

Ashley stared at him as if he were crazy.

"We're helping Liza with her pronunciation," Dave said.

"*I'm* helping her," Jack said.

Liza exhaled and tried to figure out how to settle the boys down. Only problem was, the Zombies had disconnected the part of her brain that might have been useful. The drink tasted like punch, but obviously packed a wallop.

"I can help, too," Dave said belligerently.

Omigod, what she didn't need was a brawl. In fact, if she really forced herself to focus, what she needed was to remember that both these guys were *players*. She had to quit being so flattered that the men liked her—they liked all women—and get back to her original plan which involved cutting out early and sneaking into Jack's computer.

She glanced at her watch. Damn, she'd been here over two hours already. At the rate she was going, she'd lose this opportunity—and who knew if she'd ever get as good a chance again?

She dragged her Zombie-sodden brain back into investigative reporting mode. "I hate to break things up, but between all the shoveling and the painting I've been doing, I'm exhausted. So, I'm going to take off. Why don't you guys work on vowels with Ashley?"

"I'll drive you home," Dave offered.

"No, I'll take her home," Jack said.

Absolutely amazing. Two guys fighting over her. She should have bought silky underwear years ago. "No, no. I'd rather walk. Those Zombies have my head spinning—the fresh air will do me good. Besides, Jack, these are all old friends of yours—I don't want you to cut your night short because of me."

Ashley slid in next to Jack. "Yeah, Jack, stay out a while —we never get to see you."

"But—"

"No buts." Liza slid on her jacket and pulled her mittens from the pockets. "You never get to see these people. I'll be fine. Good exercise. Besides, I already ordered you another beer," she prattled so he couldn't get a word in edgewise. "It was great meeting all of you." Waving over her shoulder, she squeezed her way to the door. Hopefully Jack wouldn't wait too long for his beer to arrive because she'd never actually ordered him one.

The frigid outside air tingled in her nose. She headed down the quiet road, sucking in a few deep breaths to force oxygen into her brain. At the sound of footfalls crunching the snow behind her, she twisted round in alarm, then giddy relief filled her at the sight of Jack. "Jack! Are you crazy? Where's your coat?"

"Just wanted to ..." He jogged the rest of the way. "Damn, it's cold out here."

"Yeah, like below zero. So what are you—?"

"Wanted to kiss you good night." He pulled her into his arms and slanted his mouth across hers. "But holy damn, it's freezing."

She let out a laugh, loose and free, and reached up to draw his head downward again. "Here, I'll warm you up," she said before kissing him long and slow.

"Sure you don't want to stay until the party ends?" Jack murmured against her mouth. "We could walk home together on this still winter night. Make a little more romance on the road."

Her knees weakened. Well, maybe—

No, no, no! As tempting as his offer was, she had to stay focused on why she was here in the first place. Right now she had a perfect opportunity to get at the information she needed. "Maybe next time." She gave what she hoped was a mysterious smile and stepped out of his embrace. "You'd better get inside before you turn into a block of ice."

"Okay, I'm holding you to it. Next time."

As he jogged back to the bar, she didn't move. He seriously wanted a next time with her? This relatively straightforward reporting assignment was beginning to get very complicated.

Giving her head a shake, she headed down the road again, speeding up from race-walker mode into full run. Her breath was coming harder after half a block, and she lamented that she didn't do this sort of thing regularly so she could maintain the pace longer. She'd have to add exercise to her list of life changes to make. She pushed herself to keep jogging, counted her steps, one, two, three, four, five ... left foot, right foot, left foot, right foot, left—

Her foot hit the ground, skidded outward on a patch of ice, and she fell, ankle twisting as she hit the sidewalk hand first, then hip. Moaning, she lay still, eyes closed. Her ankle throbbed, her hand throbbed, her hip throbbed.

At least her brain was intact. Or, as intact as it could be awash in Zombie juice.

Exhaling from between gritted teeth, she pushed herself to sitting and pulled off her mitten to inspect her hand. No abrasions and nothing seemed broken. She rubbed her bruised hip, then gingerly got to her feet and brushed the snow off her jeans. Thank God she was only a few blocks from home. Why had she ever thought investigative reporting would be fun? What had possessed her to go after this job?

She limped forward, jaw clenched tight. *Because she wanted to change her life.* Oh my God, had she succeeded. This was exactly what she'd gone searching for. The thrill of investigation, the fear of discovery, the pain of ... falling?

Okay, so she hadn't gone searching for pain. But someday down the road, long after she had flushed out Dear Cordelia, someday when she was regaling her colleagues with details of her latest exposé, she would tell this story and get a laugh. No pain, no gain, and all that stuff.

By the time she got home, she had walked most of the ache out of her ankle. Hurrying up the back steps to the house, she tossed her jacket on the kitchen table and headed upstairs. She stopped in the hall a moment to catch her breath, then opened Jack's bedroom door and flicked on the desk lamp.

The clothes he'd been wearing earlier in the day lay in a heap on the bed. She slid into the desk chair and opened his computer. "Come on baby, time to give up everything you know," she muttered. As soon as the system had booted up, she began to methodically search the saved files, reading a bit of each before moving on to the next.

A half hour passed with no forward progress, and she let out a sharp exhale. Time was wasting. She scanned the names of the remaining folders—each was a different month and each yielded nothing more than old Cordelia columns.

If what she wanted was advice on her love life, she'd be all set. But this was no help at all in her quest to connect with Cordelia.

Surely, somewhere on this computer was the information she needed. After another half hour passed with no forward progress, she slumped back in the chair and stared, dejected, at the screen. What was she missing? She'd gotten into Jack's phone *and* into his computer. The two devices were linked so she shouldn't have to check the *Contacts List* on both devices—they would be the same.

Unless. She sat up straight. Unless Jack used more than one email address. If he did, each address could have its own contact list. She clicked into the settings of his account, then let out an ecstatic gasp when three email addresses appeared: *JackGraham1*, *JackGrahamPublicity*, and *DearCordelia*.

"Jackpot!" she whispered.

Her excitement plummeted after a quick perusal of the DearCordelia address book didn't offer anything new. "How can you work for Cordelia and not have her email address, Jack? What kind of a publicist are you?"

The computer let out a couple of dings as two new messages joined a row of others in the inbox, all with subject lines like: "Help!" "Should I leave him?" "Is this love?" "How do I find my dream man?"

"How do you find your dream man?" she murmured aloud. "Well, first you find the best looking guy you've ever seen. Then you follow him halfway across the country and move into his house, ostensibly to watch his dog." She sighed. "The question, dear reader, isn't: *how do you find him*. It's how do you make him fall for you? Or in my case, how do you make him tell you what you want to know and then make him fall for you?"

She put her elbows on the desk and rested her chin in her hands, thinking. Why were the Dear Cordelia letters coming to Jack instead of going directly to Cordelia? Was it just another way he helped protect her privacy?

Wait a minute. If Jack forwarded the emails to Cordelia, her email address would be on those emails. Of course. Omigod, she could be seconds away from snagging Cordelia's email address.

She clicked open the sent folder expecting to see a long list of reader letters forwarded to Cordelia. Instead, she found a long list of emails sent to a woman at King Features, one of the big syndicates that represented newspaper columnists. Each email contained an attachment of a Dear Cordelia column.

What the hell? Jack's sent folder didn't show any reader letters forwarded to Cordelia. His inbox didn't show any completed columns received from Cordelia. So where was Jack getting the columns he was sending to the syndicate? She checked the other folders in the account.

It didn't make sense. There weren't any messages, deleted or otherwise, containing Cordelia's column. Not in the inbox. Not in the trash. Not in saved. The only place they showed up was in his sent folder.

She narrowed her eyes at the screen, then slowly turned to look at the painting on the wall, as though a change of scenery would cut through her confusion. Without turning her head back, she let her eyes slide to the computer screen.

No way.

No fucking way.

Jack Graham wasn't answering Dear Cordelia letters. *Was he?*

Holy shit. What had she just found?

Nothing—it couldn't be anything important. All he was doing was forwarding the columns once Cordelia wrote them. That was it—nothing more. Unless …

Fingers flying, she clicked back to the files on his hard drive that she had looked at earlier. Each filename was simply a date—day, month, and year—and most were for dates in the weeks ahead.

There had to be a logical explanation. Maybe he helped Cordelia with the column, or she was sick or on vacation or behind in her work ... *or nonexistent.*

Oh. My. God.

Could it be? Had she been living with Dear Cordelia these past few days? If she could find proof that Jack Graham was Cordelia, her career would be made. She'd be the investigative reporter who finally ripped the veil off Dear Cordelia.

She reveled in the possibility of triumph for a few seconds then pulled herself back to the present. She may be close, but she wasn't there yet. Hopefully Jack was having a rip-roaring good time at the bar and would stay out until it closed.

A door slammed down the hall. Her head jerked up, her mouth dropped open. She stared at the closed door, eyes widening in horror. Someone was coming down the hall and there was only one someone it could be. Jack.

She closed the open file, flicked off the lamp, and prayed Jack would go into the bathroom so she could escape his room without getting caught. Holding her breath, she stared at the door, at the knob, and watched as it turned.

21

Figure something out! her brain screamed. So she sat on the edge of the bed and smiled at Jack when he came through the door.

He stopped, taken aback. "Hi."

She kept smiling, though her stomach was jumping crazy and her brain was spinning like a puppy chasing its tail. She smiled as if being found in a man's bedroom wasn't an unusual experience for her.

His brow furrowed and his gaze slid around the room before coming to rest on her again. "What, ah, are you doing here?"

Liza swallowed, and her smile faded. There was a couple of ways out of this, but only one that would save her.

"Waiting for you." She smiled again, hopefully in that mysterious way Kristin had tried to teach her.

Head cocked slightly as though not sure he believed her, Jack slowly crossed the room. She stood before he got there. His eyes were narrowed and dark and hot, and what had seemed like a reasonable idea when it popped into her head a moment ago now was feeling like one of the worst ideas she'd ever had. She was Liza Dunnigan, for God's sake. She went on many, many, *many* dates before she even got remotely close to situations like this.

And, need she add, she never got in situations like this with men who oozed sex out of every pore on their body. Not that she hadn't wanted to get into situations like this with men like this, but ...

"But I can go," she blurted. She took a step to one side and he countered, blocking her path.

"No. Don't."

Her heart was thudding so hard she Jack could probably hear it. She should have said she was looking for an Ace bandage to wrap her ankle, not waiting for him. Why hadn't she thought of that before? What was she supposed to do now? Where was Kristin when she needed her? What did Dear Cordelia have to say about situations like this?

Cordelia? Her advice was to avoid situations like this. Don't get caught in the wrong place.

Jack's head dipped toward hers—and her brain felt as like it might explode. Cordelia? Wait, if Liza was right about Jack, she could just ask him—her—

And then his mouth covered hers and all coherent thought fled. He tasted of beer and rum and strawberries and exotic beaches in the summer—if she'd ever actually tasted an exotic beach, that is. He pulled her up against him, took her mouth fully, one hand in her hair. She let herself sink into the heat of him and thought, *omigod this guy can kiss*. Which was not really a good thing because she should probably put a stop to it and mention that Ace bandage thing.

She would. In a minute.

The hand that had been holding her head slid over her shoulder and down the side of her breast, and she shuddered as every goose bump on her body bumped to attention.

And then he slid that hand under her sweater, up the soft curve of her waist to caress her breast. His mouth was on her throat and her head was back and her skin was tight and aching for more. She really thought that maybe this was going too far and not the sort of thing she typically found herself doing but—Oh! When his lips found that spot right at the base of her neck and his hands were finding those other spots—all of them, every one—she thought maybe she would put off interrupting this for another minute or so.

Jack pushed her sweater up and pulled it over her head. His hands skimmed over her *leopard bra*.

"Liza Dunnigan, I would have pegged you for white cotton," he murmured.

Leaning into her, he pressed her tight against him and she gasped, "I graduated from cotton a long time ago."

His body pushed her against the wall and his hands held her head as he kissed her so long and hard and deep she thought her knees might give out.

She really should have bought leopard underwear years ago.

Hips still pressed to hers, Jack began to unbutton his shirt with one hand. She cleared her throat and watched his fingers undo one button after the next until his shirt fell open. She gulped as he undid his cuffs. She was far too straight for something like this. They needed to date and all that. Have awkward phone conversations. Fall in love. Make a commitment. This was just not how she did things.

"Actually, I was looking for an Ace bandage," she croaked out. "Because ..."

He tossed his shirt to the floor and she took in his broad

chest and the muscular definition of his arms. Her heart hammered. Every nerve in her body was on high alert.

"Hold that thought," he said as he took a step back from her, pulled his phone from his back pocket and tapped into a screen. Classical music flooded out of a Bluetooth speaker on the nightstand.

Jack smiled. "Now where were we?" he asked as he slid open the fly of his jeans.

Boxers or briefs? her mind whispered. She tried to force her thoughts back to her unfinished sentence.

He slid his jeans to the floor and stepped out of them. Boxers.

"An Ace bandage," he murmured as he pulled her into his arms again. "That's a new one. What do we do with it?" But then his mouth was on hers, and she forgot about the bandage as he steered her onto the bed. And somehow, there she was on her back in only her new leopard underwear—was her stomach sticking out?—and Jack Graham, man of a thousand conquests, was lying on the bed beside her, his hands moving over and under her animal-print unmentionables until she couldn't bear it any longer and moaned out loud.

Moaned. Out loud. Liza Dunnigan. *Get in control*, she admonished herself just before she sank under the erotic assault of his mouth and hands.

He shifted on top of her, their bodies separated only by the silky layer of her underwear and his boxers.

He was good at this, she had to grant him that. But she didn't need to become his thousandth conquest.

She lifted her head and tried to push up on her elbows. "The Ace bandage was for—" She gasped as he pushed her bra up, and the heady sensations rolling through her body forced her back onto the pillow. Okay, no reason she couldn't take advantage of his expertise for a few minutes longer. Then she'd put a stop to this thing. After all, it wasn't often she was able to apprentice with a master.

"We can try kinky the next time," he whispered in her ear.

Kinky? What was that supposed to mean? Oh no, he didn't think she wanted to do something with an Ace bandage, did he?

What could one possibly do with an Ace bandage?

She opened her eyes, ready to clear the whole thing up, but just then his fingers began working magic on parts of her that she swore had never before been touched like that. And his mouth was on her throat, and it had been forever—okay, her entire life—since she'd had an experience like this. Besides, she could hardly breathe, let alone speak. It crossed her very pleasure-saturated mind that investigative reporting could be a very fulfilling field, and it was probably smart for her to keep investigating this particular process.

Suddenly he rolled off her and a wave of cool air moved in to take the place where she had once been heated to a delicious degree.

"Hang on a minute." He disappeared into the bathroom and reappeared holding something behind his back.

A shiver ripped through her. It was now or never. This guy thought she was going to make love with him, and she really couldn't. They hardly knew each other after all ... this was totally wrong for her. "I really think—"

"Shh. I know, I know." He pressed something into her hand as he settled full length beside her on the bed.

Oh God, an Ace bandage.

He ran a hand up her leg from calf to thigh to breast—and every inch of her waited for more, wanted more.

"Well?" he whispered as he nibbled at her ear, his

breath warm, his voice low and seductive. His hand moved to her breasts, his touch more urgent. "What do we do with it?"

"Nothing," she murmured. "Next time."

"Ah, a woman after my own heart." On the CD player the symphony played and she sighed and gave in to what she knew she would later admit was what she'd wanted all along.

———

Jack woke the next morning with his head pounding and his mouth feeling like it was full of cotton. Eyes shut, he rolled over and caught the scent Liza had been wearing last evening.

Liza.

The memory of last night flooded back to him and he reached out to pull her into his arms—and came up empty. He opened his eyes hesitantly, squinting against the sun lighting up the edges of the window shade.

No Liza.

He drew a long, slow breath and looked at the time on his phone. Eleven in the morning. Damn. No wonder Liza was already out of bed. He let his eyelids slip shut and considered getting up but made no move to do it. The pillow felt so good cradling his aching head. Besides, any minute, Liza would surely be up to check on him. Women had a certain predictability. She'd bring him a hot cup of coffee, open the shades, and offer to whip up some scrambled eggs. Then she'd come over to the bed and commiserate about his hangover and before long they'd be making love again.

He remembered her leopard print underwear

—unmentionables, she called them—and how she must have been wearing them all day yesterday. And how he'd been clueless that Liza had a wild side.

The very thought almost cleared up his headache by itself. He rolled onto his back and put his hands behind his head in anticipation. Considering it was almost midday, Liza would have to be coming up soon.

After waiting a bit longer, he began to get antsy. His stomach growled. Well, hell. Where was the hot coffee? The scrambled eggs?

He rolled out of bed and padded down the hall naked to take a shower. The hot, powerful spray massaged his shoulders and neck, helping to cleanse away the poisons he'd ingested last night.

On second thought, it would be better if Liza came upstairs now. She could sneak into the shower with him. Nothing like a slippery, sudsy start to the day. The steaming water cascaded over him and he grinned in anticipation of the pleasures ahead.

And still Liza didn't arrive.

He stepped out of the shower and toweled off, feeling a twinge of regret that he didn't have much time left to share with Liza before he went back to Chicago. What little time they had, they should put to good use.

So where was she?

He pulled on jeans and a sweatshirt and went downstairs, glancing in every room and holding back a growing concern over her absence. She hadn't been scared off by last night, had she? What if she'd decided to move out?

The thought sent another stab of regret through him.

He went barefoot onto the front porch to look for her car, squinting at the brilliant morning. It had snowed sometime during the night, covering everything with fresh, clean coating of white that was sparkling in the bright morning sun.

Leaning over the porch rail to look down the driveway, he spotted Liza clearing away the snow, her shovel making a quiet scraping sound against the concrete. He grinned. This had to be a first; he'd never had a woman leave his bed to shovel. "Good morning," he called.

She jerked her head up in surprise. "Jack! You scared me." She walked toward him, smiling tentatively. "Good morning. How do you feel?"

"My feet are cold." He stuck a foot between the slats of the porch rail.

"Omigod, you'll get frostbite! What are you doing out here barefoot?"

"Looking for you."

She frowned slightly. "Why?"

He almost said something about being afraid she'd left and that he didn't want her to leave, but decided it sounded too needy. "You want to go out for breakfast?"

"Sure." She let out a laugh. "Or maybe lunch."

He grinned. "I need some thick black coffee and greasy fried eggs. How about you?"

"I don't need them but they sound great. Just let me finish shoveling, I'm almost done."

"You're kind of nice to have around—keep this up and I might give you a raise."

Liza tossed a shovelful of snow in his direction and the wind blew it back in her face. She let out a screech.

"Didn't you ever learn about not pissing into the wind?" He started to dance from foot to foot because his feet were going numb from the cold.

She sputtered and wiped her face with a mittened

hand. "Yeah, and haven't you ever heard that a wise man wears shoes in the winter?"

He laughed. She could give as good as she got. He was half tempted to march down to the driveway and kiss her until she was breathless. "Touché. Let me get some shoes on and I'll give you a hand."

22

Liza watched Jack go into the house, a sick feeling in her stomach. What did he think about last night? Did he have regrets?

She'd awakened early, warm and safe in his embrace, and had lain there in the dark, thinking, her emotions tangled and confused. Slipping out from under his arm, she'd rolled onto her side and watched him sleep, his chest rising and falling, his breath soft and easy. She had almost reached out to slide her hand down his arm and over his chest. Almost.

But early morning sunlight had begun to appear around the edges of the shade, and the room had grown brighter, and suddenly she'd felt a little like Cinderella the morning after the ball. Like her clothes were in tatters and her hair was a mess and one of her shoes was missing.

This was Jack Graham after all. And she was Liza Dunnigan, most recently a very practical woman. So, as much as she'd wanted to awaken him with a kiss, she'd been terrified he would open his eyes and look with horror upon her as something the mai tais had brought home.

Of course, then he'd be nice—and give her one of those lines that both of them knew wasn't true. Like: *I'll call you.* Or: *We should stay in touch.* Or worst of all: *That was a mistake, let's forget it even happened.*

After what they'd shared last night, the thought of being rejected had been enough to make her grab her clothes and flee the room. Which was just as well because somewhere between his room and hers she'd had a sudden epiphany about the game she was playing—and she wasn't impressed.

She had moved into Jack's house on a lie, had broken into his phone and computer, and then slept with the guy— all in the name of investigative reporting. What kind of a person did stuff like that? Not her.

Not the old her anyway. Her stomach began to tumble.

"Sleep well?" Jack's voice jerked her out of her thoughts.

She nodded.

"So did I. Best night's sleep I've had in a long time." His eyes locked with hers for a long moment, almost too long. "Thanks."

Liza felt faint. He was thanking her? Had she just provided a service? "Glad I could help." *Glad she could help?* What kind of idiocy was that?

"So am I." Jack lifted a shovel from a nail on the garage wall and began to help clear the walk.

———

Mary and Diane waved from a booth along the far wall of the coffee shop.

"Join us, why don't you." Mary scooted over in her seat. "Diane, come over by me so they can sit together."

"Oh, that's not necessary," Liza said.

"No, no trouble at all." Diane moved to the other side, then slid her plate with a club sandwich and fries across the table.

Sit, sit," Mary said, fluttering one hand. "Do you want some bacon?" She held a piece up as Liza scooted into the booth and Jack followed.

"I'll eat it," Jack said. "I'm starving."

"Doesn't that belong in your sandwich?" Liza nodded at the BLT on Mary's plate.

"I'm supposed to keep my sodium intake down."

"Did you two have fun last night?" Diane asked.

Clearly there were no secrets from the ladies next door.

Jack nodded as he crunched on the bacon. "Too much fun," he said with a wince.

"How was Ashley?" Diane whispered at Liza as Jack accepted another slice of bacon from Mary.

"About the same," Liza said.

"You'd better watch her—"

"Watch who?" Jack asked.

"Jack, would you be a dear and get me some mayonnaise?" Mary smiled at him.

He slid out of the booth and went to the counter.

"Now, back to Ashley," Diane said. "She wants Jack. But nothing would be a worse match. We know Jack—"

"And we know Ashley—"

"And so does every man in town, if you get what I mean," Diane said in a low voice.

"She's not that bad," Mary said.

"Okay, fine, but she isn't right for Jack." Diane took a bite of her sandwich. "Whenever Jack's in town, she comes hanging around."

Liza had no doubt what Ashley came around for. The same thing Jack went to see Ashley for. She blanched. She hoped she hadn't simply taken Ashley's place—same service in Coldwater, new girl.

"We have to be careful about what we say, though. Jack thinks we're being—" Mary's voice dropped lower, "—busybodies. But we think you and he—"

Jack set a small bowl of mayo on the table and slid into the booth. The waitress came up behind him, and poured them each a cup of coffee. "You two want something to eat?"

As soon as they finished placing their orders, Diane began talking again. "Any news about CJ?"

Jack shook his head.

"Don't lose hope. Dogs wander away all the time and come back when you least expect it," Mary said as she spread some mayo on her BLT.

"Yeah, but at some point I have to be realistic. How long could an old dog survive in this weather?"

"She has that fur coat," Mary said. "And an extra layer of fat."

"Maybe even two," Diane added.

"I'm more worried because of her age."

Mary frowned. "Age is just a frame of mind."

Diane nodded. "You're only as old as you feel."

"Old is as old does," Liza chimed in with a grin.

Diane waved a finger. "You'll find her, I just know it."

"Well, it better be soon, because I've got clients I keep putting on hold. I can't stay here much longer."

"When you didn't go back a couple of days ago, all your clients were fine," Diane said around a mouthful of sandwich.

"Yeah, but—"

"You couldn't leave without knowing about CJ, could you?" Mary asked in alarm.

Jack shook his head. "She's been gone almost forty-eight hours. Much as I hate to say it, I'm beginning to lose hope."

"What would your grandmother think, you deserting her dog?" Diane shook her head sternly.

Jack blew out a breath. "I'm not deserting her, but at some point soon, I have to get back. I'm about to reschedule an important appointment for the second time." He took a sip of coffee. "What I'm thinking is that Liza could stay at the house for a while, and if CJ is found, then she'll just become the caretaker." He looked at her. "If you want to, that is."

He was talking about going back to Chicago again? Already? She had to figure out if he was Cordelia, quick. And if he wasn't, then she had to figure out where Cordelia was. She was probably closer than anyone had ever gotten to the truth about Cordelia. Which meant she had to forget everything that had happened between them. Forget that he was a really nice guy. *Forget that she had apparently abandoned her ethics in order to get this story.*

The waitress arrived with their food and tucked the bill under the saltshaker.

Diane dabbed her mouth with her napkin. "Well, you two eat. We have to get going. Errands to run. Come on, Mary."

As the two women went to the register to pay, Mary turned back to admonish them from ten feet away, "Now, don't gulp your food or you'll get indigestion."

"When they're ready to leave, they just get up and go, don't they," Liza said with a grin.

"They're like that. Try talking to Diane on the phone sometime. As soon as she says what she called for, she hangs up. No chitchat. Accomplish the goal, then move on."

Might be a lesson for her to take to heart. Stay focused.

Put an end to all this ... *chitchat* ... with Jack and concentrate her energy on finding Cordelia.

It shouldn't matter what happened between them last night. It shouldn't matter if Jack was a nice guy or not. It shouldn't matter that the philosophy she seemed to be operating under—*the end justifies the means*—was the opposite of what she'd always believed. She had information to find, a future to create, and she needed to get it done and move on.

23

As she came in the front door, Liza scooped up the envelope lying on the floor beneath the mail slot and handed it to Jack. "You've got mail," she said playfully.

He tore it open and pulled out a single sheet of paper, his expression changing from mild interest to surprise to anger. "What the hell is this? A ransom note for the dog?"

Liza took the paper from him. The words, *We have CJ We'll be in touch,* were scrawled in large sloppy printing across the unlined sheet. "This has to be a prank. Probably kids who saw our lost dog signs," she said as her mind went into overdrive. What if someone else had discovered Jack was Cordelia and figured he had plenty of money to pay a ransom. Maybe someone else was about to scoop her scoop.

Ridiculous. After all these years, there was no way two people would have figured out at exactly the same moment that Jack and Cordelia were the same person. It probably wasn't even true; all she had was circumstantial evidence. Still, the sooner she got to the bottom of the question, the better off she'd be.

Jack threw his keys on the dining-room table and his

jacket over the back of a chair. "This is bizarre. Kids or not, I'm calling the police." Five minutes later, he hung up the phone, discouraged. "No help there. He said if we get another note with an actual ransom amount to call back. Otherwise, it's probably a prank. Kids who saw the signs."

"Do *you* think it's a prank?"

Jack shrugged. "If she ran away and someone found her, you'd think they'd be happy to give her back. Who would want to keep a fat, old basset hound with a bulging eye?"

"Who slobbers," Liza said.

"And sheds," Jack added. "Seriously, what motive would someone have to keep CJ other than to get a ransom?"

Liza crossed the room. "Remember that waitress yesterday? The *think tank* one? She said someone might have taken CJ for ransom."

"She also said people think my grandmother had a lot of money. Which she didn't."

"Yeah, but you know how rumors work. Your grandmother set up her dog with a pretty sweet living situation. Maybe people think you inherited a bundle. Are you secretly rich?" Liza held her breath, hoping he'd say something that might give her a clue about Cordelia.

He let out a snort. "Hardly."

Unless he actually was Cordelia. Then he undoubtedly had a lot more money than he was letting on. Liza dropped onto the couch. "Did your grandmother have any enemies? We need to make a list of suspects."

"Even if she did, why would they wait three years to kidnap the dog? CJ could have kicked off before now and the opportunity would be lost."

"We should talk to the neighbors again. See if anyone noticed someone skulking around."

"This is unbelievable." Jack went to the window, then turned to face Liza. "Unless ... I can't believe I'm about to say this ... maybe one of the candidates for the caretaker's job took her."

"Because they got really attached to her during the interview?" Liza tried not to sound incredulous.

"No, Watson. Because they want the job."

"Jack," Liza said calmly, as though talking to a child. "Why would anyone think stealing the dog would get them the job? That's sort of like stealing the ice cream machine to make Dairy Queen hire you. It's not logical."

"Bingo. I wouldn't exactly say I had a slew of logical candidates."

"Oh, really?" She raised her eyebrows.

He held up a hand and smiled. "Except you, sweetheart, except you." He sat beside her on the couch and put an arm around her shoulders. "You were a welcome relief after the other applicants."

"Okay, so let's think about those candidates? Did any seem remotely criminal-like?" she said brightly, shifting to break physical contact and look directly at him.

Big mistake. His eyes didn't look at all like he was thinking about dognappers—they looked like he was thinking about last night.

Just like she was.

But she couldn't go there—she had a job to do, information to find. She was changing her life and just because last night was ... the most incredible experience she'd ever had and another step toward the new Liza—

He reached for her, bringing her next to him again. Her brain faltered. Just because last night—

And then his lips touched hers and her brain shut down and she surrendered to the moment.

She leaned into him, kissed him back long and hard, took hold of his shirt to pull him closer. And when finally they broke apart, breathless, all she could think was, *oh my God, what if he really was Dear Cordelia?* What would she do then?

No more kissing, no more nothing until she knew for sure either way. Otherwise, she would be a basket case. She drew a hand across her lips. "So, ah, really then, which of the candidates might be suspects?"

Jack threw his head back and laughed. "Okay. We'll stay on topic. First on the list should probably be yesterday's waitress, the one who brought up the idea of ransom."

"I agree."

"As for applicants, I haven't interviewed that many yet. There was a chain-smoker, and the college girl who arrived right after you did, and some woman who decided the whole place needed redecorating," he said. "There were others who I eliminated during the phone call phase."

"And they all seemed like they all wanted the job—I mean, *really* wanted it?"

He nodded. "Dog lovers, one and all."

"Okay. Did anyone get mad because they didn't get the job? What about Ashley? She seemed pretty upset you didn't hire her."

"Ashley just gets—she would never—" Jack stood abruptly and crossed the room, shoving his hands in his jean pockets. "You know what? I should have thought of this before."

"Ashley might have CJ?"

"Maybe. Hell, more than maybe. She's been adamant about wanting the job. And last night she said—she thought CJ would come home if you were gone." He winced.

"What's that supposed to mean? I'm the reason CJ ran away?"

"I think she was trying to imply you're the evil stepmother," he said teasingly.

Liza let out a snort. "The dog hasn't known me long enough to draw that conclusion."

"I think we both agree CJ had no reason to hate you."

"But she did have reason to hate Ashley and the boys. You could tell the minute they arrived—she was always trying to get away from them. Especially that youngest one."

"So you're saying CJ ran away out of fear that Ashley was going to become the caretaker?"

Liza grinned. "Works for me."

"We won't share that theory with the police. Let's go see if the ladies spotted anything unusual while we were out." Jack shrugged into his jacket and headed for the door.

Five minutes later, they were talking to Diane on her front porch. A blustery wind raced across the yard and swirled the top layer of snow into the air. "Dognapped?" Diane reached into her sleeve for a tissue just as a big sneeze escaped her. She blew her nose, then pushed open the door and shouted. "Mary, come quick. CJ's been kidnapped!"

As Mary came out the door, Jack handed her the ransom note. "We found this in the mail slot. Must have been delivered while we were gone. Did you notice anyone around the house this morning?"

"Well, there was the meter reader from the power company," Mary said after a moment.

"Right. But did you see anyone suspicious?" Jack asked.

"I'm just saying, maybe he wasn't a meter reader."

"Okay. What did he look like?"

"A bit like you, except in a gas company uniform." Mary

wrapped her arms around her waist for warmth. "Said even though the meters are automated, they have to manually check once every two years."

Jack shook his head. "I think he's a meter reader."

"You asked if we saw anyone unusual," Mary said defensively. "Haven't seen a meter reader around in a long time."

"Probably two years," Jack muttered.

"How about unusual cars?" Liza asked.

Both women shook their heads.

"We just got home ourselves. We were running errands." Diane wiped her nose again. "This cold is going to be the death of me," she muttered.

"We'll keep an eye out for shady characters. I'm freezing." Mary went into the house.

"I'll never get well if I stay out here." Diane followed Mary in.

"Well, thanks for your—" The door clicked shut. "—help," Jack said. He rolled his eyes at Liza. "That was productive, don't you think?"

"It's cold. They're old. Diane's sick. Let's go check with the other neighbors."

Two hours later they'd learned nothing to help with their investigation, but now knew plenty of neighborhood gossip, including every ailment being experienced on either side of the street.

As Liza started up the front steps, Jack pulled open his car door. "I'm going to run over to Ashley's," he said. "See if she knows anything. Wish me luck."

"Good luck." Omigod, Jack was leaving her alone in the house again? What a miracle; if she worked fast, maybe she'd be able to dig out the answers she needed before he got back. She raced upstairs, electrified and terrified over the possibility of getting at the truth.

As much as she wanted to get this scoop, part of her hoped she was wrong about Jack being Cordelia. She liked him. A lot. He was a decent guy, a good man. So even though she would give anything to break this story, she dreaded being the person who ultimately exposed Jack's secret to the world.

She slipped into the chair at his desk and turned on his computer, speed-dialing Kristin as she waited for the computer to boot up. After what felt like about a hundred rings, Kristin finally answered.

"Thank God you're there!" Liza said on a breath.

"What's the matter?"

"Nothing. Well, everything. I got into Jack's computer—"

"Fantastic! Did you get an address for Cordelia?"

"No—"

"Phone number?"

"No—"

"Email?"

"No, will you let me—"

"Liza, you're running out of time!"

"You don't have to remind me. I'm aware every day how little time I have."

"So? Have you got *anything*?"

She thought of what she'd found on Jack's computer last night, and what had happened between them afterward. "I think so."

"Well? Lay it out. The suspense is killing me."

"I don't know for sure. I mean, I could be wrong. This could be a false lead and all that—"

"What is it?" Kristin almost shouted.

"Do you think Jack Graham could be Dear Cordelia?"

Laughter exploded from the earpiece. "Not on your life."

Liza felt the flood of relief. She was so glad she'd called Kristin. "Why not?"

"Why not? You've read Dear Cordelia's book. He doesn't do anything the book says. He's a player. He lives his life completely different from the way Cordelia advises people. No way is Jack Graham writing that column."

She hadn't quite thought of it like that.

"What made you think he was Cordelia?"

Liza scrunched up her face. "It was just a thought—I didn't actually take it seriously. It's just he's got all these files, questions people sent to the column, even has answers to the questions."

"That doesn't mean he's writing the answers. Maybe Cordelia emails her finished columns to him to proofread or forward to the different newspapers or something."

"Yeah, I thought that, too." Liza clicked her way into Jack's email. "There's another thing, though. An email address—a separate one. It's DearCordelia—"

"Yeah?"

"It seems to be the inbox where people send their letters and questions to Cordelia."

"Maybe Jack screens the questions for her."

"And there are finished columns that haven't even run yet."

Kristin exhaled. "It's probably just another way he's helping his client. If you actually think this could be something, that Jack really is Cordelia, you'll need rock-solid proof. Don't let your imagination take you on a flyer."

"I know. I know. I better get at this—I don't know how long he'll be gone. I'll text you if I find anything."

Liza turned her attention to Jack's computer and began to methodically search his files, noting two new documents had been created yesterday. She clicked each one open and skimmed the contents. Both were upcoming advice columns written by Cordelia; one letter made her pause.

Dear Cordelia,

I'm thirty-two and have fallen hard for a guy that I'm not sure feels the same way about me. We have a lot of fun, he's very attentive when we're together, charming even. But he's dated a lot of women and I can't shake the feeling I may end up just being one in a long line of many. Do guys like him ever settle down or am I wasting my time?

Dating a Player

Liza sat back in the chair. Change the writer's age, and this letter could almost be about her and Jack. She scrolled down to Cordelia's reply:

Dear Dating,

There are a lot of reasons why men don't settle down. Some get bored easily, or are perfectionists, or are protecting themselves from a broken heart, or even hiding something. As to whether you're wasting If you think you're wasting You're not wasting time if you Try to look at this from his point Maybethe best thing for you to do is Maybe he really does like you

. . .

Hmm, typos everywhere. Obviously, Cordelia was still working on her answer to this one. Very suspicious that it was saved on Jack's computer. But it wasn't anywhere near rock-solid proof that Jack was Cordelia. For all she knew, Cordy could have emailed it to him because she needed help coming up with a response. After all, it did seem like a topic he could totally relate to.

She closed the file and started searching through saved emails, opening and scanning only those with subject lines that seemed pertinent to her quest. But none of them contained helpful information—no contact info for Cordelia, no details to support the theory that Jack and Cordelia were the same person.

Spotting an email he'd saved from his grandmother, she hesitated. The subject line, *love never fails*, could be relevant to Cordelia. But probably not. More likely this email was just his grandmother gently chiding Jack about his playboy ways and disinterest in settling down.

Curiosity nipped at her. She wondered what kind of advice Jack's grandma had given him about women? About settling down? Had he been dating someone she hoped he would marry? Her finger twitched on the touchpad. She knew she should let this email go. It was undoubtedly a private communication, not part of her investigation. But how would she know unless she looked?

She vacillated a second longer, then shoved aside her guilt over prying into Jack's life and clicked the message open:

Dear Jack,

It's late and I can't stop thinking about our call tonight. I took Cordelia Jane out for a walk and her sad basset face made me remember a sad little boy named Jack who blossomed when he finally came to a place where he was loved. Don't be so hard on yourself. These have not been wasted years.

You help people find love. A finer thing you couldn't do. When you are very old, you will look back and know that your life had purpose. If you have helped even one relationship grow stronger, or one couple find the love they seek, then your time has been well spent. Love never fails.

I know you never meant the column to be forever. I'm glad you're finally going after the career you always wanted. Be content. Keep the faith.

All my love,
Gram

Oh. My. God. She'd been right.

24

CORDELIA JANE WAS A BASSET HOUND. DEAR CORDELIA
was Jack.

Liza blinked to clear the tears blurring her eyes. She'd
gone looking for proof and she'd found it. Jack and Cordelia
were the same person.

So now what? All she'd wanted was to get an interview
with Dear Cordelia, a chance to prove she was good enough
to be an investigative reporter. Instead, she'd uncovered
blockbuster news that could skyrocket her career—and
explode Jack's life.

Suddenly she wanted to get as far away from this room
as she could. She closed the computer and went
downstairs, paced from the living room to the kitchen and
back again.

So what did she do now? Stay the course? Turn Jack's
life upside down by exposing his secret to the world? He'd
trusted her. And she'd lied to him about why she was in
Coldwater, had broken into his computer, and invaded his
privacy. She drew a slow shuddering breath.

She had to think. But not here. She couldn't think in the

place where she'd spun a web of lies—and there were reminders of Jack everywhere she turned.

————

Jack tried to figure out how to ask Ashley if she'd taken CJ without sounding as if he were accusing her of dognapping. It felt a bit like trying to balance on a thread.

"Thanks for stopping over." Ashley handed him a Coke, then dropped onto the couch beside him, shoulder to shoulder, thigh to thigh. "We've hardly seen each other while you've been back this time."

"I feel the same way. That's why I'm here," he lied. It took a measure of self-restraint to hold himself back coming right out with, "Do you have the dog?"

"I should be mad at you, the way you've been ignoring me. In fact, I *was* mad at you. But then I decided you had a lot on your mind with all this CJ stuff." She smiled. "And I forgave you."

"Thanks." He resisted the urge to roll his eyes. "I just stopped to let you know I've got to get back to Chicago."

"Already? What about CJ?"

"Liza will be staying at the house a few days in case she shows up." Hopefully this revelation would lead the discussion in the right direction.

"Well, that's a problem. CJ won't come back if she's there. I already told you—the poor dog probably ran away just to avoid her."

"Ashley, the dog can't open the gate."

She blinked. "All I know is if I were a dog and that was the caretaker you hired for me, I would be hightailing it out of town as fast as I could."

He decided to let her *if I were a dog* remark slide. "That

isn't just sour grapes about you not getting the caretaker job, is it?"

"What?"

"When you say CJ would come home if Liza was gone, you sound like someone who knows where the dog is."

Ashley pushed herself to standing. "Are you accusing me of stealing your dog?" she asked in a shocked voice.

"You wanted the job pretty bad—"

"I wouldn't steal CJ to get it," she snapped. "Anyway, if the dog is gone, there is no job. Stealing the dog wouldn't help me get the job at all."

"It would if Liza left."

Ashley's eyes flashed. "I can't believe this. After all these years, after how close we've been, I'd think you'd know me better than that.

Jack tried to gauge whether she was telling the truth or not. Yeah, of course she was. Stealing the dog was way outside Ashley's capabilities. Especially since she had four kids who took up all her time. "Okay, sorry. I'm sorry. I'm just getting desperate."

She dropped down beside him again. "You want to know what I think? If you really want to find CJ, ask Liza."

He barked out a laugh. Liza blamed Ashley. Ashley blamed Liza. "I'll bite. What's her motive?"

"She's afraid you'll go back to Chicago. So she took the dog to make you stay."

"Why would she care if I went back to Chicago?"

"Men are so stupid." Ashley tipped up her chin. "She wants you."

Jack shook his head. "I don't think so."

"Oh, I know so. You'd be a great catch—handsome, good job, money—she actually thinks she might be able to land you."

"No."

"Oh Jack, think about it. You offer her the job, then you say you're going back to Chicago, and suddenly! Shock! The dog is missing. She knew you were planning to leave."

"Uh, yeah."

"That's when the dog disappeared—right?"

He nodded.

"There's your thief."

"One problem. Liza couldn't have stolen CJ because I was with her when the dog disappeared." *Making out on the couch.*

"Then she's got a partner."

"Ash, you're reaching now."

"Truth is always stranger than fiction. Where did she come from anyway?" She pointed a finger at him and nodded.

"Chicago."

"Uh-huh. Just like you. What a coincidence. Someone from Chicago just happened to come to Coldwater and apply for a job as the dog's caretaker?"

"Not exactly," he said defensively.

Ashley let out a snort. "Close enough, I bet."

It was more like ... *someone who worked for the Chicago Sentinel just happened to come to Coldwater for a job at the culinary institute and thought the house was for sale and then applied for a job as the dog's caretaker.*

She was right; it did sound pretty coincidental. He took a big swallow of Coke. Ashley had no idea he was Cordelia, no idea that there was a bigger reason a newspaper reporter would want to get to him. Shit. This better not be about Cordelia. It couldn't be. No way. Liza couldn't have ulterior motives.

He started for the door.

"Mark my words," Ashley said. "She's got designs on you. And she's got someone helping her set you up." Her words followed him outside.

Jack drew a deep breath of cold air as he walked to his car. He didn't want to believe the worst about Liza. Sometimes unbelievable coincidences just happened. Sometimes life was stranger than fiction. It was possible that Liza was just a woman—an incredible woman—who used to work in the food section of the Chicago Sentinel. Nothing more.

He was halfway home before he admitted to himself that, yeah, the dog disappeared only a few hours after he'd told Liza he was going back to Chicago the next day. And, okay fine, they found a ransom note this morning not long after he'd again brought up returning to Chicago.

It could be coincidence. *Could be.*

Except, the night Liza had come to dinner with the ladies next door, she'd spoken as if she still worked at the paper—and then corrected herself. He'd chalked it up to the fact that she'd only recently quit her job there.

But what if she hadn't.

Suddenly, everything about Liza seemed suspect. Had she really been waiting for him in his room last night? Or had she been searching for information about Cordelia and said the only thing that made sense when he surprised her?

Not Liza. She couldn't be like so many others.

He exhaled sharply. Until this moment, he hadn't realized how hard he'd fallen.

Hold on. He was jumping to conclusions, finding Liza guilty based on the accusations of a jealous woman. Liza couldn't be faking everything—quitting her job, joining the culinary institute, wanting to buy a house. She'd gone to a meeting at the institute just yesterday, a fact that would be easy enough to check.

In fact, it all would be easy to check. Just two phone calls would clear everything up—one to the newspaper to see if she was still an employee, and the other to verify her status at the culinary institute.

He pulled the car to the curb. Everything about him—his livelihood, his reputation, his budding sports agent business—could be on the line right now. For his own protection, he had to make sure Liza was everything she said she was.

Swiping open his phone, he looked up the number for the human resources at the Maine Culinary Institute. Using calm, professional voice, he explained that he was a landlord in Coldwater and needed to verify the information submitted on a rental application. Could they confirm that Liza Dunnigan had taken a position on staff?

After what seemed like an inordinately long wait, the woman returned to the phone. "No one by that name has been hired recently," she said, clearly confused. "Are you sure you called the right school? Maybe she's been hired at the University of Maine."

Stunned speechless, he could only nod. Liza didn't have a job at the culinary institute?

"Sir?"

"Uh, yeah, UMaine. You're right. Actually that's what the application says. Don't know what I was thinking. Sorry to bother you."

He ended the call and stared at the phone. Fear nipped at the edges of his mind, tried a full-frontal assault on his consciousness, but he shoved it back.

Not his Liza.

Of all the women who had been in his life, all the casual

relationships he'd had with gorgeous, fun women, he'd always been able to keep himself mentally free of entanglements.

Until now.

In a sense, it was probably poetic justice. Here he was, falling for a woman who probably not only didn't want him, but was hoping to bring about his downfall.

He went to the Chicago Sentinel website and scrolled through the staff email list until he spotted Liza Dunnigan's name under the Lifestyles section. His heartrate sped up. Damn.

Still, maybe the site administrator was behind on making updates. Maybe deleting Liza from the staff listing was on his to-do list of. He called the newspaper's main phone number and asked for Liza. Seconds later, Liza's voicemail message kicked in and he had his answer: "You have reached Liza Dunnigan. I'm out of the office the next two weeks chasing down a big story, but I'll be checking email—"

He shut off the phone and tossed it onto the passenger seat. Liza wasn't moving to Coldwater. She wasn't looking to buy a house. She wasn't going to work at the culinary institute.

Without a doubt, Liza Dunnigan was after what every reporter seemed to want these days.

Cordelia.

He'd been set up. My God, all the years he'd been so diligent about keeping this secret, and he'd almost been found out by a reporter from the food section.

He went into the house, gripping the phone in his fist. Since when did food section reporters get sent undercover to do investigative reporting? Was Liza planning to create a new dish and name it after him? Cordelia Casserole?

Not even funny. She was probably working with that guy from the *Sentinel* who had been calling him for weeks. Damn, but their plan had been pretty brilliant. They'd probably known he was looking for a caretaker for CJ, but instead of applying for the job, she'd laid out that story about moving to Coldwater and wanting to buy the house. By not initially applying for the job, she could stall about accepting it, thereby forcing him to stay in Coldwater so she had more time and opportunity to find the information she wanted.

He shook his head. He'd looked into her eyes and swallowed every bit of her story—hook, line and sinker. Hell, he'd even invited her to live in his house so she could get to know CJ better. She must have had a real laugh over that one.

Ashley was probably right. Liza was working with someone—that other reporter—who took the dog so Jack would be forced to stay in town.

And then there was last night. He blew out a sharp breath. Obviously, Liza hadn't been waiting for him like she'd said. No way.

He'd stupidly disabled the password on his computer while he was here because he didn't think he had to worry about security in his own home. No doubt, Liza discovered that last night. She hadn't been waiting for him in his room —she'd been digging around in his computer. *That incredible night they'd shared had been an act.*

"I should have known," he said aloud to the empty house. "After all these years writing that column, I should have been able to tell that something wasn't right with her."

He went to the front window and looked out, not really seeing. Liza had fooled him completely—and he never got fooled. She was good, no question about it. But to be that good, she had to be completely without scruples.

Now he knew why she'd really come to Maine—to find out the truth about Cordelia. The question was, had she?

Every cell in his body wanted to throw her out of his house the minute she got back. And every inch of his heart was betraying him—because all it wanted to do was take her in his arms. But he could do neither. Not until he learned for certain he was right about why she was here—and whether she'd gotten what she'd come for.

He pushed his hands into his pockets and settled in to wait for her return.

25

HALF AN HOUR LATER THE FRONT DOOR OPENED, AND Liza stepped into the room along with a blast of frigid air, her cheeks rosy, her eyes sparkling from the cold. "Hey," she said, grinning. She hung her jacket on the coat tree.

The warmth on her face made his stomach roil. "Where'd you go?" he asked.

"Just walking, wanted to get some fresh air, clear my head. Sometimes I get a little stir crazy in the winter."

He looked at her a moment, just looked. He wished he could just lay out his questions and that she'd have a logical explanation for everything. But he knew it wouldn't work that way. She'd already proven she had no qualms about lying. Which meant he had to handle her with kid gloves if he was going to get at the truth.

"I have to head back to Chicago. Work beckons," he said. "I'm just not optimistic we're going to find CJ—not after so many days."

"Oh Jack, I'm sure she's okay. We'll find her. Don't give up yet."

She was so certain. Which she would be, of course, if

she was responsible for CJ's disappearance in the first place. His heart hardened. No doubt the dog would show up just as soon as Liza went back to Chicago and filed her story.

"If she does, the ladies will let me know. I'm going to close up the house and put it on the market. You'll have to find somewhere else to live." He paused a moment. "That is, unless you're still interested in buying?"

"Oh, ah, I might be, maybe ..." She looked a little stricken.

She wasn't the only one feeling a little stricken right now.

"Last week, you said you wanted to buy the house," he said, taking a perverse pleasure in how discomforted she seemed.

"I did. But you're catching me off guard. I'd sort of put the home-buying idea to rest when I began to seriously consider taking this job with CJ"

"No CJ, no job," he said flippantly. "I suppose you could stay here a few days until you find another place. Be pretty hard to start a new job and be homeless at the same time."

Liza nodded. "Thanks, I'd appreciate that."

What a liar. Screw the kid gloves. "You're starting your job next week, right?"

She nodded again, her smile fading.

"Because the oddest thing happened." He strolled across the room and turned to face her. "I talked to the culinary institute today. They said you aren't on their staff. You haven't been hired there. And I'm wondering what exactly that might be all about."

Liza's eyes widened, then she flashed a sheepish smile. "The thing is, I'm actually not on staff yet. I'm going to be working on developing recipes for a cookbook with them, and they'll be putting me on payroll by spring."

He marveled at how easily the falsehoods came out of her. Bitter disappointment coursed through him.

She pressed her lips together, and he remembered what had been like to kiss those lips, to feel Liza's soft body beneath his own, her breath mingling with his— He rammed the memory into the darkest corner of his mind and drenched it in anger. "You want to tell me what you were really doing in my room last night?"

He willed her to tell the truth, to come clean, to apologize, to tell him that she loved him—where the hell had that come from? To tell him she loved him? *As much as he loved her.*

Fuck. This was rich. He'd had fallen in love with a woman whose goal it was to betray him. If this were a movie, he'd laugh at the ridiculousness of it.

Liza shook her head. "I told you last night."

"You sure? Because I also called the Chicago Sentinel. Seems you still work there, just taking two weeks off to chase down a big story."

Liza paled. "I can explain."

"Explain what? That you're doing a story on Dear Cordelia?" He held his breath, giving her a chance to deny the accusation, an opportunity to prove him wrong.

Liza gasped. "Oh Jack, I didn't mean to ... I'm so sorry."

His hope deflated. He'd been right about her. "You're sorry? Sorry for lying to me? Or sorry for getting caught?" He leaned toward her, mentally crushing all his feelings for her under a hard heel of contempt. "What did you learn about Cordelia, Liza? I have a right to know."

She stared at him, her dark eyes wide and welling with tears.

"You've lied about everything else. At least you owe me the truth on this."

She raised her chin and looked at him defiantly. Even then, he had to hold himself back from reaching up to brush the tears off her cheeks. "You're Cordelia," she said as though daring him to deny it.

For a flicker of a moment, he felt grudging admiration for what she'd accomplished. He walked to the window and looked at the gray day, at the white flakes wisping from the clouds trying to work themselves into a real snowfall. "Congratulations, you win the grand prize. Yes, I'm Cordelia. I have to hand it to you. You're good." He faced her, eyes narrowed. "What do you get out of it? A big raise? Recognition? A promotion?"

She flinched a little at the last one.

"A promotion? You're getting a promotion for this story?" he asked, resentment in his voice.

"I'll get my things." She started toward the stairway, and he stepped into her path.

"You *are* writing a news story, correct?"

She stared at him a long time before nodding.

"Well, make sure you put something in your article about what it's like to—screw—Cordelia." He knew he was being crude and didn't care. "In every sense of the word."

Anger flashed in her eyes. "Maybe I'll recommend that Cordelia read her own book. She might especially benefit from the chapter about honesty."

"Oh, the pot calling the kettle black, is it?"

Liza tried to step past him, and he grabbed her arm. "Who the hell are you anyway?" he demanded.

She pulled away and ran up the stairs. Jack watched her go, then went into the kitchen, popped open a beer and chugged half of it down.

A few minutes later, he heard Liza's footsteps on the stairs. He leaned against the doorjamb in the entry to the kitchen and watched her hurry toward the front door, suitcase in hand. "Aren't you forgetting something?" he called pleasantly.

She turned, her expression wary, her body language telegraphing flight. "What?"

"Where's my grandmother's dog?"

"How should I know?"

"Oh, come on. You had someone grab her to make me stay in Coldwater."

Her eyes widened. "No I didn't."

Jack walked toward her. "Look, Liza, the jig is up. I've figured everything out. Tell me where CJ is and I won't call the police."

"You actually think I took the dog?"

"You or an accomplice."

Liza's jaw dropped, and she quickly recovered. "I don't know where she is. You may think I'm the lowest possible human being on the planet right now—and who knows, maybe I am. But I'm not so low that I would kidnap a dog— or be part of a scheme to do that. No one I know took the dog. *I don't know where CJ is.*"

She tugged open the door and strode outside. Jack stood in the doorway, watched as she opened the trunk to her rental car and hoisted her suitcase inside. The wind swept a chill through him and he welcomed the cold, happy to be feeling something other than revulsion.

———

Liza slumped into her seat at the airport gate and stared out the window, unseeing, as she waited for her plane to board.

She had accomplished the impossible. She'd gotten the story that reporters all over the country would have given their left arm for. So why didn't she feel victorious?

In her mind she replayed her last conversation with Jack, saw again the disgust in his expression when he'd confronted her just a few hours ago. An ache welled up deep in her chest.

She'd gotten the story and lost the guy.

Well, now there was a delusion if she'd ever seen one. Jack had never been hers to lose. All he'd wanted was a caretaker for the dog and a short-term fling. She'd known that from the beginning.

Just as all she'd wanted was the information that would enable her to get promoted into a new job. Oh all right, and to live happily ever after with the man of her dreams. Too bad the man of her dreams turned out to be the same guy whose pockets she'd decided to pick. Kind of destroyed any chance at happily ever after.

This was priceless. Her first real assignment as an investigative reporter, and she fell in love with the subject. It would be a long and painful career if she made a habit of this.

She thought of never kissing Jack again and a knot formed in her throat. If she had taken the job as caretaker at least she would have had contact with him on a somewhat regular basis. Maybe they would have had a chance—

Oh my God, she was a raving lunatic. This was what she'd come to? Confusing a made-up story with reality?

And all because of Jack Graham.

She tried to work up some righteous indignation. If he hadn't always been so damn secretive about his client—okay, himself—this never would have happened. At some point with some reporter all he would have had to do was have *Cordelia* provide written responses to a list of questions. Hold a Q&A session on Facebook. Something. With everything in written form, no one would ever know he was Cordelia. But it would have removed some of the aura of mystery that surrounded the column and Cordelia—and reporters wouldn't have been working overtime to get to Cordelia.

Clearly, Jack had no one to blame but himself. So how come she didn't feel like celebrating? How come she felt like a cheat, a swindler, a con artist? She let out a sigh.

Self-righteous wasn't working because Jack wasn't the person at fault here. She was. She could complain all she wanted that he'd been putting one over on his readers for years. But the bottom line was, she had calculatingly gone into his life and deliberately lied about, well, pretty much everything. What had happened to her ethics?

She pulled out her phone and punched in her cousin Annie's number, hoping someone who'd known her all her life could help her find herself again.

"Liza!" Annie's voice bounced happily. "How's investigative reporting going?"

"Not so good. I think I'm lost."

"Where are you? In the middle of nowhere?"

A chortle bubbled up from Liza's belly. She pulled it back. "I think you just nailed it." She clenched her teeth to hold back the pressure building inside, the laughter squeezing her lungs. The corners of her mouth whipped into a manic smile and a laugh screeched out of her. Another burbled out after that one, and then another, until tears were spilling over her cheeks.

"Liza?" Annie asked.

She gasped for breath and forced herself to calm, only to be overcome again. As the hilarity spewed from her mouth and the tears rolled from her eyes, she gave up trying for self-control.

That's when she realized she was no longer laughing, but crying.

"Liza? You okay?"

She sucked in a breath and wiped her eyes roughly with her hands, saw the mascara on her fingertips and didn't even care that she probably seemed insane to the other travelers waiting at the gate. "I'm fine. God, I'm sorry," she murmured.

"Oh, Liza...did he end it—or did you?"

"It's not that—I mean, we weren't really even dating—not really. I don't actually know what we were doing." She let out a sigh. "He ended it."

"What happened? Are you sure it's really over?"

Liza considered what she had done to Jack. She didn't expect to be hearing from him unless it was to bring a lawsuit against her for breach of trust or implied contract or some such lawyerly thing. "I'm sure. It's over. Done. Finished. Complete. I did a pretty serious thing."

"Whatever it was, I know you. It couldn't have been that bad."

"Trust me, it was." She let out a sigh. "Annie, I don't who I am anymore. "

"Whatever it was...if you could change it, would you?"

Liza rested her head against the seat and contemplated the question. Would she give up the certain promotion into her dream job in exchange for the uncertain possibility of having Jack Graham in her life?

Certainty versus uncertainty. A bird in the hand versus two in the bush, and all that stuff. "I don't know," she finally said. "I don't know that I ever meant anything to him anyway."

A long silence settled between them. She closed her eyes.

"Have you thought about apologizing?" Annie asked.

Eyes still shut, Liza shook her head. "I don't think *I'm sorry* will solve this one. It's too complicated. Besides—" Besides what? The truth was, for once in her life she wanted things on her own terms. She wanted to apologize and still file the story. She wanted Jack to love her even if she exposed his secrets.

Fat chance of that. Her actions had ensured she'd lost any chance of ever having a relationship with Jack.

A voice boomed out of the PA system, the announcement she'd been waiting for—that her flight to Chicago was beginning to board.

"Liza?" Annie asked.

"Yeah. I have to go. My plane is boarding."

"Okay, hey listen, it'll be all right. Don't forget what Grandpa used to say—"

"Right. *It's always darkest before the storm.* I feel a lot better knowing a storm's coming."

"*Dawn.* He meant *dawn.* Call me if you need me."

"Thanks, Annie." She shut off her phone and headed for the line forming at the gate.

It made no sense to keep dwelling on this. She'd taken this assignment knowing that if she got the information she needed, she would write the exposé. And even after Kristin warned her not to get personally involved, she'd convinced herself that everything she was doing with Jack was only to get a story. She'd known in her head that it was all about the job.

The problem was, her heart never got the message.

26

"What do you mean Liza went back to Chicago?" Diane's face was a perfect picture of shock. She cast a glance at Mary. "We thought she was going to be the caretaker."

Jack shook his head. "She left yesterday. Can I come in?"

Diane held up her index finger. "Just one minute—"

Mary nodded. "We just need to pick the place up a bit."

The door slammed before he could assure them he didn't care what the house looked like. "Okay, then. I'll just wait out here," he said to the lion's head door knocker. Bored, he crossed the porch and looked down the street at the old Victorian homes lining both sides. He felt surprisingly calm considering that Liza Dunnigan's exposé would soon explode his well-ordered life.

He heard the door open behind him and turned to find both women in the doorway, winded.

"Okay!" Diane said on a gasp. "Everything is just—"

"Spiffy," Mary said. "Tip-top. Neat as a pin."

Diane nodded. "Shipshape."

Jack looked from one to the other. Guilty. They were guilty of something. Concealing a lascivious hobby they'd taken up? Hiding men? He thought of Ernie and wasn't sure he wanted to know. Who cared what they were up to? He had enough problems of his own.

He hunched his shoulders against the cold. "Great. Can I come in?"

"Yes, indeed." Diane stepped back to let him pass and stumbled into Mary.

"We were just having coffee—would you like a cup, Jack? It's fresh." Mary didn't wait for an answer before disappearing through the swinging door into the kitchen.

"Okay," he said. He sat on the brocade sofa while Diane perched on a chair flanking the hearth. She sneezed and blew her nose. Her eyes watered and she patted at them with a tissue.

"You should see a doctor. Maybe you have a sinus infection," he said.

She waved a hand dismissively. "I'll be fine soon. These things never last long."

Mary returned with a steaming mug of coffee for Jack, then settled into the chair on the other side of the hearth. Both women sipped their coffee and looked at him impassively. They looked like folk art bookends, somehow up to no good.

"Now, what happened with Liza? Will she be coming back?" Mary asked.

"No. I don't expect we'll ever see Liza Dunnigan again. Except on the evening news."

Diane let out a gasp. "What did she do?"

"Is she in jail?"

No, but it might be a good place for her. He shook his head. "Nothing like that. She ..." How did he tell them?

Even *they* didn't know he was Cordelia. "Turns out she wasn't actually moving here to take a new job."

"She wasn't?" they asked in unison.

"Actually, she wasn't moving here at all. It was a front. She was working on a news story for the *Chicago Sentinel*. Created a whole cover story about moving here so she had a reason to get close to me."

The women tittered. "That seems to be a common problem for you, doesn't it?" Diane asked. "Women doing silly things to get your attention."

He rolled his eyes. "She wasn't here because she wanted a relationship with me. What she wanted was information ... was trying to uncover a secret I've kept for a long time. And she succeeded. That's why I'm here right now. To let you know that, within the next couple of days, a big story will probably break about me ... and Dear Cordelia."

Diane blinked at Mary and Mary blinked at Diane, then both looked at him.

"You mean that you're Cordelia?" Diane finally asked.

"You know?"

The two women nodded like bobbleheads.

"For how long?"

Mary shrugged. "Gosh, almost ten years now."

"Ten years?" The words burst out of Jack. "Since the beginning?"

"Just about." Mary took a swallow of coffee.

"My grandmother told you?"

Diane smiled. "Not exactly. Do you remember when you used to call home looking for help answering questions? Sometimes your grandmother would ask our advice because she didn't know how to answer either."

"It didn't take long for us to put two and two together," Mary said leaning forward. "Once we saw some of our advice show up in Cordelia's column, we came right out and asked your grandmother."

"She swore us to secrecy."

"You two were Dear Cordelia, too?" Jack rubbed the back of his neck and shook his head. He'd been giving romantic advice to America based on the input of three old women in Coldwater, Maine. "You've known all these years and never said a word."

Mary nodded. "We figured at some point, when you were ready, you'd tell us. We also figured at some point you'd take your own advice and settle down."

"Find yourself someone to love and who loved you—"

"And start a family and tie the knot—not in that order, of course. Figured, with all those girls in Chicago, surely one would be the right one." Mary shook her head. "They were all so ... pretty and fashionable and—"

"Young—"

"Yes, but lovely—"

"And flighty." Diane frowned and shook her head in disapproval.

"And sophisticated and worldly." Mary frowned back at Diane.

"And young and gold-diggerish. Admit it."

Mary sighed. "Yes, I suppose so."

"Suppose so? We've had this discussion a million times." Diane clucked her tongue. "Looks aren't everything and Jack knows it. Why do you suppose he never married any of them? Right, Jack?"

He held both hands up in surrender. "Why I'm not married isn't going to be our discussion today."

Diane ignored him. "When Liza came into the picture, she just seemed like, well, no need to mince words—perfect for you."

Her words lay bare the wound in Jack's heart. Liza *had* been different from any woman he'd ever met. Or so he'd thought. Why the hell did she have to turn out the same as the rest after all?

"Who cares if she found out you're Cordelia?" Diane said. "You couldn't keep it a secret forever. It had to come out sometime."

"She lied about everything."

Diane flipped one hand up as though to say *so what?*

"I can't believe you're so forgiving," he said. "What would you say if I told you I think she had something to do with CJ's disappearance?"

"Liza?" Mary's eyes grew wide.

"Ashley actually thought of it. At first I thought she was crazy—"

"Jealous, more like it," Diane muttered.

"But considering everything else Liza did to get Cordelia's story, I'm beginning to think she may be right."

"Did you ask Liza?" Mary squeaked out.

Jack nodded. "She denied it—had the audacity to act hurt. I guess I'll have to let the police know."

"I wouldn't." Diane blew her nose. "You see, I don't have a cold. I have allergies."

"The cops won't care about that," he said. Her words worked their way into his mind, turned over and over onto themselves until suddenly he realized what she was saying.

"Allergies," he said, standing.

She nodded.

How the hell could he be so blind? Or stupid? *Or maybe just falling in love.* "Allergies. Of course. You're allergic to dogs, Diane," he said as he crossed the room, then turned back. "I've known about your allergies forever. You two dognapped CJ."

Diane leapt to her feet. "Don't be upset. Jack. We didn't mean to cause any harm."

"Dognapped sounds so harsh," Mary said in a soothing voice. "We just gave her a little vacation ..."

"I can't believe—"

"We only did it to help you," Mary said.

"Help me? Help me what? Lose my mind?"

Diane bent to straighten the magazines on the coffee table. "We were giving you and Liza the time ... to get to know one another."

Mary nodded. "You said you were going back to Chicago. We had to do something to make you stay—"

"She seemed like such a nice girl." Diane said. "And pretty, too. Maybe not as quite as sophisticated—"

"But certainly not a bit flighty—"

"And not too young either," Diane added.

Jack closed his eyes. Liza may be pretty and not flighty and not too young and fun to be with and approachable and incredibly appealing and— "Ladies, I think you've forgotten something. She's a fake and a liar and about to expose me to the world. *Against my wishes.* That makes her a jerk."

Diane sniffed. "Well, we didn't know all that then."

"I still think she's perfect for you," Mary said. "People do things for their jobs. Look at you, Jack. You pretend to be an old woman."

"I don't pretend to be her, I just use her name."

"That's pretending," Mary said.

"Some might call it lying," Diane added.

"Why is it I suddenly feel like the bad guy?" Jack frowned. "You're supposed to be on my side."

"We are. But Jack, maybe if you'd have put forth some effort, you know, romanced her a little, she would have stayed."

"And you two could have gotten married—"

Married? "Time out, ladies. Reality check. If Liza had agreed to stay, I would already be back in Chicago. And she would be in Coldwater. No romance, no love, no marriage."

"Not with CJ missing." Mary gave him a smug smile.

Jack snorted. "The ransom note was a nice touch."

"Mary remembered it from an old movie," Diane said. "Seemed like the perfect solution."

"Oh yeah, it was perfect."

"Who would have guessed Liza was a reporter?" Mary wrapped both hands around her coffee mug. "She did seem so right for you."

The ache Jack had buried resurfaced for a moment. There were millions of women in the world, millions of women who could replace Liza Dunnigan—if he felt like looking. He just didn't think he'd feel like looking for a long time.

"So where's CJ? I'll take her home. Give Diane's allergies a rest."

Mary pointed at the ceiling. "We carried her upstairs when you came to the door."

"She's so fat and her legs are so short, she can't do the stairs very well," Diane said with a frown.

Jack trudged up the stairs. He'd found the dog, Liza was an undercover reporter, he didn't have a caretaker, Dear Cordelia was about to be exposed, he'd probably lose his chance to succeed as a sports agent, and there was a gaping hole in his chest where his heart once was.

Things were looking up.

27

Two days after leaving Coldwater, Liza sat at her kitchen table, reading the food section of the *Chicago Sentinel* as she had every Sunday for the past seven years. Since she'd been gone two weeks, it was really fun to read the section when she hadn't played a part in putting it together.

Mmm, one of the features was beurre blanc, a wine sauce with shallots, bound with butter and served over black sea bass. Her mouth watered. It sounded like something romantic she could make for Jack.

Except she'd never be making dinner for Jack again. The thought hit like stab, and she pressed her lips together against the pain.

She flipped the page and spotted a story about football menus *guaranteed to score big*. That was supposed to have been her story—someone else had obviously written it while Liza had been gone.

Her shoulders drooped. Of course someone else had written it; with so many reporters looking for work these days, they would easily be able to replace her.

Who cared anyway? She was on the verge of filing a story exposing Dear Cordelia's identity. She should be overjoyed; she would never have to work in the food section again.

This was her new life. She was the new Liza. She'd succeeded. She'd changed herself into someone exciting and mysterious and different.

She just wasn't sure she liked herself anymore.

She went over to her desk and picked up the neatly printed pages from the printer tray. Plopping sideways into a chair, she reread the first draft of her article, hand editing with a red pen in the margins as she went along.

When she finished, she held the sheets in her flat hand as if weighing them on a scale. These pages were like gold to her—they were integral to her future as an investigative reporter.

The fact that she'd discovered what so many others had failed to learn would probably do wonders for her career. Respect like she'd never seen before would likely come her way from people in all walks of the industry. Who knew what lay ahead for her? Maybe job offers. Maybe *The New York Times*. Maybe network news. Well, maybe not that. Regardless, she was about to get a chance at the future she'd always dreamed of.

At Jack Graham's expense.

She stared at the pages and relived what it had been like to kiss him, to hold his hand, to talk with him and laugh. She remembered his smile, the one that made her feel as if she was the most important person in the world, the smile that she'd first seen when he opened the front door the day she arrived at his house with a cockamamie scheme that had actually worked. The smile she'd fallen in love with.

In love with. It was about time she admitted it to herself.

She'd fallen in love with Jack Graham that day. He'd opened the front door and smiled at her and everything had changed—including her. As much as she'd tried to deny it to herself these past few days, as much as she tried to bury it beneath rational thoughts and logical evaluations of what she had done, she knew it was true. She loved Jack Graham. She would probably love him forever.

And he hated her. With good reason. Tears bit at the back of her eyes. She'd destroyed her chance with him.

Not that a guy like him ever really picked someone like her anyway. She was always the girl who did the homecoming decorations—not one of the chosen few on the Court.

She set the sheets on the coffee table and reached for her phone. Kristin answered after a few rings. "Omigod, what happened to you?" she asked. "Why aren't you answering my texts?"

Liza smiled just hearing her friend's voice. No matter what happened, Kristin would always be there for her. "So much has happened—"

"Just tell me—is he or isn't he?"

Liza squeezed her eyes shut to force away the tears. She looked at the story, neatly printed on clean, white sheets of twenty-pound paper. Boring white paper. Very practical. But the paper was only the backdrop. The words were what mattered. And what a set of words this was. All she had to do was turn this story in, and she would never be called *boring* again.

"Or *practical*." She didn't realize at first that she'd said the words aloud.

"Practical? What does that have to do with Cordelia?"

"Nothing." She picked up the top sheet of her article and examined it. "Kristin, isn't it amazing how plain white paper can become something valuable just because of what's on it?"

"Yeaahh."

"Kind of like life, don't you think? We all start out as blank sheets of paper. But what makes us valuable is what gets written on our souls and in our conscience." A chill rippled through her. The words on the pages of her life didn't always have to be predictable. But they had to be true to who she was.

"Liza? Girl?" Kristin said. "What are you talking about? You're scaring me a little."

Liza set the page back on the pile. From one perspective, turning in the story was the right thing to do. The smart thing to do. After all the work she'd done, after all the lies she'd told, after falling in love with a guy she could never have, it was only logical that she turn the story in and grab the brass ring with both hands.

Yep.

But then, this wasn't just Cordelia's or Jack's story—it was her story, too. She could write whatever she wanted on the blank pages of her life. She'd already decided to change her life; just because people expected certain behavior from her didn't mean she had to oblige them.

"Hellooo? Liza, are you there?" Kristin sounded frantic. "Damn, did this call drop?"

"I'm here, I'm here."

"What's going on? He's Cordelia, isn't he?"

Liza picked up the pages and went into the kitchen. When Jack confronted her, he'd asked, *Who are you?* At the time, she hadn't known how to answer. Now she knew.

She was the woman who would never betray him.

"Jack Graham? No. I was wrong. He's not Cordelia."

"What?" Kristin was incredulous. "You seemed all but certain two days ago. What happened?"

"That's why I didn't answer your texts. It took me that long to dig out the information. He works so closely with Cordelia ... and I was rushing as I looked at his files that first day. I was in such a hurry and so determined to be right that I jumped to the wrong conclusion. Big time."

Kristin let out a protracted groan. "I can't believe this. Did you at least find out where she is so you can get an interview?"

Liza opened a cupboard drawer and pulled out a book of matches. "Nope. After all that time in Coldwater, I didn't actually find out anything. It was a big bust." She lightly crumpled the pages, put them in the sink, then lit a match and touched it to the paper.

"Liza, I'm devastated. I had headlines all written—*First Lady of the Lovelorn is Actually a Man.* Or *Dear Cordelia Is Actually Dear Cornelius.* And my favorite: *Love Is a MANy Splendored Thing.*"

Liza snorted out a laugh. "Based on those, it's probably good I didn't get the story. You'd better stick to writing about cooking."

"That's it then? You're done?"

Liza watched the paper curl and burst into flame, the typewritten words dissolving as the paper changed from white to black and then into ash. "Yeah. I think my dreams just went up in smoke," she said, mildly amused that she could joke about it.

"You're sounding way too cavalier. What the hell happened?" Kristin asked, bewildered. "You wanted out. You wanted to change your life. You were on the verge of succeeding. Something's out of whack here. What happened?"

"I like the food section."

"You hate the food section."

"Correction. I used to hate the food section. Now I look forward to working there with my friends." Liza smiled.

"You fell in love."

She hesitated. "No, I didn't."

"Oh God, I've got this. Totally. You can't tell me the truth about Cordelia because you fell in love with the guy. Are you two getting married? Lalalalalala! Oh I can't believe this, *you fell in love with Jack Graham, the player!*" She chortled gleefully.

Liza laughed despite the pain she felt at the truth in Kristin's words. "Absolutely not. There's no love going on here. In fact, I doubt if Jack Graham and I will ever speak again."

"Lovers' spat?"

"No. He has his life, I have mine. Maybe you haven't noticed, but Jack Graham and I don't move in the same social circles in Chicago."

"You're kidding. Why, this is absolutely the first I've heard of that." Kristin laughed again.

"Haha."

"So tell it to me straight. I want you to say the words— I'm not in love with him."

Liza pressed her fingers to the bridge of her nose to keep the tears burning in her eyes from spilling onto her cheeks. "I'm definitely not in love with him."

"And you didn't get the story."

"No. I didn't get the story."

Kristin heaved a long-suffering sigh. "Okay, whatever you say. I'm sure the boss will be happy to hear you're sticking around."

"Feel free to let him know. I've got to give Mr. Klein a

call and tell him I failed—just like everyone else. He can reassign the story back to that guy who was on it before."

She hung up the phone and rinsed the small pile of black ash down the drain. A scrap of charred paper remained, and she picked it up and read the only words still legible through the gray: *of integrity*. In the article, she'd written that Jack Graham was an honorable man.

She wondered whether he would he say the same about her. Instantly, she knew the answer was no.

Determined to remove all vestiges of the assignment from her life, she deleted the Cordelia file from her computer and emptied the computer's garbage can so no one short of a computer expert would ever be able to retrieve the exposé she'd written. A weight lifted off her. Even though it was Sunday, she called Mr. Klein's office number and left a voicemail saying she had failed to get anywhere on the Dear Cordelia story and thanking him for giving her the opportunity to try.

Then she rested her elbows on her desk, dropped her head into her hands and thought about Jack. A lump lodged in her throat. She'd found her bachelor next door—and she'd lost him.

How had it come to be that, of all the dreams she'd ever had, a life with Jack was what she wanted most of all. And it was the one dream she knew would never come true.

28

"JACK, IT'S GOOD TO HAVE YOU BACK."

He looked up from his computer and smiled at the young woman who had stepped into his office to set the mail and morning newspaper on his desk.

"It's too lonely around here when you're gone," she said.

"Things got a little more complicated in Coldwater than I expected." As he picked up the newspaper, a knot formed in his gut. It had been over a week since Liza left Coldwater. Every day since then he'd expected her Dear Cordelia exposé to appear in the paper. It bothered him that the paper hadn't contacted him for a comment, hadn't called to verify that Liza's story was true, but if they were going to do a half-assed job of reporting, there was nothing he could do about it.

"But it's all fixed now?"

Everything but his heart. "Yeah. Got a caretaker all settled in. Turns out the ladies next door knew someone from their church, and it all fell into place." After they'd been caught dognapping in order to do matchmaking, those sweet ladies couldn't do enough to help him find someone to take the job.

His assistant smiled and made eye contact with him. "Well ... if you need me, I'll be at my desk." She waited another beat before stepping out of the room, long honey-blond hair swinging across the back of her tight sweater that was tucked into her equally tight pencil skirt. Nice to look at. But young. Way too young.

Diane and Mary were right. He needed someone like Liza. Hell, turned out the joke was on him. Once he realized he no longer wanted a rotating door of beauties coming and going, once he realized he just wanted one woman, that's when he discovered the woman he wanted didn't actually want him.

He used to believe true love didn't exist. Now he just believed it didn't exist for him.

He shoved the mail to the side and opened the main section of the newspaper, scanning the pages for a story about Dear Cordelia. When he reached the editorial section at the end, he sat back in his chair. Huh. He would have thought he warranted Section A at least. A quick check of the rest of the paper didn't turn up a story either.

What the hell? When was this story going to break? He was beginning to think that waiting and nervous anticipation were worse than the actual disclosure would be.

The intercom beeped on his desk phone. "Jack, there's a guy on the phone from the *Chicago Sentinel*," his assistant said. "Same guy who was calling about Cordelia before you went to Coldwater. You want to talk to him?"

Finally they were calling for his comments. Why it took so long for them to get to this point was anybody's guess. Who cared? The fact was, they were on the phone now.

Maybe they'd gathered all sorts of other information about his past, what he'd been doing in the years before he started the column, and had lots of shit to ask about.

"Yeah, I'll talk to him." For a couple of seconds he considered telling the guy that Liza had made up the story to make a name for herself, that none of it was true. But he couldn't do it. The time had come for the truth—no more running away from Cordelia.

Muscles tense, he picked up the phone. "Jack Graham."

"Mr. Graham, this is Tom Calloway from the *Chicago Sentinel*. Thanks for taking my call. I'm calling—"

"I know why you're calling."

"Right. I guess you would know by now. It's about Cordelia."

Jack felt a stab of irritation. So Liza got the story, and now she was too afraid to face him to get his comments? Bullshit. She had no qualms sleeping with him as a means of getting at the information she needed, but she sent in some other guy for the kill? No way. Let her finish the story. If they wanted his comments about Dear Cordelia, Liza would have to call him.

"Why isn't Liza Dunnigan calling on this story?" he asked abruptly.

"Oh." The reporter sounded taken aback. "Well, it was originally assigned to me. She just took it over for a couple of weeks while I was on vacation."

Jack frowned. "You mean they took her off the story once you were back?"

"Yeah. It was my assignment."

"So she isn't even getting credit for it?" Jack couldn't keep the surprise out of his voice. Liza did all the work and this guy was going to get the accolades? What kind of newspaper was this?

"She did what she could while I was gone, but it's always been my story—"

"Will her name even be on the byline as a contributor?"

Several seconds of silence greeted him. "Uh, would you like her name on the byline?" the reporter asked slowly.

"I think she deserves it," Jack said.

"Okay. Sure. I can talk to my editor. I'm sure he'll agree that if you grant us an interview with Cordelia, we can put Ms. Dunnigan's name on the byline with mine."

"You want an interview?"

"R-right. That's what I've been calling for all along." He sounded confused.

Jack sat back in his chair, stunned into silence.

"Mr. Graham?" Calloway said. "If you like, Ms. Dunnigan can accompany me on the interview."

"With Cordelia?" he managed to choke out. "The columnist Cordelia?" He knew he sounded really stupid, but he had to buy some time to figure this out.

"Right. I'm sorry, I didn't realize you and Ms. Dunnigan had connected on this story. I thought she had no luck at all reaching you." The reporter's words started coming faster. "Like I said, I'm sure my editor would bring her right back on for the interview. We'd love to have it in time for Valentine's Day. How does this Thursday sound?"

Liza didn't turn him in. *She didn't tell the newspaper. She didn't file a story.*

Calm slid over him followed by regret so deep it hurt.

"Mr. Graham, are you there? Would you like Ms. Dunnigan to be present at the interview?"

Jack snapped back to attention. "Cordelia doesn't do interviews."

"But I thought—"

"No interviews—"

"But Ms. Dunnigan can be there, I guarantee it," he said almost desperately

"I'm sorry, Mr. Calloway, Cordelia doesn't do interviews. She likes her privacy. Have a nice day." Jack set the phone back in its cradle and didn't move for a long moment.

Liza hadn't done it.

He spun his chair so he could look out the window. Though the weather was as gray and blustery as the day he'd gotten the call that the caretaker had died, suddenly it felt as if the sun was shining.

Liza had succeeded in digging up the information that every media outlet in America had been trying to get for years. And she hadn't used it. She'd earned herself a promotion—and she'd given it up.

He wanted to call her. To ask why. To thank her. To look at her face again, to touch her hair, to kiss her ... to love her.

Oh, God, did he love her.

He almost felt giddy. Almost. What an idiot he'd been, always insisting there was no such thing as true love. Since when was he an expert anyway? Suddenly it felt great to be so wrong.

Diane was probably right—who cared if the world knew Cordelia was a man? If he lost out on the opportunity to represent certain overly macho sports figures because of it, well, their loss. With the right PR, he could probably turn this to his advantage. He'd have to think it through, but there were probably benefits to having a sports agent who had a good understanding of the human psyche.

He steepled his fingers and tapped them against his lower lip. Liza's had needed an interview with Cordelia to get a promotion.

No problem. It just so happened he had an *in* with Cordelia.

Five minutes later he was on the phone with the Sentinel's editor, Bill Klein. "*The* Dear Cordelia? The advice columnist *Cordelia* wants to give an interview to the *Sentinel?*" Klein sounded stunned.

"Yes, but there are some stipulations."

"Absolutely. Whatever she wants."

"The interview will be with Liza Dunnigan."

"Liza?" Klein asked.

"Don't you know who she is?"

"Oh sure, yeah, I know. It's just she's in the—"

"Food section. I know. Nevertheless, that's who Cordelia wants to meet with." Jack kicked back in his chair, enjoying this immensely.

"Works for us. Is there any chance Cordelia would be open to doing this before Valentine's Day?"

"That's her goal."

Klein audibly exhaled. Jack smiled; it felt kind of good to make this guy's day.

"Great. Is there a specific location where she'd like the interview to take place?" Klein asked. "Here in the office? A restaurant?"

"As you know, Cordelia's very private. She asked that the interview take place in my apartment, so she knows her privacy is guaranteed. I hope that's all right."

"Fine. Absolutely fine. Can I send a photographer?"

Jack smiled. "She's agreed to the interview only. But no pictures."

"No problem. Just had to ask. How about questions—is anything off limits? Can Ms. Dunnigan ask about her childhood, education, family ...?"

"She can ask. I'll leave it up to Cordelia whether she'll answer." Jack looked at the calendar on his desk.

"Great. And a date. Does she have a date in mind?"

"How about Friday night, seven-thirty." He gave the man his address. "Cordelia requested a dinner interview. She finds meetings less stressful with strangers when there's something to do. Oh, and tell Ms. Dunnigan there's no need to dress up—casual, jeans would be fine." *Leopard underwear would be a nice touch.*

"Fantastic. I'll set it up. Mr. Graham, thank you. Tell Cordelia we'll do a great job. We'll do a story that makes her proud." He sounded like a man who'd just won the lottery.

"Oh, there's just one more thing. Would you tell Ms. Dunnigan that Cordelia asked her to bring along an Ace bandage?" He grinned at the silence that followed.

"An Ace bandage?"

"Right. You know, those brown elastic bandages you wrap around injured knees and twisted ankles?"

"Yeah, I know what they are. Just curious ... what does she want it for?"

Jack held back a laugh. "Who knows? She's got quite an eccentric streak. I've learned it's always good to humor her, though. Especially since she's granting this interview."

"Absolutely. Absolutely. Ms. Dunnigan will be there Friday night at seven-thirty—Ace bandage in hand."

29

LIZA TOOK OFF HER GLOVES AND STEPPED TO THE FRONT desk in the lobby of Jack's posh apartment building. She smiled at the stone-faced uniformed man sitting at the counter, and swallowed down her fear. "I'm here to see Jack Graham," she said with as much confidence as she could muster.

"Ms. Dunnigan." A smile softened his features. "He's expecting you—twenty-second floor, number 2226, go on up." He gestured toward the elevators.

She pressed the button and looked at the dial above the door. Both elevators were up around the twentieth floor. She closed her eyes and tried to calm her pounding heart.

By now Jack had to know she hadn't filed the story she'd uncovered. So what did he want with her? Was he really going to give her an interview? Was he still angry about her deception? She would give anything to go back and make different decisions, but life seldom gave you those kinds of second chances. The woman on the plane had asked, *if she could change what she'd done, would she?* At the time, she hadn't known how to answer. Now she knew.

She touched the Ace bandage in her purse; her cheeks heated at the memory of the night she'd first brought it up. Maybe Jack had asked her to bring it along as a way of telling her she was forgiven, that they could be friends. It was almost too much to hope for. She mentally rehearsed what she wanted to say to him—how sorry she was for what she'd done, how much she appreciated him giving her this opportunity, how hopeful she was that they could put the past behind them.

The elevator doors opened with a *ding*, and she stepped inside, reaching the twenty-second floor faster than she expected. Leave it to Jack to live in a place with warp speed elevators. She stopped in front of his door and wiped her damp palms on her wool jacket. Her knees felt like pipe cleaners ready to collapse at the slightest pressure, and she considered making a run back to the elevators.

Instead, she lifted her hand and knocked.

And then the door swung open and Jack was before her, smiling one of those smiles that stole all coherent thought from her brain. For a moment she was transported back to the day she'd arrived on his grandmother's front porch.

He was wearing jeans again, and a crewneck sweater over a T-shirt. But he wasn't wearing rag wool socks this time. Nope, it wasn't the same. This time he was barefoot. She remembered her feet tangling with his that night—

She looked into his face. "Hi."

"Come on in. I'm glad you could come." He stood back to let her pass.

"Me too," she squeaked out, forgetting every other thing she'd planned to say. Well, no one would ever call her too sophisticated, that was for sure. Thank God *she* wasn't giving advice to the lovelorn—no one's relationships would ever last.

Jack hung her coat in the front closet and led the way to the kitchen. "I just opened a bottle of cabernet—you want a glass?"

"Sure." The nearness of him almost made her shiver, and she stepped into the living room to put some distance between them. Her gaze roamed across the room, taking in the rich tan leather sofa, the beautiful rug and hardwood floor, a gas fire burning in the hearth. Beautiful and comfortable—like she had felt when she was with him.

At some point, soon, she had to apologize. She wasn't so afraid to do that; it was the conversation afterward that she dreaded.

"This place is gorgeous." She went to the windows facing east, overlooking Lake Michigan. "The view during the day must be amazing."

"Yeah. One of the benefits of success." He handed her a glass of wine. "I ordered Chinese. You want to get started on the interview while we wait? I've got some plans for later."

Liza's heart wrenched. He had later plans? So, despite wine and dinner, this was all business for him.

He gestured toward the sofa and they each took a seat—at opposite ends.

She looked at him. "So why me, Jack? After everything I did to you, why would you give this interview to me?"

He didn't answer for a moment, as if considering her question. "I'm going to hold off answering that for a bit."

She pulled small digital recorder from her bag, along with a pencil, pad of paper, and the list of questions she and the editor had worked up. Her fingertips touched the Ace bandage, and she felt her color rise. If he'd asked her to bring that thing to torture her, he was succeeding wildly.

"Do you mind if I record the interview?" she asked. "I'll

also take some notes, just in case any of the recording ends up unintelligible."

"No problem."

"I've got a list of questions, but we don't have to follow them if you want to go in a different direction. It's mostly just to get us started, or help out if the conversation stalls." Though her stomach was churning, she gave him a confident smile. No way was she going to let him know the effect he had on her.

He smiled, his blue eyes crinkling in the corners, those amazing blue eyes that made her feel like anything was possible, including love with a man like Jack Graham. God, she was stupid.

"Questions seem like the best way to go for me." He took a sip of wine

She nodded and looked down at the page; the questions blurred in front her eyes. Maybe she should apologize first, get that out of the way so she could relax. Her heartrate went into triple time and she chickened out. She'd work the apology in later.

"I guess the best place to start is at the beginning," she said. "What made you start writing Dear Cordelia?"

"I was in college and broke. Got a job writing classified ads at a local shopper paper to make a little extra money." He gave a self-deprecating laugh. "*Little* is the definitive word. Anyway, their local advice columnist had retired, and I saw opportunity. A chance to make a few more bucks. But I was smart enough to know they'd never hire a college guy to write an advice column."

He paused to sip his wine, and she quickly finished taking down his words.

Jack shifted to face her more directly. "The paper was

struggling financially, as all papers are these days, and they hadn't picked up another advice column. So I mentioned this woman I knew, Cordelia, who was brilliant at relationship advice, and her price was a fraction of what they'd been paying for the other woman. Suggested she might be good at doing a column and she'd even offered to do it free for a while, as a test. If they didn't like the columns she submitted, they didn't have to run them." He shook his head. "I made an audacious move and was lucky as hell. Dear Cordelia got popular fast and started getting picked up by other papers."

Liza looked up from her note taking. "So, did you tell the newspaper that you're Cordelia?"

"Nope. Cordelia, has never been an employee of the paper. I was her agent, so all checks came to me from them and every other newspaper that picked up the column—and I paid Cordelia."

Liza nodded. "How old were you? Twenty? How could a young man with virtually no life experience answer all the questions people have about love and relationships?"

He laughed. "It wasn't easy. I based a lot on what I saw around me, families I knew. I'm a good observer—got to see a lot of different types of interactions every time I changed foster homes. When I got stumped, I turned to my grandmother. She was an incredible help. And I just learned last week that the ladies next door were helping her when she couldn't come up with an answer." He dropped his head back against the couch and looked up at the ceiling. "Turns out America's been relying on romantic advice from three old women in Maine and a twenty-something guy who started the whole thing to make some money. How's that for an angle?"

"That's an angle all right." An angle that would pretty much destroy the column if it ever got out. Despite the fact that Jack was telling the truth, that he was handing her a breakout story, Liza wanted no part of it. She looked at him and knew she couldn't do it. "I just don't know. It's a great story about you, Jack Graham. But about Cordelia? She sounds shallow and unromantic." Liza frowned. "Really, Jack. Cordelia has to say something else. Something more like: *My late husband, Edward, and I had a wonderful marriage, and I wanted to help others find the kind of lasting love we had.*"

"Her late husband, Edward?"

"Well, no one knows anything about Cordelia, so she might as well have a late husband. Makes her more real, more relatable as the purveyor of advice for the lovelorn."

Jack frowned. "What are you doing? I'm telling the world that I'm Cordelia."

"And I'm telling you not to. This is your livelihood, Jack."

"Yes. And this is my decision, too," he said, annoyance in his voice. "I've thought this through, Liza. I'm prepared to give a tell-all interview."

"So give one. I'm here to interview Cordelia—not Jack Graham. This interview should be about who Cordelia is and what she stands for—not how Jack Graham pulled the wool over everyone's eyes."

"Liza—"

"Find someone else to tell your story to then. I won't do it." She set her jaw.

He just looked at her. "You'll be an accomplice."

"I've called myself worse," she said softly. She turned away and began to speak again. "*We were never blessed with children, and after Edward died, I found myself alone, remembering the love we'd shared. So, I contacted a local newspaper and offered to provide advice to couples searching for romance in their lives. It has been such a rewarding experience knowing that I can bring people together this way, help them find their soulmates."*

Jack shook his head. "Kind of fluffy, isn't it?"

"When it comes to romance, people love fluffy," Liza said. "They want to know Cordelia is drawing on personal experience to help them solve their relationship troubles."

"They do?"

"Imagine what they would think if they found out Cordelia is a single guy who started doing this for the *cash,* who kept doing it to make more cash, and has never been in love in his life."

"What makes you think he's never been in love?"

Liza rolled her eyes. "You, Jack. You're a player."

"Point taken. Is there a problem with that?"

She died inside a little. Well, it wasn't as if she didn't deserve it. "No. But Cordelia can't be a single guy who's known for great success with the ladies."

"Sounds bad, huh?"

"Beyond bad."

"You're sure about this—me not telling them I'm Cordelia?"

"More sure than I've been about anything in a long time."

He gave her a slight nod. "Okay. What's the next question?"

Liza read off the sheet: "Do people ever write back and tell you how your advice has helped them?"

"Sometimes. But you know, it's the same as anything else—you usually hear from the complainers not the satisfied customers."

He wasn't getting it yet. "Wrong answer," she said with a sigh.

"It's the truth."

"Not for Cordelia. She would say something like this ..." Liza straightened her shoulders, lifted her chin, and splayed one hand across her chest like a prim, older woman. "I *often hear from couples telling me how I have helped them improve their relationship, or find the love of their life. I live vicariously through each of those letters, reliving the love Edward and I shared.*"

She smiled. "What do you think?"

"It's too much. I don't think even Cordelia would be that mushy."

"Okay, then you fix it. And it better be something more romantic than you get emails from disappointed readers."

Jack blinked. "Fine. You win."

"It's not about winning. It's about making sure Cordelia lives up to her reputation. You've been helping people for ten years—don't pull the rug out from under them now. See what I'm saying?" She looked at the list of questions. "Okay, next. What's the most romantic love story you've had a hand in?"

"You'll have to refuse to accept it, you know."

She slanted a look at him sideways. "Accept what?"

"The award they'll want to give you for being the first reporter to bring in an interview with Dear Cordelia."

"What? Oh, you mean because the story's a bunch of lies?"

He nodded.

She grinned. "Okay, I'll turn it down. Now ... what's the most romantic love story you've had a hand in?" *Say that it's me,* her brain whispered, and she shoved the thought away.

Jack settled into the cushions, one arm resting across the

back of the couch. His eyes caught hers, and she wrenched her gaze away to protect her heart.

"Let me think on that one," Jack said. "I have a couple of questions I'd like to ask first."

Oh, here it came. The third degree about what she had pulled in Coldwater, questions about her character, her integrity, her deception.

But that was okay—it had to be okay. She could handle this. After all the lies she'd told, she owed him answers to whatever questions he had. Answers, and the apology she had yet to make.

She should have apologized right away like she'd planned. "Sure. It's your interview," she chirped too brightly.

"Two questions really," he said. "About Coldwater."

Her stomach tumbled.

"Why did you make love with me that night? And why didn't you file the story?"

Liza felt like throwing up. She'd expected Jack to ask about both things, but now that the moment of truth had arrived, she just wanted to run away. All her planned answers disappeared. Did she tell him how he made her feel? That she made love with him because she'd been falling in love with him? That she was probably already been in love with him when it happened, but had been too dumb to realize it at the time?

God, she sounded like a lovesick groupie. She couldn't say any of that; he probably heard it from other women all the time.

"Why did I make love with you?" she repeated weakly. "I was caught in your room, and didn't want you to know the real reason I was there. So at that moment it just seemed logical to say I was waiting for you."

He cocked his head, watching her intently.

She faltered under his gaze. "It's a reasonable reason."

"For a guy. But for you, Liza Dunnigan, an excuse about spraining your ankle and looking for an Ace bandage would have sufficed."

"I didn't think of that until—it was too late."

"So the only reason you made love with me was because you got caught in my room?" His eyes locked with hers.

"No ... yes! Isn't that a good enough reason?"

"Sure. Absolutely. And the news story about Cordelia? Why didn't you file the story that would have made your career and gotten you out of the food section?"

Liza quietly sighed. *Because I realized I love you. And even though I know I can never have you, I can't bear to hurt you.* "Oh. Well, I thought, actually I knew, I'd been totally unfair about it." Weakest answer on earth, but maybe he'd let it slide.

"Unfair? How so?"

Her cheeks heated. "You know, by sneaking into your bedroom and telling you I wanted you. I was using you to get the story I wanted—"

"You were using me?" Jack's voice, soft and low, sent tremors through her core. "Are you saying you really didn't *want* me?"

"Yes—I mean no—I mean—I don't know." She turned away, mortified. "Look. I'm really sorry. I came here intending to apologize the minute I arrived, and I wimped out. You have no idea how much I regret what I did to you— what I almost did to you. I'm sorry."

Jack's eyes narrowed, and he slid across the sofa until his thigh touched hers. "Let me make sure I have this right. You made love with me because you didn't want to get caught in my room. And you didn't file the story because you made love with me."

She turned toward him. It took everything she had not to lean into him and press her mouth to his. "Y-yes, that's right." His eyes bored into hers and defensiveness rose up inside her. "Surely there's not something wrong with that?"

"No. No. It's just I was hoping that ... maybe your reasons why you did the one or why you didn't do the other ... might have something to do with how you feel about ... me?"

Time seemed to stop. "What do you mean?" she asked cautiously.

He reached a finger up and began to play with the hair above her ear. She couldn't breathe.

"I made love with you that night, Liza, because I wanted to make love with you. And I was hoping ... you felt the same."

She looked at his mouth. *Don't kiss him,* her brain screamed. *Talk. Talk to him. Make sure you're not just hearing what you want to hear.*

"I did want you," she whispered.

"And the story? Why didn't you file the story?" His voice, still low and soft, had taken on a more insistent tone.

She shook her head.

"At the very least, you owe me the truth on this subject, Liza."

She met his gaze, looked him straight in the eye, and pushed practical, predictable Liza away for good. "Because I love you." Silence hung over them for what seemed like an entire lifetime.

And then his arm was around her shoulders and his mouth was on hers, kissing her gently, so gently that she couldn't stand it and had to grab the front of his shirt and pull him up against her hard. When they broke apart, Jack brought a hand up to caress her cheek.

"I have to tell you," he said. "I fell in love with you that first day, when you were sitting all alone at my grandmother's dining room table trying to find just the right way to sit."

Excuse me? "Could you repeat that, please?"

"What part?"

"The beginning."

"I fell in love with you—"

"You love me?"

He nodded.

"But I'm not beautiful. I'm not tall or fashionable, and I'm—" She couldn't bring herself to say *practical*. "Sensible. Or I used to be anyway."

"Shhh. You're so beautiful I dream of you at night. And you're fashionable in an honest, unpretentious way. And I like sensible—it beats flighty any day."

"But—"

"No more buts. And no more questions. I've made up my mind and nothing you say will change it."

He kissed her ear, her hair, her throat. Liza closed her eyes and let her head drop back against the sofa. "What did you want the Ace bandage for?" she asked.

"I don't know. I thought maybe you could show me what you had in mind the other night. I was intrigued."

"My ankle—it was for my ankle."

"Bondage?" he murmured against her lips.

She laughed. "Omigod, no. I twisted my ankle."

He kissed her again, hard, as if he couldn't get enough of her. When they came up for air, she pushed back far enough so she could see his face. "What about the rest of the interview?" she asked only because she thought she should and not because she really cared if she asked the guy another question about writing an advice column for the rest of her life.

"You'll get your story," he said, eyes dark and seductive. His hands slid under her sweater around her waist. "Cordelia loves to give interviews."

EPILOGUE

LIZA WALKED ACROSS THE HARDWOOD FLOOR, HER footsteps echoing in the empty room. She opened the sliding door, stepped out onto the patio twenty-two stories in the air and remembered her first time in this apartment—the night she'd come to interview Cordelia. The view of Lake Michigan was breathtaking today, sparkling blue beneath a flawless sky, the water dotted with sailboats. The heat of summer surrounded her, and a soft breeze touched her cheek and ruffled her hair.

Behind her she could hear Jack on the phone, his voice growing louder as he drew near. "I'm sorry, but she was very adamant about this." He stepped onto the patio and put his arm around Liza's shoulder as he spoke. "She's chosen to retire the same way she wrote the column—quietly and privately. No interviews. I'm sorry. Thanks for the call."

He shut off the phone and pressed a kiss to Liza's forehead. "Two weeks since Cordelia announced her retirement and the calls have dwindled to almost nothing. I feel like a free man. What are you doing out here?"

"Letting the baby enjoy the view one last time."

Jack laughed and set a hand on Liza's very rounded belly. She put her own hand on top of his and looked up into his eyes, this man she loved with all her heart, this man she had married two years ago.

"You still want to do this?" she asked.

"Have a baby?" he teased.

"No. Move to Coldwater."

He looked out over the lake. "Yeah, this is one hell of a lifestyle to give up, isn't it? Gorgeous views. High-class neighbors. Great restaurants. No lawn to mow, no snow to shovel, no gutters to clean out. Always something happening, never a dull moment." He glanced at her. "And, did I mention the gorgeous views?"

Liza nodded.

Jack stepped forward and rested his hands on the railing as he gazed outward. "Yep. No backyard for kids to play in, no driveway for basketball, no garage door to hit a tennis ball against. No front porch for us to sit on after dinner and watch dusk fall and the fireflies come out. No nosy neighbors to treat our kids like they're their own. No deserted roads to make romance on."

Liza caught her breath, remembering.

Jack turned. "Any second thoughts for you?"

She shook her head, her emotions welling up inside.

He took her hand and gave it a squeeze. "It's still unanimous. I've had enough of crowds and elevators and smog and rush, rush, rush. Come on." Still holding her hand, he led her through the empty apartment and into the hall. The door snapped shut behind them and he bent to brush her lips with his own. "Let's go home."

———

If you enjoyed this book ... I would be forever grateful if you would post a review on the sight where you bought it.

———

The fifth book in the *Bachelor Next Door* series, **KISSING ON THE CORNER**, is Annie's story. Please enjoy the following excerpt.

Excerpt from
KISSING ON THE CORNER
The Bachelor Next Door, book five

Chapter One

Nick hadn't seen Annie since the week after their wedding —six years ago last month.

She'd married him, just as they'd agreed. Had left him a week later, just as they'd agreed. And he'd filed for divorce, just as they'd agreed.

He cleared his throat and tapped his fingers on the steering wheel as he practiced aloud a new version of the speech he had been working on for days now. "Annie, our divorce was never finalized. I left the country and never followed up with the lawyer to make sure everything got done."

She was a practical sort, Annie was. She'd probably offer him a cold lemonade, and they'd have a laugh over how irresponsible he once had been. Then she'd sign the new set of papers he'd brought with him, and he'd kiss her on the cheek when he left. And they'd go back to life the way it had been for the past six years.

Unless, of course, she'd remarried.

He pulled his Range Rover to a stop in front of a big pale-yellow Victorian house, and lifted his sunglasses to squint at the sign in front.

Unless of course, he'd made her a bigamist.

Bailey House Bed & Breakfast. He drew a breath. This was the place, exactly where the old woman at the gas station on the edge of town said he would find it. Small-town Wisconsin at its finest.

He shoved open the car door and stepped out into the late afternoon summer sun. A crumbled fast-food bag and a toothbrush dropped out onto the pavement. He scooped them up and tossed them onto the passenger seat.

Why was he nervous? Annie would still be Annie. Whether she'd married or not, all she had to do was sign the papers and they'd slip back into their lives—no one the wiser. Well, no one but her *other* husband … and the judge who would have to remarry them … and a couple of witnesses—

He buried those thoughts and headed across the walk and up the stairs to the wide front porch, noting the paint just beginning to peel on the old wood. There were layers of old buildup underneath, layers that would make this place a nightmare to scrape and paint. Thank God he wasn't the owner.

He jabbed the doorbell and put a pleasant expression on his face. After a long minute without a response, he pushed the bell again. Maybe he should have called instead.

No, it was bad enough they were still married. It would have been far worse to tell her that over the phone.

Suddenly the door swung inward, and Annie stood before him in cutoffs and a T-shirt. Barefoot. Radiant. Deep blue eyes shining. Tawny blond hair pulled back into a ponytail, a grin on her face as though she were ready to take on the world.

Annie.

He couldn't remember the Annie he knew, the waitress in the all-night coffee shop, looking so gorgeous.

"Hey, Annie," he said.

Her eyes widened. Her grin disappeared.

An older woman's voice floated down the hallway from somewhere behind her. "Tell Vivian I'll be right out."

"Get out of here," Annie said in low voice. "Now."

What? He took a step toward her. "I know this is a surprise, but I need to talk to you."

The older woman spoke again, her voice closer, louder, with each word. "Annie, dear, I'll be back in time to help you flip the mattresses."

Panic stole over Annie's face—panic that was instantly replaced by an expression of fierce determination. In one nearly seamless movement, she launched herself out of the doorway and into his arms and began to kiss him like he was the long-lost love of her life.

She pressed herself against him as if willing him to put his arms around her, and for a brief stunned moment, he pulled her close and returned the kiss. Then his brain kicked into gear and he took her by the arms and pushed back a bit.

"What—" he choked out.

"Good heavens!" the older woman screeched as she came through the doorway and spotted Annie in his arms. "He's here!"

Behind her, a gold-and-black, watermelon-shaped mutt bounded out onto the porch and began to bounce around them, barking incessantly.

Nick tore his gaze from Annie and focused on the diminutive gray-haired old woman; every line in her soft face angled upward from her joyous smile. Almost dancing with excitement, she reached up to tug his head down and kiss his cheek.

And the dog just kept barking as if he'd spotted the bone of his dreams.

"Chester! Quiet! Chester!" Annie shouted.

"I'm Luella!" the old woman cried over the chaos.

"Be quiet!" Annie grabbed hold of the dog's collar and dragged him toward the door.

"So happy to finally meet you. You look just like your picture," Luella said in a voice still loud and high. "I've been the inn's housekeeper for twenty years. I keep your Annie from overworking herself, what with that little bun in the oven."

Bun? His heart seemed to slow. *Pregnant? Husband?*

He shifted his gaze to Annie just as she snatched up the squirming dog and spun around, the desperate expression on her face now a mixture of horror and hope.

Bigamist?

Her eyes locked with his.

"I, ah—" he stammered.

Behind him a car horn blared and he jumped, startled. He turned as the driver slammed on the brakes of her silver Lincoln and skidded to a halt just inches behind his SUV.

"Oh! Vivian's here!" Annie almost screamed in panicked glee. "You don't want to be late for Women's Club." She shoved the dog into the house and pulled the door shut before he could escape.

Luella shook her head. "That old lady. Always has to make a grand entrance."

The blue-haired woman at the wheel laid on the horn once more, and then a third time.

"Oh! She's in fine form today." Luella patted him on the arm. "I'll just have to find out everything later. Just wait until Vivian hears the news."

She headed down the steps. "I believe this calls for a glass of wine with our supper, don't you think?"

"Have two," Annie called. "Take your time."

Luella glanced back at Nick and grinned. "Oh yes, dear.

I see what you mean. We'll make it a long meal." She'd hardly gotten into the car and closed the door before it sped off, leaving the faint smell of burning rubber in its wake.

"Good God," Annie muttered. "This is going to be all over town in half an hour."

"What the hell is going on?"

She sighed and shook her head. "You might as well come in. Want a lemonade?"

At least he'd been right about one thing. "Sure."

As Annie pushed open the front door, the dog leapt toward them, whining excitedly, tail whipping from side to side as it nuzzled Nick's legs in greeting.

"Just ignore him, he'll calm down." She led the way to a big, bright kitchen filled with the sugary, buttery-rich scent of chocolate chip cookies baking.

"I always have homemade cookies for the guests. I want them to think of Bailey House as *home* while they're here." Annie took a pitcher of lemonade from the refrigerator and a couple of tall glasses from a cupboard. "Bake up a fresh batch every couple of days so the cookie jar is always full."

She handed him a glass of lemonade, slice of lemon floating on the top, and he took a seat at the old oak table in the center of the room. The tall windows facing south opened to the kind of view most people only dreamed of having—a long expanse of lawn sloping gently toward a sandy beach on a lake that looked to be surrounded by pristine forest.

A moment later, Annie set a plate of warm cookies on the table and slid into the chair opposite him. The dog collapsed on the floor beside her, apparently exhausted from expending so much energy the past five minutes.

"I guess I owe you an explanation," she said.

He waited.

She looked down at her hands, clasped together on the table. "Two years ago I bought this B & B with the money you gave me. Well, first I went to college so I could learn how to run a business. Then I found this place." Her voice quivered and she reached down to rub the dog's head. "It's a great little town ..."

Enough with the color commentary. What about the bun in the oven? "Annie—are you pregnant?"

Her expression shifted as though the question caught her completely off guard. She looked like she was about to say something and stopped herself, then drew a slow breath and exhaled. Avoiding his eyes, she stared at the ceiling for a long moment before finally bringing her gaze back to rest on him. She bit her lower lip and made a futile gesture with one hand, as though the motion might give him an answer.

He raised an eyebrow.

She nodded.

Shit. "Married?"

"No."

He let out a breath. At least he hadn't made her a bigamist. He picked up a cookie. "So where's the father?"

She locked eyes with him, and he waited. A charged silence seemed to fill the room.

"I'm looking at him," she finally said.

Buy KISSING ON THE CORNER today.

To receive news about upcoming books, giveaways, and special offers join Pamela Ford's mailing list at pamelaford.net

ABOUT THE AUTHOR

PAMELA FORD is the award-winning author of contemporary and historical romance. She grew up watching old movies, blissfully sighing over the romance; and reading sci-fi and adventure novels, vicariously living the action. The combination probably explains why the books she writes are romantic, happily-ever-afters with plenty of plot—and often, lots of laughter.

After graduating from college with a degree in Advertising, Pam spent many years as a copywriter and freelance writer before inserting a plot twist in her career path and writing her first book.

Pam has won numerous awards including the Booksellers Best, the Laurel Wreath, and a gold medal IPPY in the Independent Book Publisher Awards. She is a National Readers' Choice Awards finalist, a Maggie Awards finalist, a Kindle Book Awards finalist, and a two-time Golden Heart Finalist.

Sign up for Pam's mailing list at: www.pamelaford.net
Contact: pamelafordbooks@gmail.com
Facebook.com/pamelafordbooks
Instagram.com/pamelafordbooks